SONIC
THE HEDGEHOG
ARCHIVES VOLUME 18

IAN FLYNN, PATRICK "SPAZ" SPAZIANTE, JIM AMASH, KARL BOLLERS, SAM MAXWELL,
HARVEY MERCADOOCASIO, DAVE MANAK, JON D'AGOSTINO, RAMONA FRADON, COLLEEN DORAN,
FRANK GAGLIARDO, KEN PENDERS, PAUL CASTIGLIA, CHRIS ALLAN, BARRY GROSSMAN,
PAM EKLUND, VICKIE WILLIAMS, JEFF POWELL, & STEVEN BUTLER

cover by
PATRICK "SPAZ" SPAZIANTE

SPECIAL THANKS TO ANTHONY GACCIONE & CINDY CHAU @ SEGA LICENSING

SONIC THE HEDGEHOG ARCHIVES, Volume 18. Printed in USA. Published by Archie Comic Publications, Inc., 325 Fayette Avenue, Mamaroneck, NY 10543-2318. Sega is registered in the U.S. Patent and Trademark Office. SEGA, Sonic The Hedgehog, and all related characters and indicia are either registered trademarks or trademarks of SEGA CORPORATION © 1991-2012. SEGA CORPORATION and SONICTEAM, LTD./SEGA CORPORATION © 2001-2012. All Rights Reserved. The product is manufactured under license from Sega of America, Inc., 350 Rhode Island St., Ste. 400, San Francisco, CA 94103 www.sega.com. Any similarities between characters, names, persons, and/or institutions in this book and any living, dead or fictional characters, names, persons, and/or institutions are not intended and if they exist, are purely coincidental. Nothing may be printed in whole or part without written permission from Archie Comic Publications, Inc.
ISBN: 978-1-936975-07-5

ARCHIE COMIC PUBLICATIONS, INC.
JONATHAN GOLDWATER, publisher/co-ceo
NANCY SILBERKLEIT, co-ceo
MIKE PELLERITO, president
VICTOR GORELICK, co-president/e-i-c
BILL HORAN, director of circulation
HAROLD BUCHHOLZ, executive director of
publishing/operations
ALEX SEGURA, executive director of
publicity & marketing
PAUL KAMINSKI, executive director of
...ation editor
...stant editor
...on manager
...ator cover colors
...consultant
...roofreader

TABLE OF CONTENTS

Sonic the Hedgehog #69
"A DAY IN THE LIFE"

Sonic is back home, and that means it's time to catch up with friends and family, and take it easy for a while -- right? Wrong! The convicts of the Devil's Gulag are free, and they're gunning for their common enemy: Sonic!

Tales of the Freedom Fighters Part III
"WEATHERING THE STORM"

Lupe and the Wolf Pack are pinned under ruins during a terrible storm, and are now the keepers of a pair of orphaned Overlander girls. Lupe must come to a decision over their fate, and the fate of her pack.

Sonic the Hedgehog #70
"SAVING NATE MORGAN"

The convicts of the Devil's Gulag have kidnapped Nate Morgan! King Acorn assigns the Secret Service to save the day, but Sonic's not going to sit this one out! The frantic showdown gets even more heated as a mysterious force makes its play.

"STATUE OF LIMITATIONS"

Sonic takes a wild ride of self-reflection as his past adventures -- both victories and failures -- come back to haunt his dreams.

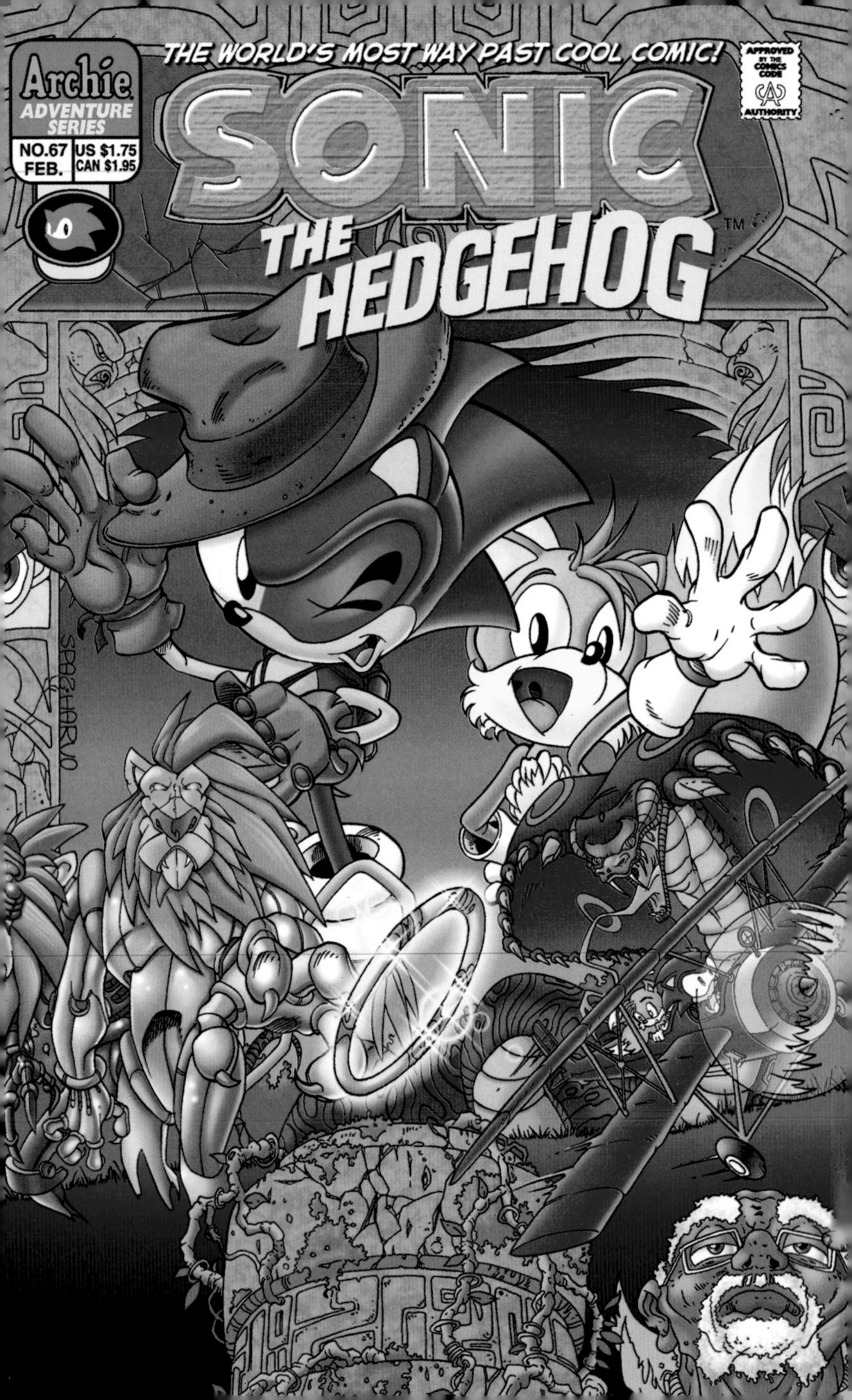
THE WORLD'S MOST WAY PAST COOL COMIC!
Archie
ADVENTURE SERIES
NO.67
FEB.
US $1.75
CAN $1.95
APPROVED BY THE COMICS CODE AUTHORITY
SONIC
THE HEDGEHOG
TM
SPAZ

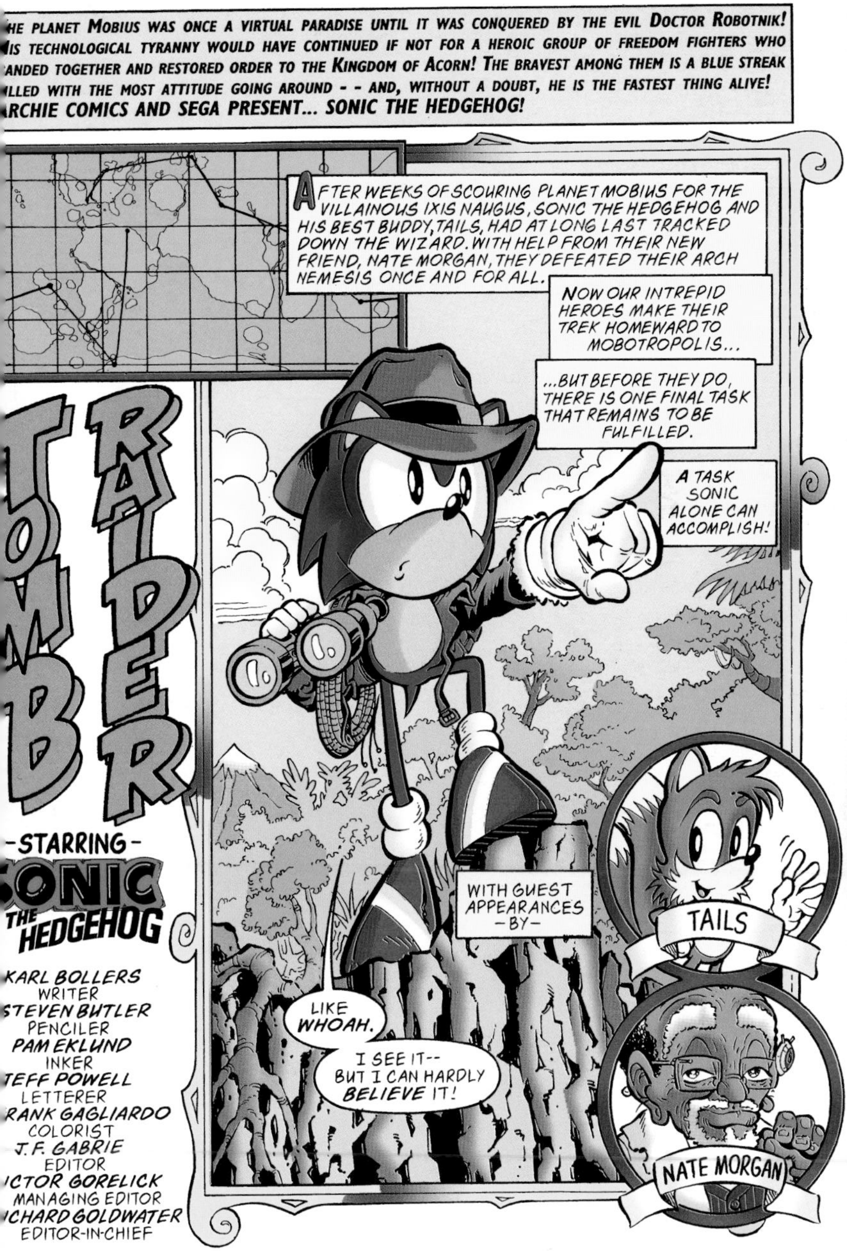
HE PLANET MOBIUS WAS ONCE A VIRTUAL PARADISE UNTIL IT WAS CONQUERED BY THE EVIL DOCTOR ROBOTNIK! IS TECHNOLOGICAL TYRANNY WOULD HAVE CONTINUED IF NOT FOR A HEROIC GROUP OF FREEDOM FIGHTERS WHO ANDED TOGETHER AND RESTORED ORDER TO THE KINGDOM OF ACORN! THE BRAVEST AMONG THEM IS A BLUE STREAK ILLED WITH THE MOST ATTITUDE GOING AROUND - - AND, WITHOUT A DOUBT, HE IS THE FASTEST THING ALIVE!
RCHIE COMICS AND SEGA PRESENT... SONIC THE HEDGEHOG!
AFTER WEEKS OF SCOURING PLANET MOBIUS FOR THE VILLAINOUS IXIS NAUGUS, SONIC THE HEDGEHOG AND HIS BEST BUDDY, TAILS, HAD AT LONG LAST TRACKED DOWN THE WIZARD. WITH HELP FROM THEIR NEW FRIEND, NATE MORGAN, THEY DEFEATED THEIR ARCH NEMESIS ONCE AND FOR ALL.
NOW OUR INTREPID HEROES MAKE THEIR TREK HOMEWARD TO MOBOTROPOLIS...
...BUT BEFORE THEY DO, THERE IS ONE FINAL TASK THAT REMAINS TO BE FULFILLED.
A TASK SONIC ALONE CAN ACCOMPLISH!
OMB RAIDER
-STARRING-
ONIC THE HEDGEHOG
KARL BOLLERS WRITER
STEVEN BUTLER PENCILER
PAM EKLUND INKER
TEFF POWELL LETTERER
RANK GAGLIARDO COLORIST
J. F. GABRIE EDITOR
ICTOR GORELICK MANAGING EDITOR
ICHARD GOLDWATER EDITOR-IN-CHIEF
WITH GUEST APPEARANCES -BY-
TAILS
NATE MORGAN
LIKE WHOAH.
I SEE IT-- BUT I CAN HARDLY BELIEVE IT!

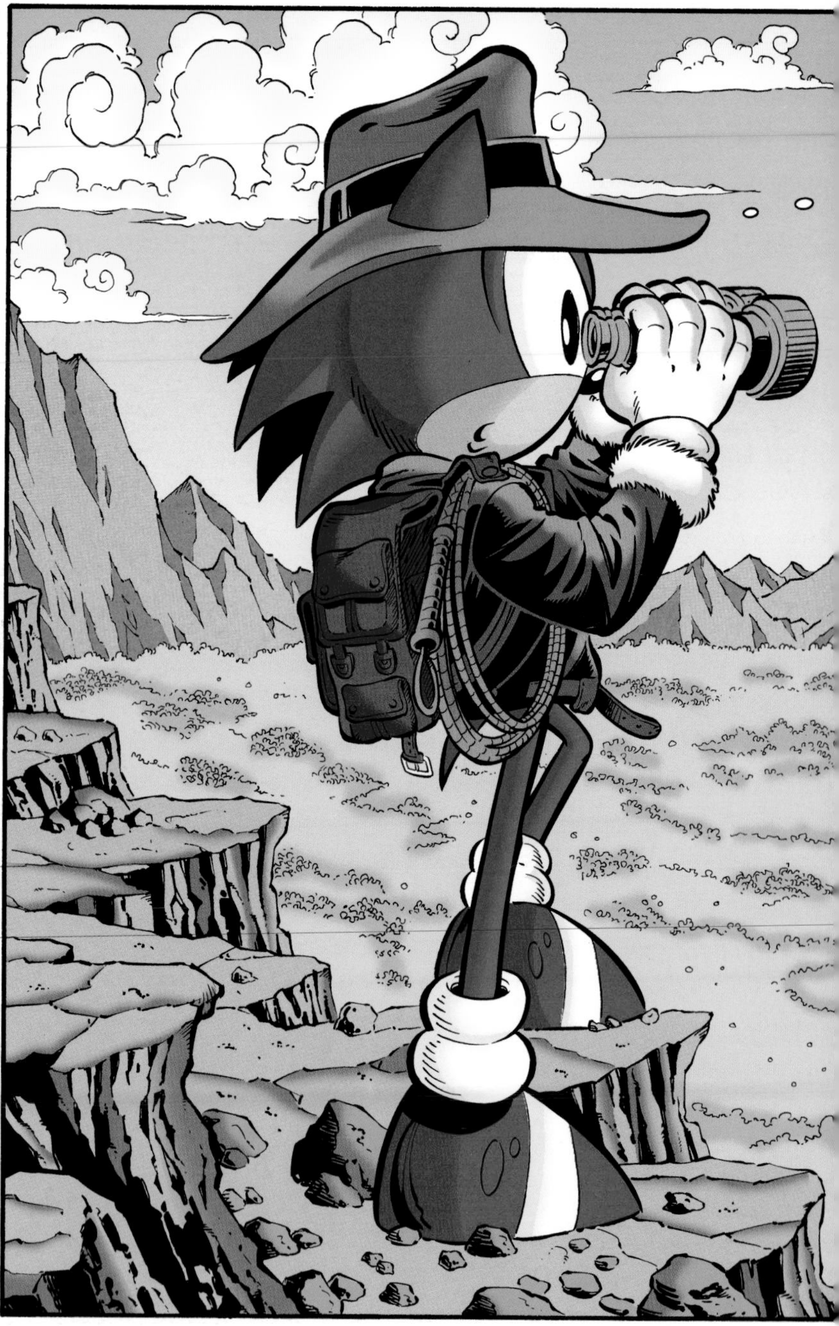

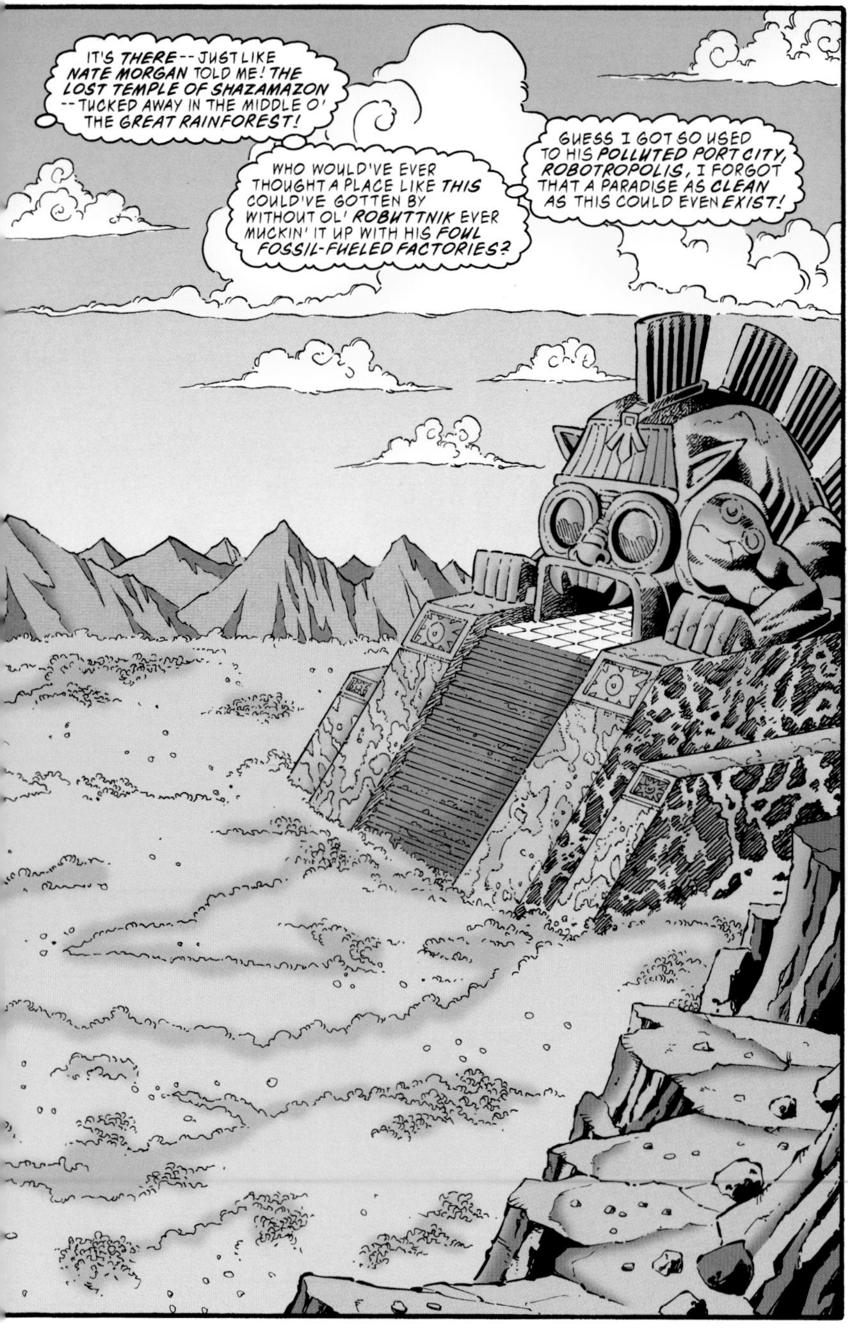
IT'S THERE -- JUST LIKE NATE MORGAN TOLD ME! THE LOST TEMPLE OF SHAZAMAZON -- TUCKED AWAY IN THE MIDDLE O' THE GREAT RAINFOREST!
WHO WOULD'VE EVER THOUGHT A PLACE LIKE THIS COULD'VE GOTTEN BY WITHOUT OL' ROBUTTNIK EVER MUCKIN' IT UP WITH HIS FOUL FOSSIL-FUELED FACTORIES?
GUESS I GOT SO USED TO HIS POLLUTED PORT CITY, ROBOTROPOLIS, I FORGOT THAT A PARADISE AS CLEAN AS THIS COULD EVEN EXIST!

THE SCENERY'S HAPPENING IN A *WAY PAST COOL* WAY, BUT FOR NOW I'D BETTER *JUICE* ON OVER TO THE TEMPLE AND *SIGHTSEE* LATER!

TAILS AND I *NEVER* EXPECTED TO SEE *THIS* PART O' THE PLANET WHEN WE LEFT *MOBOTROPOLIS* TO FIND *IXIS NAUGUS!**

THERE WAS NO WAY ON *MOBIUS* WE COULD'VE PREDICTED *HALF* O' WHAT'S GONE DOWN *SINCE!*

* AS SEEN IN SONIC ARCHIVES VOL. 15--ED.

TRIPLE-S SPIN!

" I HAD TO *HAND* IT IXIS-- FOR AN EVIL *WIZARD* BENT ON TAKIN' OVER *EVERYTHING* HE SURE KNEW HOW TO KEEP A LOW *PROFILE!*

WE HADN'T SEEN *HIDE* NOR *HAIR* O' HIM UNTIL WE GOT TO THE *SOUTHERN TUNDRA*-- THE *BOTTOM* O' THE WORLD!*

"MATTER O' FACT, WE HADN'T SEEN ANY *OVERLANDERS** SINCE ROBUTTNIK BIT THE BIG ONE AND WE SENT HIS ASSISTANT, *SNIVELY,* OFF TO THE *DEVIL'S ISLAND GULAG...***

* Humans
** BACK IN SONIC ARCHIVES VOL. 13 --ED.

"...BUT *NATE MORGAN* WASN'T LIKE *ANY* OVERLANDER *I* EVER MET! HE WAS THE *CREATOR* OF ALL THE *POWER RINGS*** ON THE GLOBE!

"OH, HE SURE *TALKED* A GOOD TALK WHEN HE SAID HE ONLY *CARED* ABOUT HIMSELF AND HIS OWN ('OWN' BEING HIS BEST FRIEND *EDDY THE ABOMINABLE SNOW-BOT*)

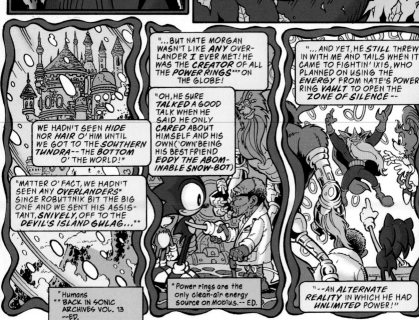

* Power rings are the only clean-air energy source on Mobius.-- ED.

"...AND YET, HE *STILL* THREW IN WITH ME AND TAILS WHEN IT CAME TO FIGHTIN' IXIS, WHO PLANNED ON USING THE *ENERGY* FROM NATE'S POWER *RING VAULT* TO OPEN THE *ZONE OF SILENCE* --

"--AN *ALTERNATE REALITY* IN WHICH HE HAD *UNLIMITED* POWER!"

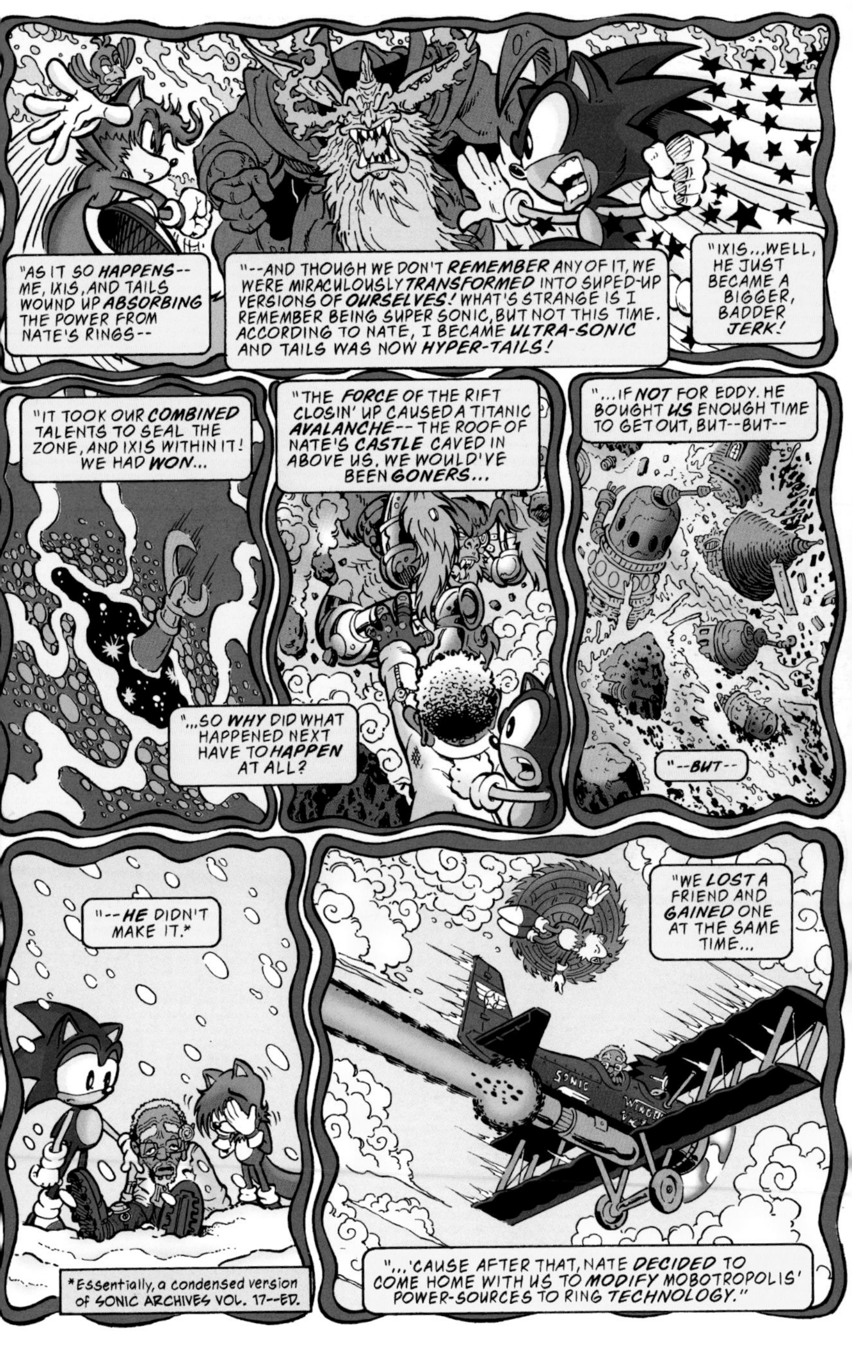
"AS IT SO HAPPENS-- ME, IXIS, AND TAILS WOUND UP ABSORBING THE POWER FROM NATE'S RINGS--
"--AND THOUGH WE DON'T REMEMBER ANY OF IT, WE WERE MIRACULOUSLY TRANSFORMED INTO SUPED-UP VERSIONS OF OURSELVES! WHAT'S STRANGE IS I REMEMBER BEING SUPER SONIC, BUT NOT THIS TIME. ACCORDING TO NATE, I BECAME ULTRA-SONIC AND TAILS WAS NOW HYPER-TAILS!
"IXIS...WELL, HE JUST BECAME A BIGGER, BADDER JERK!
"IT TOOK OUR COMBINED TALENTS TO SEAL THE ZONE, AND IXIS WITHIN IT! WE HAD WON...
"...SO WHY DID WHAT HAPPENED NEXT HAVE TO HAPPEN AT ALL?
"THE FORCE OF THE RIFT CLOSIN' UP CAUSED A TITANIC AVALANCHE-- THE ROOF OF NATE'S CASTLE CAVED IN ABOVE US. WE WOULD'VE BEEN GONERS...
"...IF NOT FOR EDDY. HE BOUGHT US ENOUGH TIME TO GET OUT, BUT--BUT--
"--BUT--
"--HE DIDN'T MAKE IT.*
*Essentially, a condensed version of SONIC ARCHIVES VOL. 17--ED.
"WE LOST A FRIEND AND GAINED ONE AT THE SAME TIME...
SONIC
"...'CAUSE AFTER THAT, NATE DECIDED TO COME HOME WITH US TO MODIFY MOBOTROPOLIS' POWER-SOURCES TO RING TECHNOLOGY."

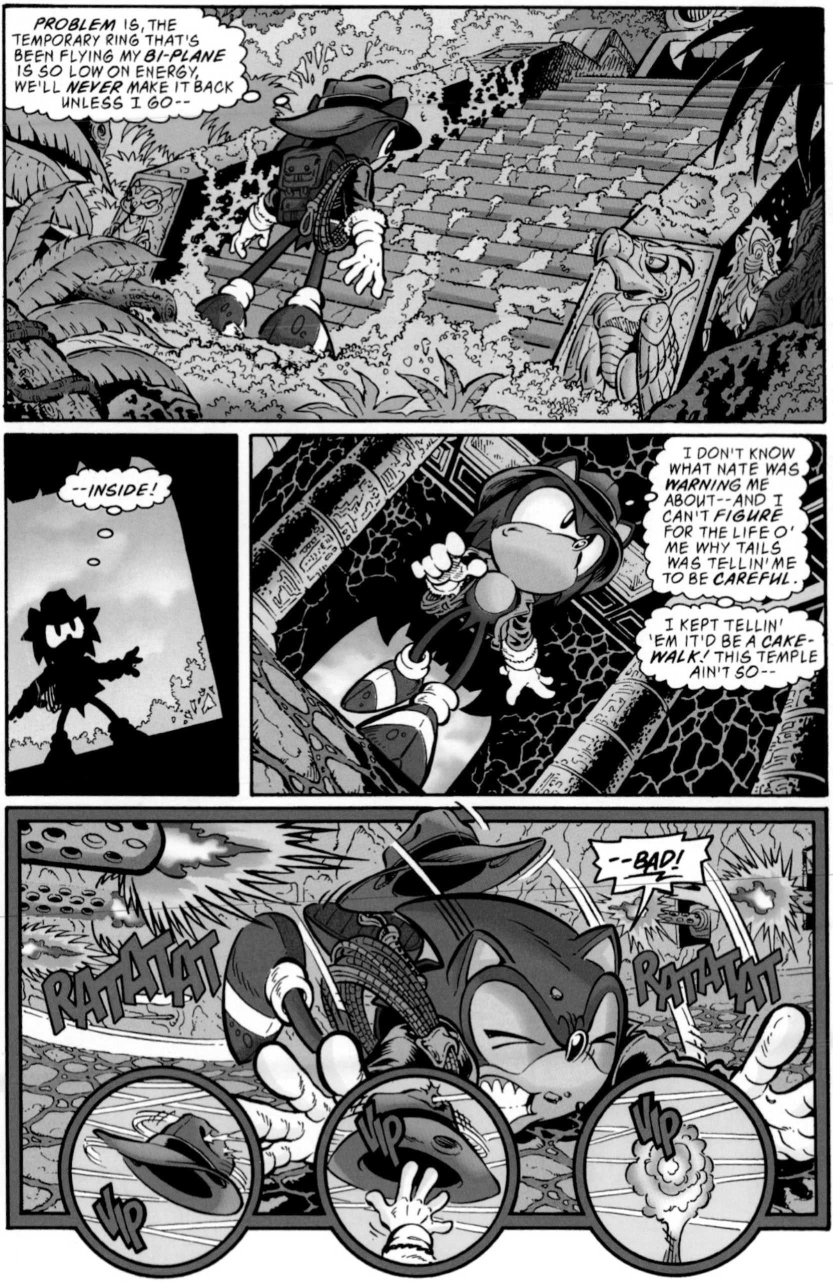
PROBLEM IS, THE TEMPORARY RING THAT'S BEEN FLYING MY BI-PLANE IS SO LOW ON ENERGY, WE'LL NEVER MAKE IT BACK UNLESS I GO--
--INSIDE!
I DON'T KNOW WHAT NATE WAS WARNING ME ABOUT--AND I CAN'T FIGURE FOR THE LIFE O' ME WHY TAILS WAS TELLIN' ME TO BE CAREFUL.
I KEPT TELLIN' 'EM IT'D BE A CAKE-WALK! THIS TEMPLE AIN'T SO--
--BAD!
RATATAT
RATATAT
VIP
VIP
VIP

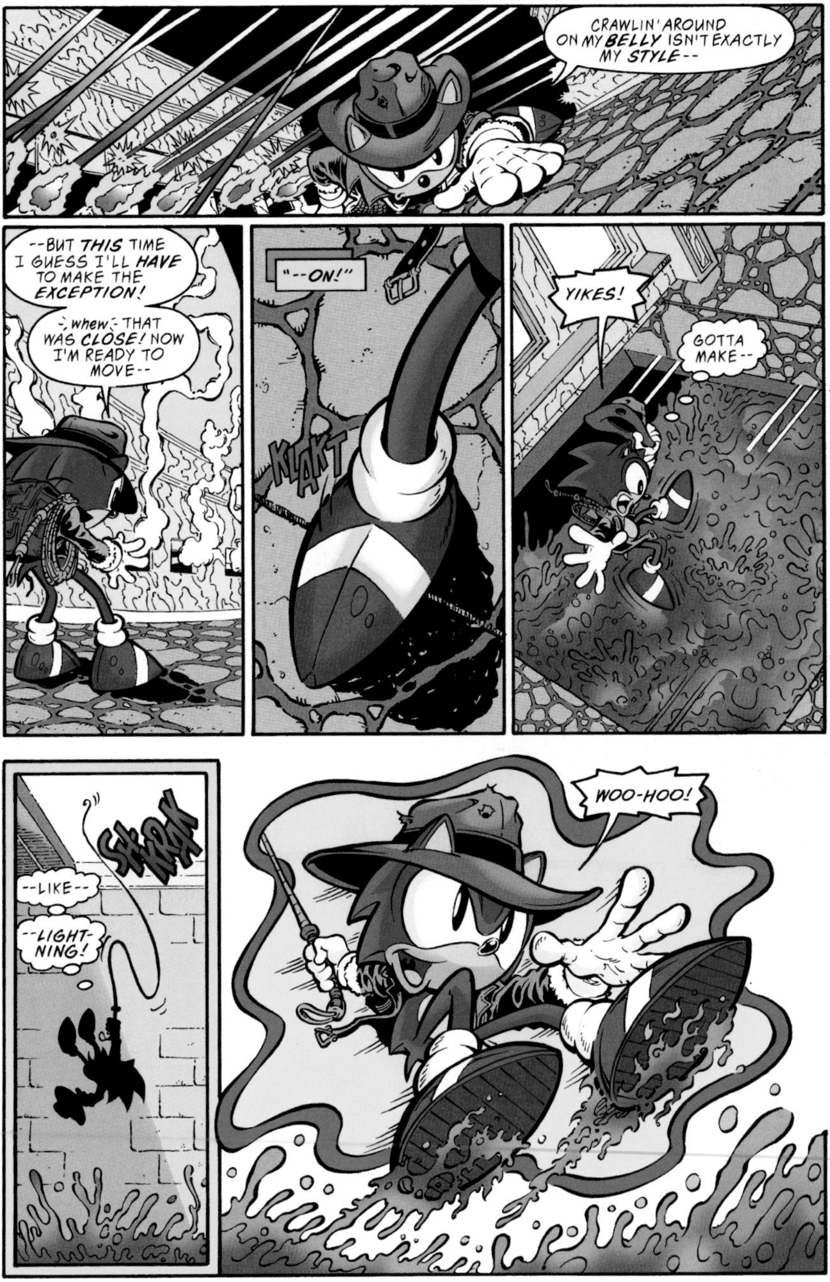
CRAWLIN' AROUND ON MY BELLY ISN'T EXACTLY MY STYLE--
--BUT THIS TIME I GUESS I'LL HAVE TO MAKE THE EXCEPTION!
whew THAT WAS CLOSE! NOW I'M READY TO MOVE--
"--ON!"
KLAKT
YIKES!
GOTTA MAKE--
SHRAK
--LIKE--
--LIGHTNING!
WOO-HOO!

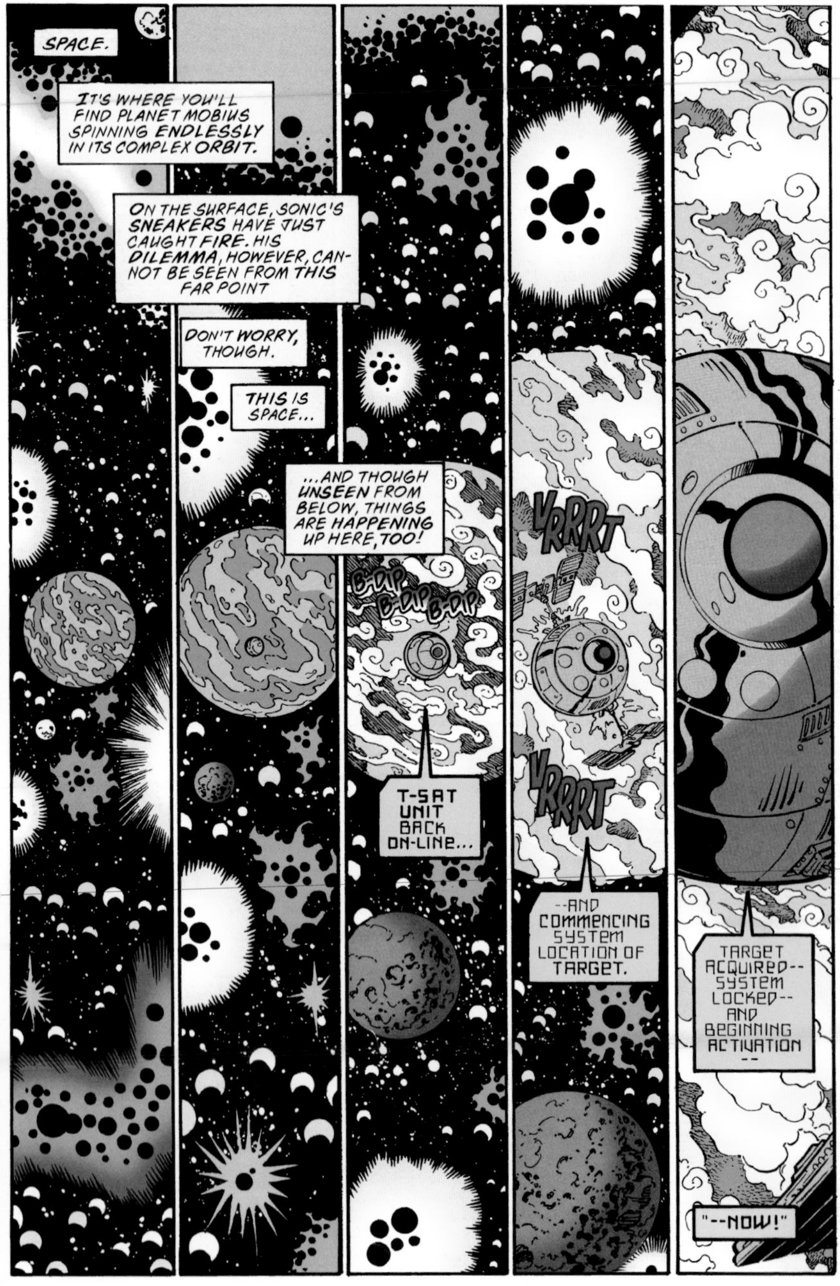
SPACE.
IT'S WHERE YOU'LL FIND PLANET MOBIUS SPINNING ENDLESSLY IN ITS COMPLEX ORBIT.
ON THE SURFACE, SONIC'S SNEAKERS HAVE JUST CAUGHT FIRE. HIS DILEMMA, HOWEVER, CAN-NOT BE SEEN FROM THIS FAR POINT
DON'T WORRY, THOUGH.
THIS IS SPACE...
...AND THOUGH UNSEEN FROM BELOW, THINGS ARE HAPPENING UP HERE, TOO!
B-DIP B-DIP B-DIP
T-SAT UNIT BACK ON-LINE...
VRRRT
VRRRT
--AND COMMENCING SYSTEM LOCATION OF TARGET.
TARGET ACQUIRED-- SYSTEM LOCKED-- AND BEGINNING ACTIVATION --
"--NOW!"

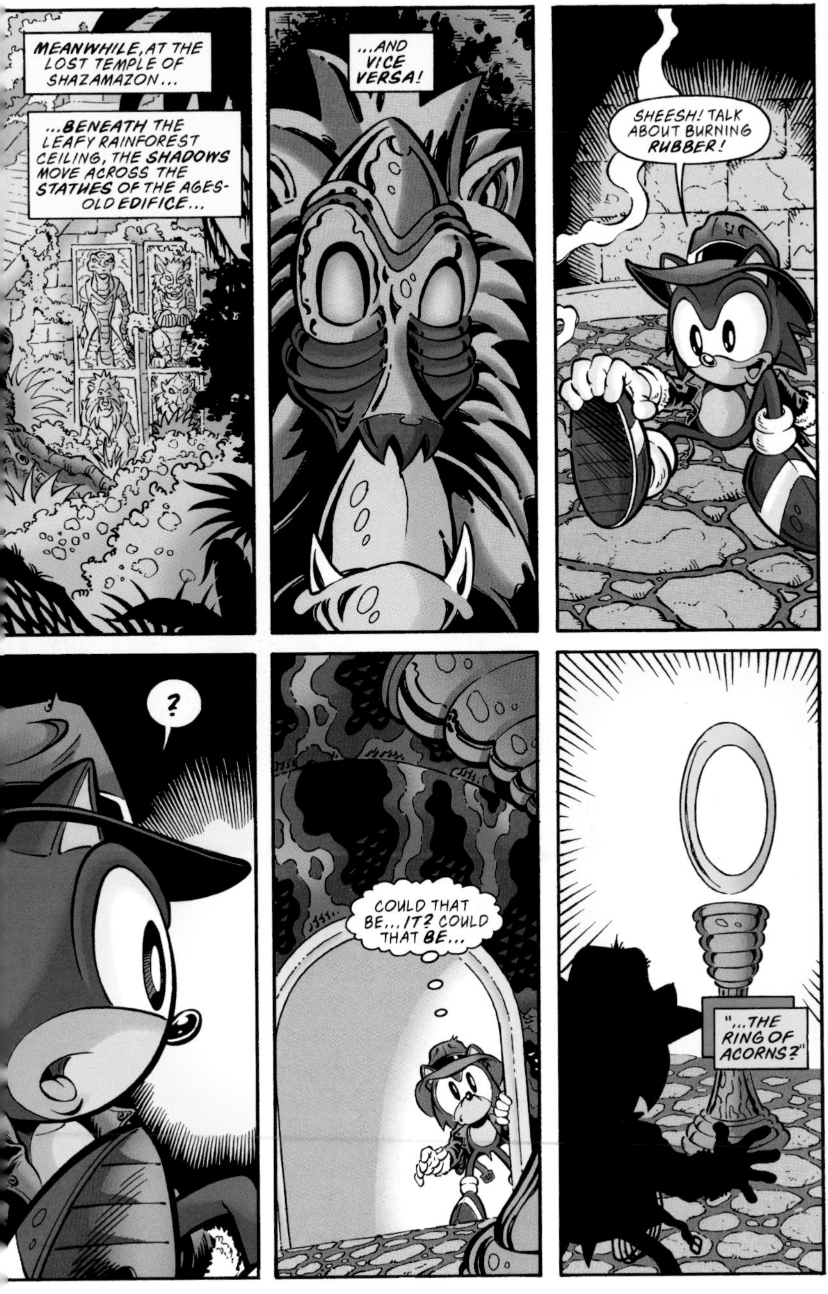
MEANWHILE, AT THE LOST TEMPLE OF SHAZAMAZON...
...BENEATH THE LEAFY RAINFOREST CEILING, THE SHADOWS MOVE ACROSS THE STATUES OF THE AGES-OLD EDIFICE...
...AND VICE VERSA!
SHEESH! TALK ABOUT BURNING RUBBER!
?
COULD THAT BE... IT? COULD THAT BE...
"...THE RING OF ACORNS?"

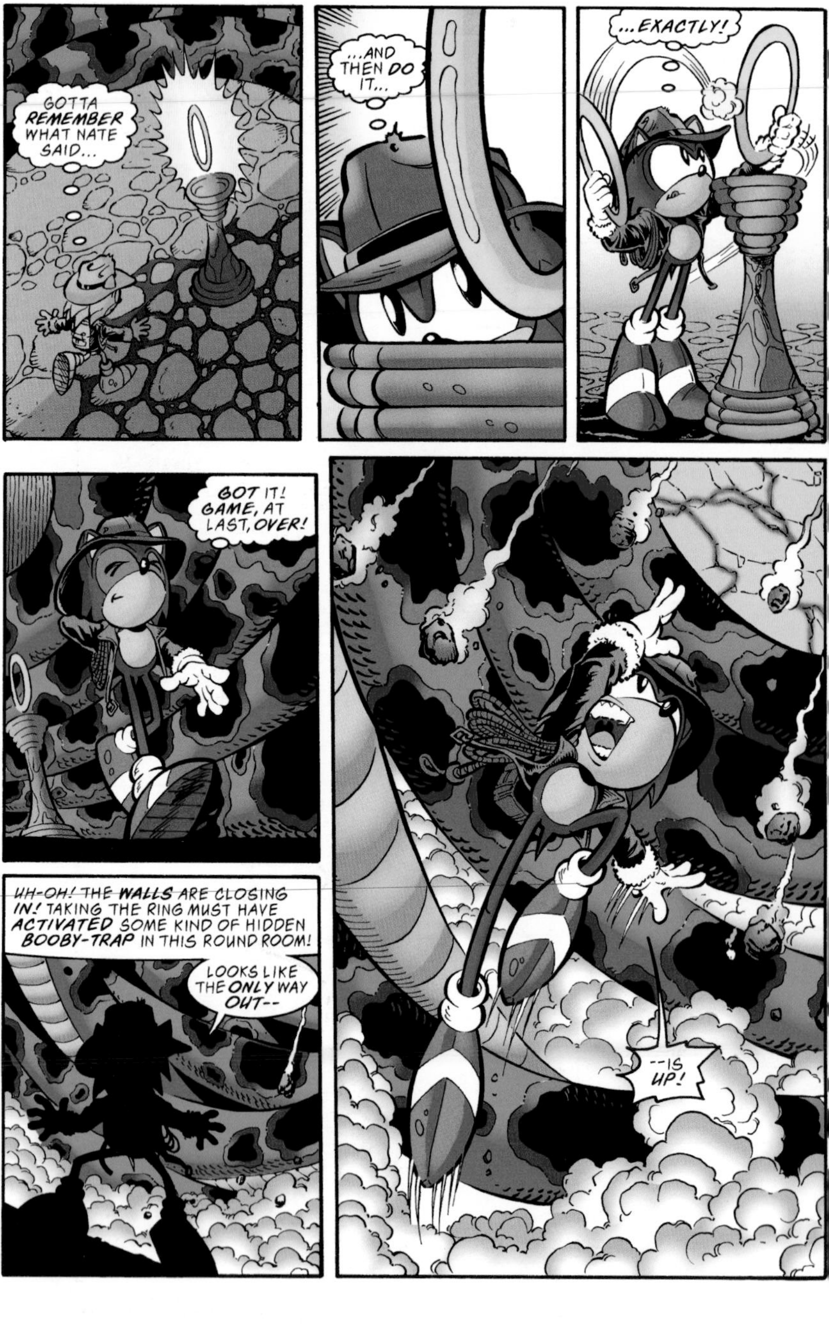
GOTTA REMEMBER WHAT NATE SAID...
...AND THEN DO IT...
...EXACTLY!
GOT IT! GAME, AT LAST, OVER!
UH-OH! THE WALLS ARE CLOSING IN! TAKING THE RING MUST HAVE ACTIVATED SOME KIND OF HIDDEN BOOBY-TRAP IN THIS ROUND ROOM!
LOOKS LIKE THE ONLY WAY OUT--
--IS UP!

BONUS PIN-UP

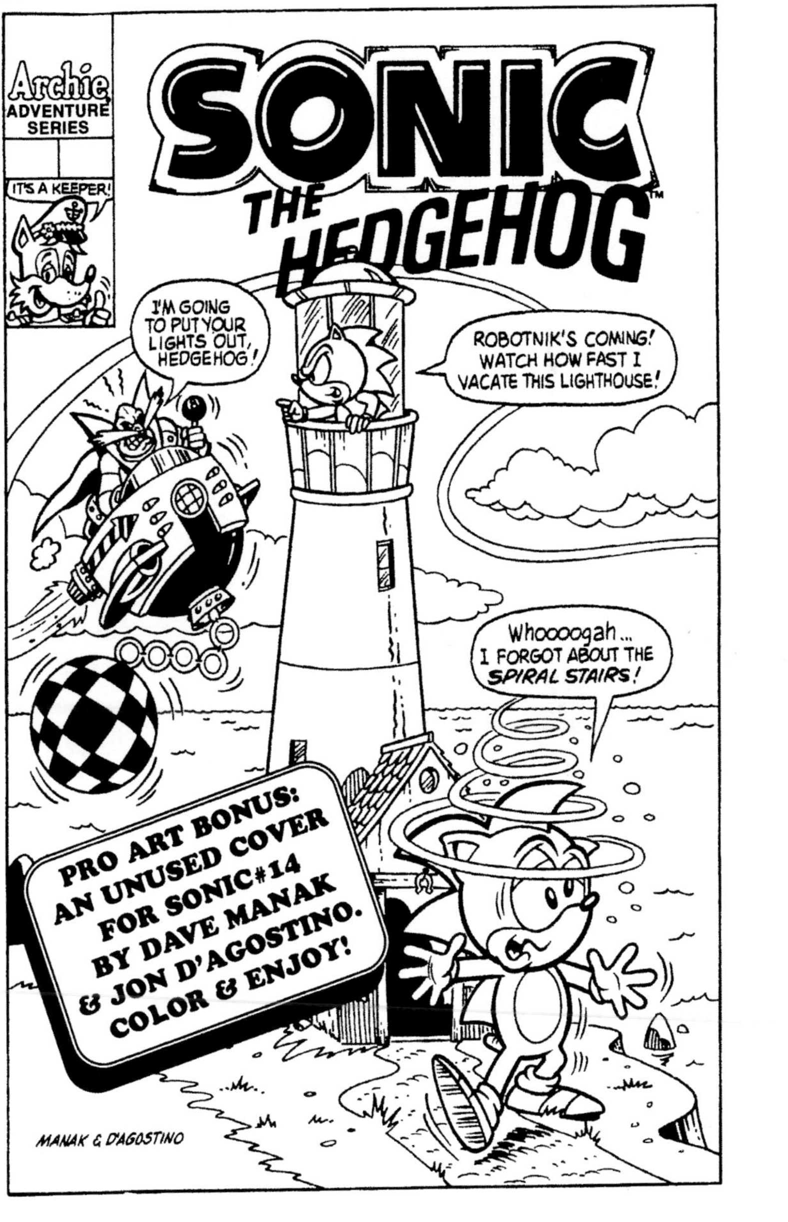

Archie ADVENTURE SERIES
IT'S A KEEPER!
SONIC THE HEDGEHOG™
I'M GOING TO PUT YOUR LIGHTS OUT, HEDGEHOG!
ROBOTNIK'S COMING! WATCH HOW FAST I VACATE THIS LIGHTHOUSE!
Whooooogah... I FORGOT ABOUT THE SPIRAL STAIRS!
PRO ART BONUS: AN UNUSED COVER FOR SONIC#14 BY DAVE MANAK & JON D'AGOSTINO. COLOR & ENJOY!
MANAK & D'AGOSTINO

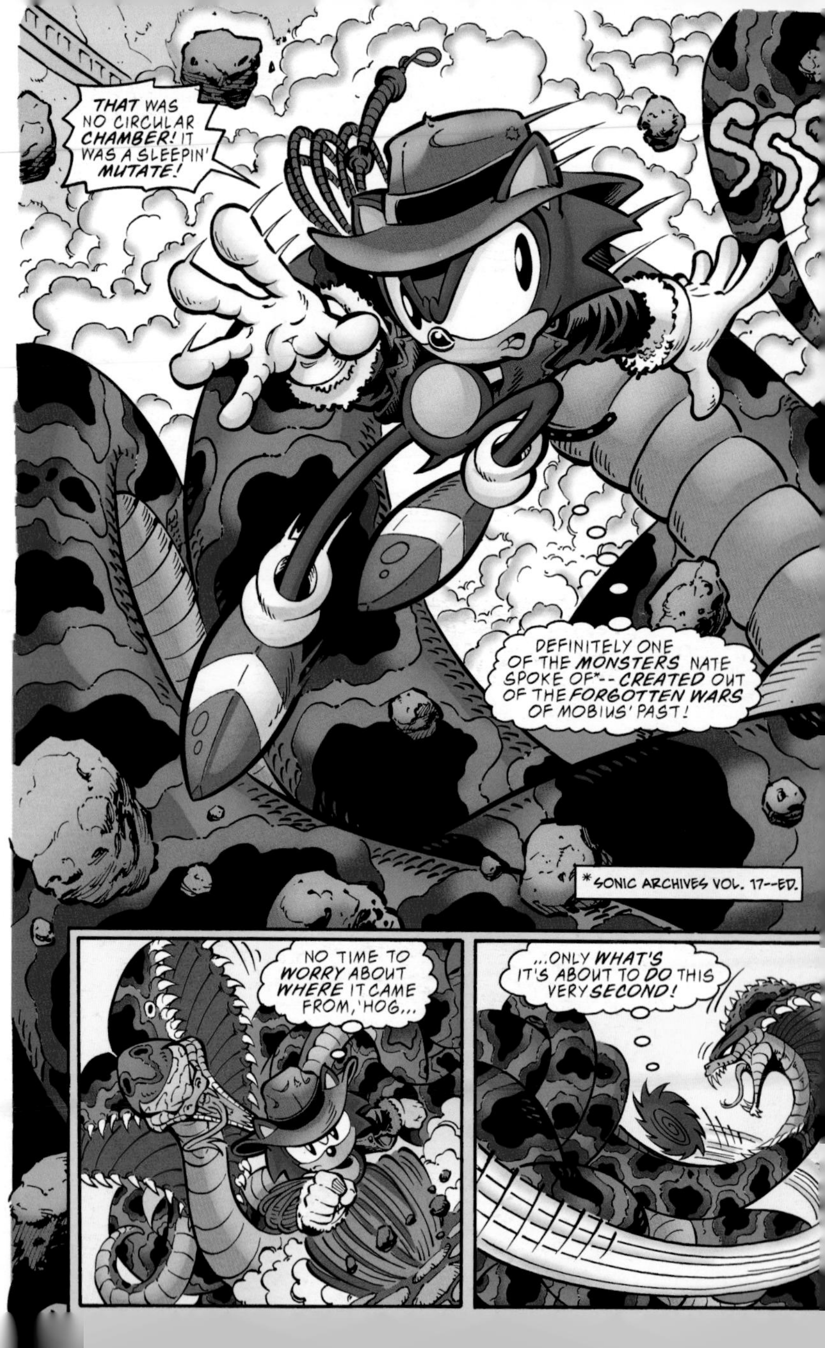
THAT WAS NO CIRCULAR CHAMBER! IT WAS A SLEEPIN' MUTATE!
SSS
DEFINITELY ONE OF THE MONSTERS NATE SPOKE OF*-- CREATED OUT OF THE FORGOTTEN WARS OF MOBIUS' PAST!
*SONIC ARCHIVES VOL. 17--ED.
NO TIME TO WORRY ABOUT WHERE IT CAME FROM, 'HOG...
...ONLY WHAT'S IT'S ABOUT TO DO THIS VERY SECOND!

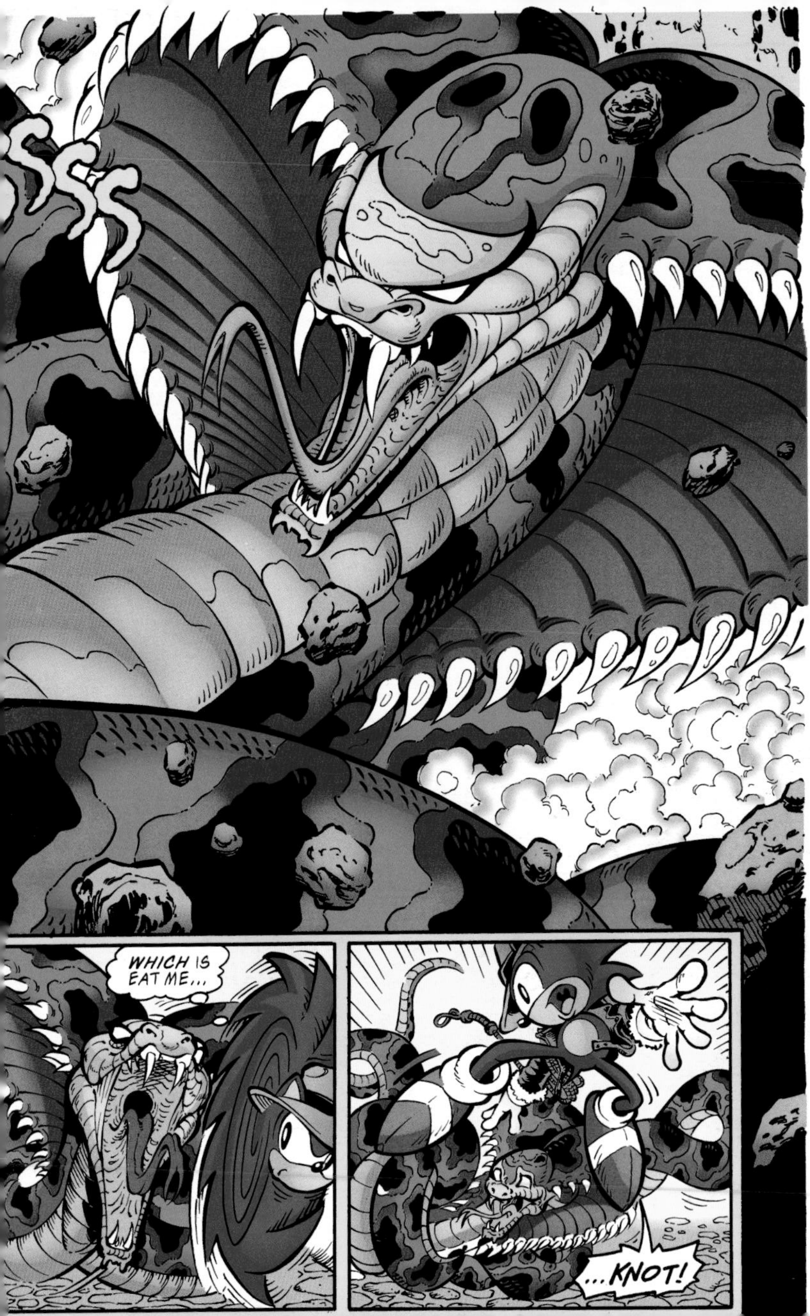
SSS
WHICH IS EAT ME...
...KNOT!

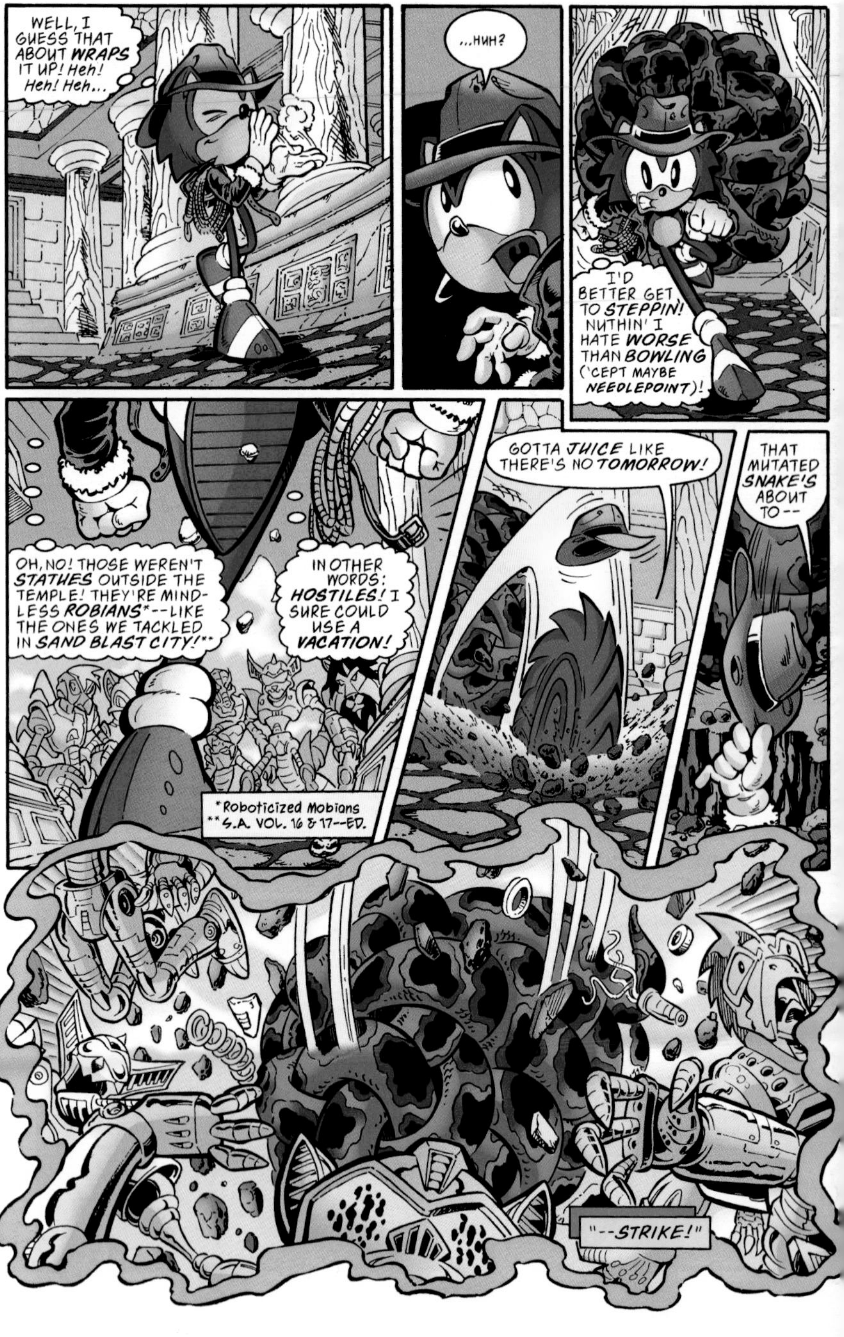
WELL, I GUESS THAT ABOUT WRAPS IT UP! Heh! Heh! Heh...
...HUH?
I'D BETTER GET TO STEPPIN! NUTHIN' I HATE WORSE THAN BOWLING ('CEPT MAYBE NEEDLEPOINT)!
OH, NO! THOSE WEREN'T STATUES OUTSIDE THE TEMPLE! THEY'RE MINDLESS ROBIANS*--LIKE THE ONES WE TACKLED IN SAND BLAST CITY!**
IN OTHER WORDS: HOSTILES! I SURE COULD USE A VACATION!
*Roboticized Mobians
**S.A. VOL. 16 & 17--ED.
GOTTA JUICE LIKE THERE'S NO TOMORROW!
THAT MUTATED SNAKE'S ABOUT TO--
"--STRIKE!"

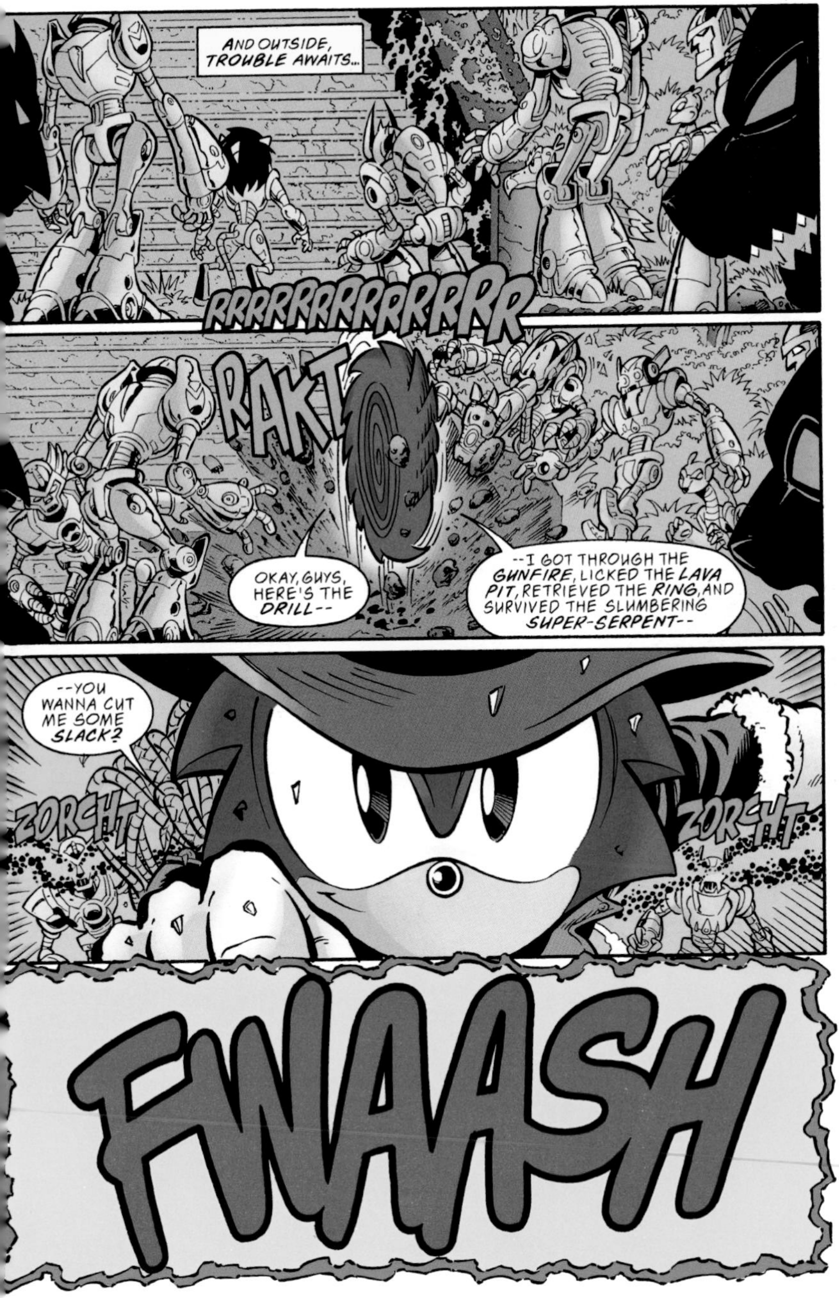
AND OUTSIDE, TROUBLE AWAITS...
RRRRRRRRRRRRRRR
RAKT
OKAY, GUYS, HERE'S THE DRILL--
--I GOT THROUGH THE GUNFIRE, LICKED THE LAVA PIT, RETRIEVED THE RING, AND SURVIVED THE SLUMBERING SUPER-SERPENT--
--YOU WANNA CUT ME SOME SLACK?
ZORCHT
ZORCHT
FWAASH

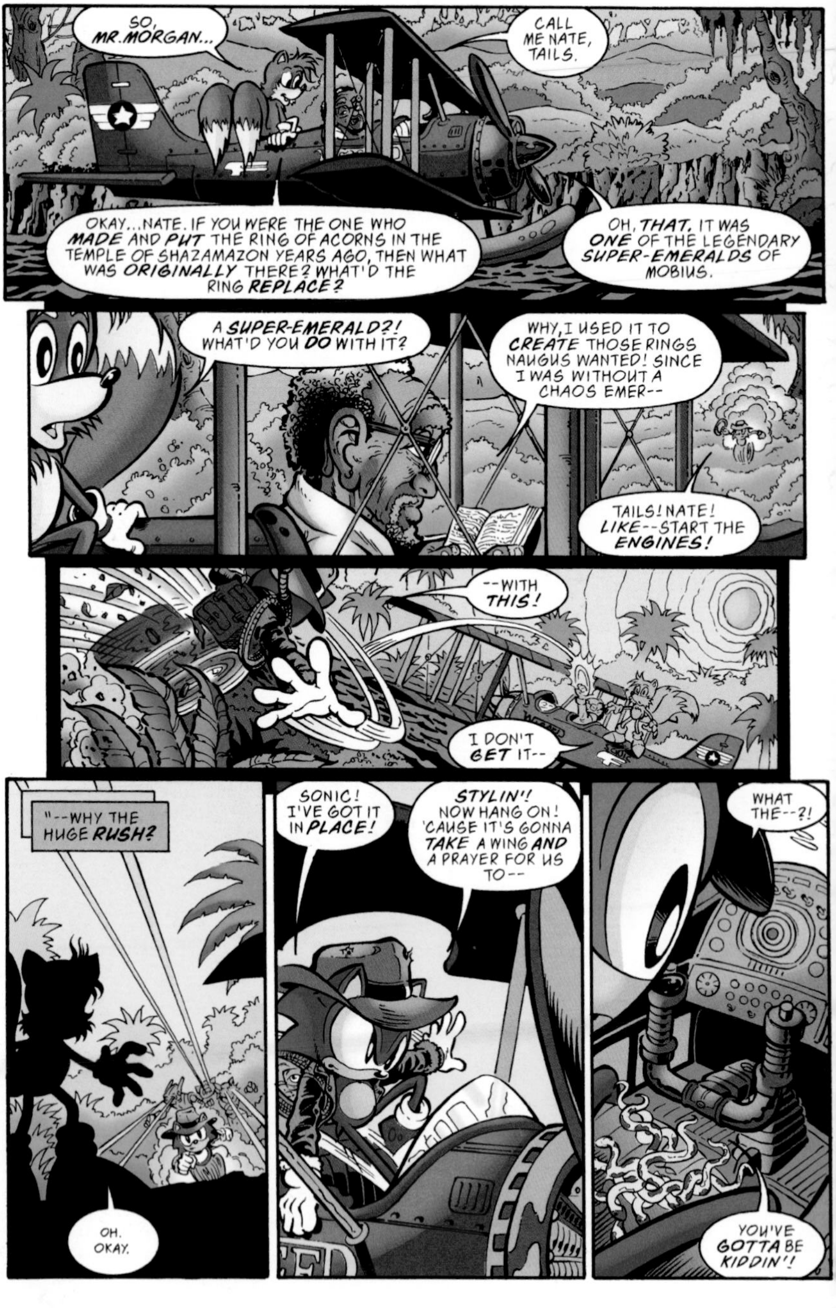

SO, MR. MORGAN...
CALL ME NATE, TAILS.
OKAY...NATE. IF YOU WERE THE ONE WHO MADE AND PUT THE RING OF ACORNS IN THE TEMPLE OF SHAZAMAZON YEARS AGO, THEN WHAT WAS ORIGINALLY THERE? WHAT'D THE RING REPLACE?
OH, THAT. IT WAS ONE OF THE LEGENDARY SUPER-EMERALDS OF MOBIUS.
A SUPER-EMERALD?! WHAT'D YOU DO WITH IT?
WHY, I USED IT TO CREATE THOSE RINGS NAUGUS WANTED! SINCE I WAS WITHOUT A CHAOS EMER--
TAILS! NATE! LIKE--START THE ENGINES!
--WITH THIS!
I DON'T GET IT--
"--WHY THE HUGE RUSH?
OH. OKAY.
SONIC! I'VE GOT IT IN PLACE!
STYLIN'! NOW HANG ON! 'CAUSE IT'S GONNA TAKE A WING AND A PRAYER FOR US TO--
WHAT THE--?!
YOU'VE GOTTA BE KIDDIN'!

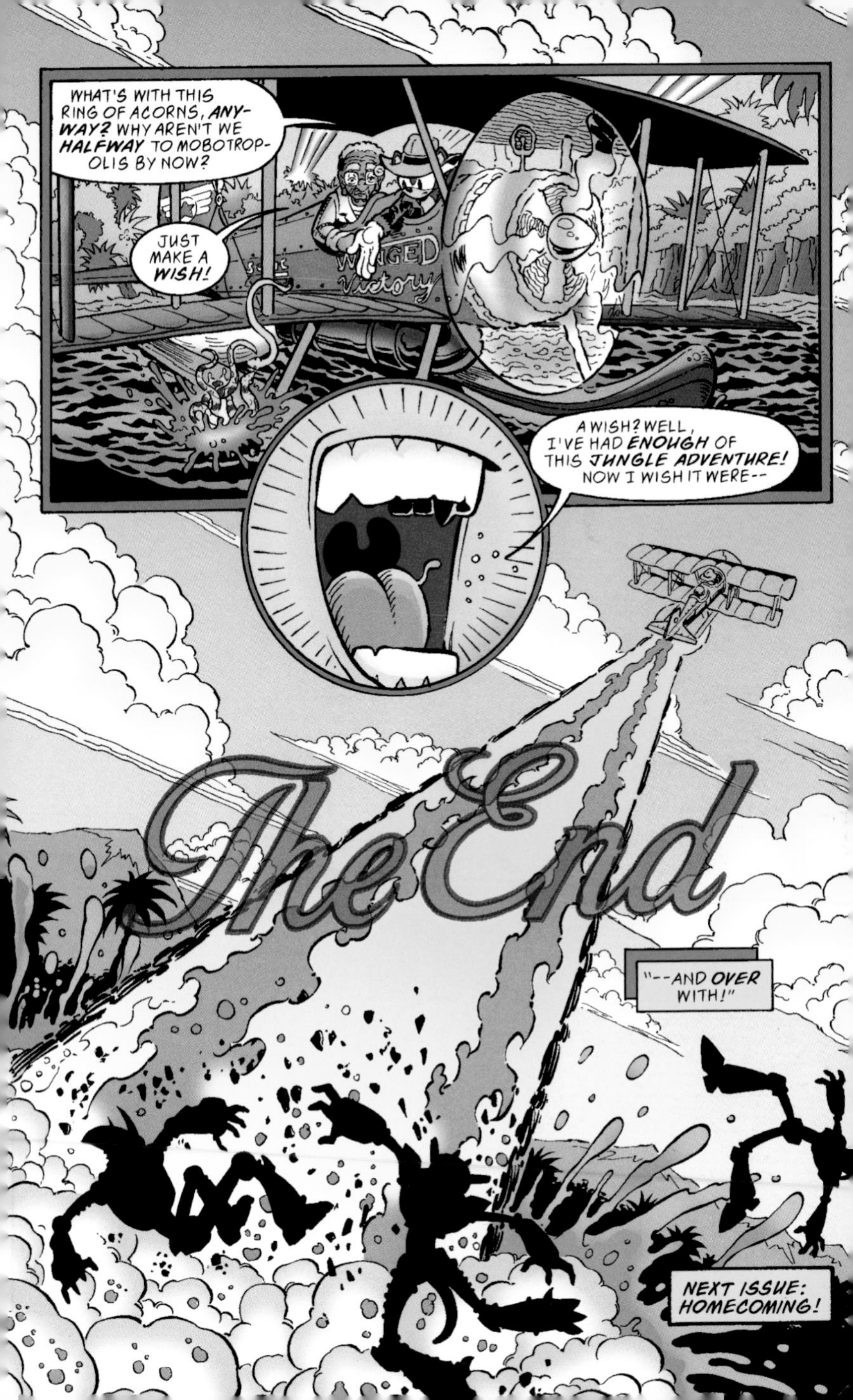
WHAT'S WITH THIS RING OF ACORNS, ANY-WAY? WHY AREN'T WE HALFWAY TO MOBOTROP-OLIS BY NOW?
JUST MAKE A WISH!
WINGED Victory
A WISH? WELL, I'VE HAD ENOUGH OF THIS JUNGLE ADVENTURE! NOW I WISH IT WERE--
The End
"--AND OVER WITH!"
NEXT ISSUE: HOMECOMING!

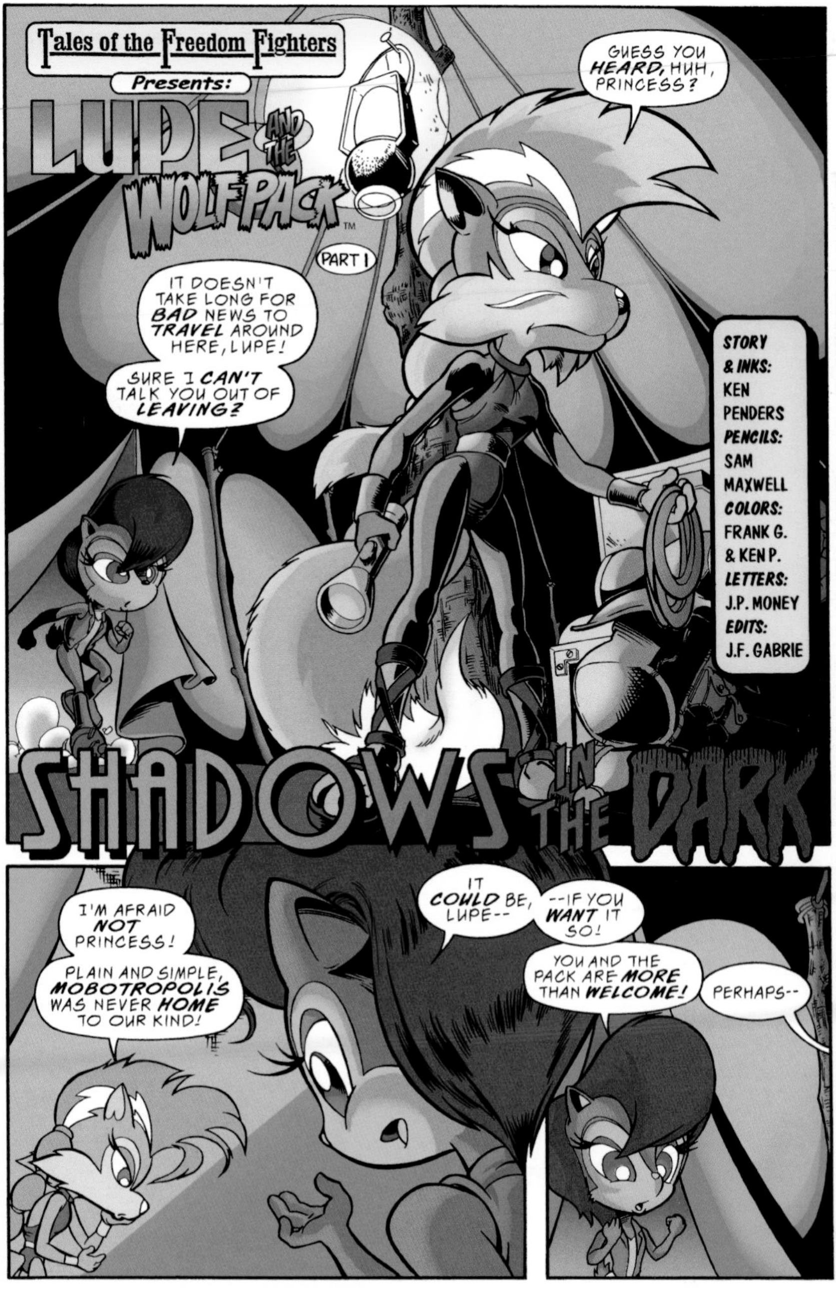
Tales of the Freedom Fighters
Presents:
LUPE AND THE WOLF PACK™
PART 1
GUESS YOU HEARD, HUH, PRINCESS?
IT DOESN'T TAKE LONG FOR BAD NEWS TO TRAVEL AROUND HERE, LUPE!
SURE I CAN'T TALK YOU OUT OF LEAVING?
STORY & INKS: KEN PENDERS PENCILS: SAM MAXWELL COLORS: FRANK G. & KEN P. LETTERS: J.P. MONEY EDITS: J.F. GABRIE
SHADOWS IN THE DARK
I'M AFRAID NOT PRINCESS!
PLAIN AND SIMPLE, MOBOTROPOLIS WAS NEVER HOME TO OUR KIND!
IT COULD BE, LUPE--
--IF YOU WANT IT SO!
YOU AND THE PACK ARE MORE THAN WELCOME!
PERHAPS--

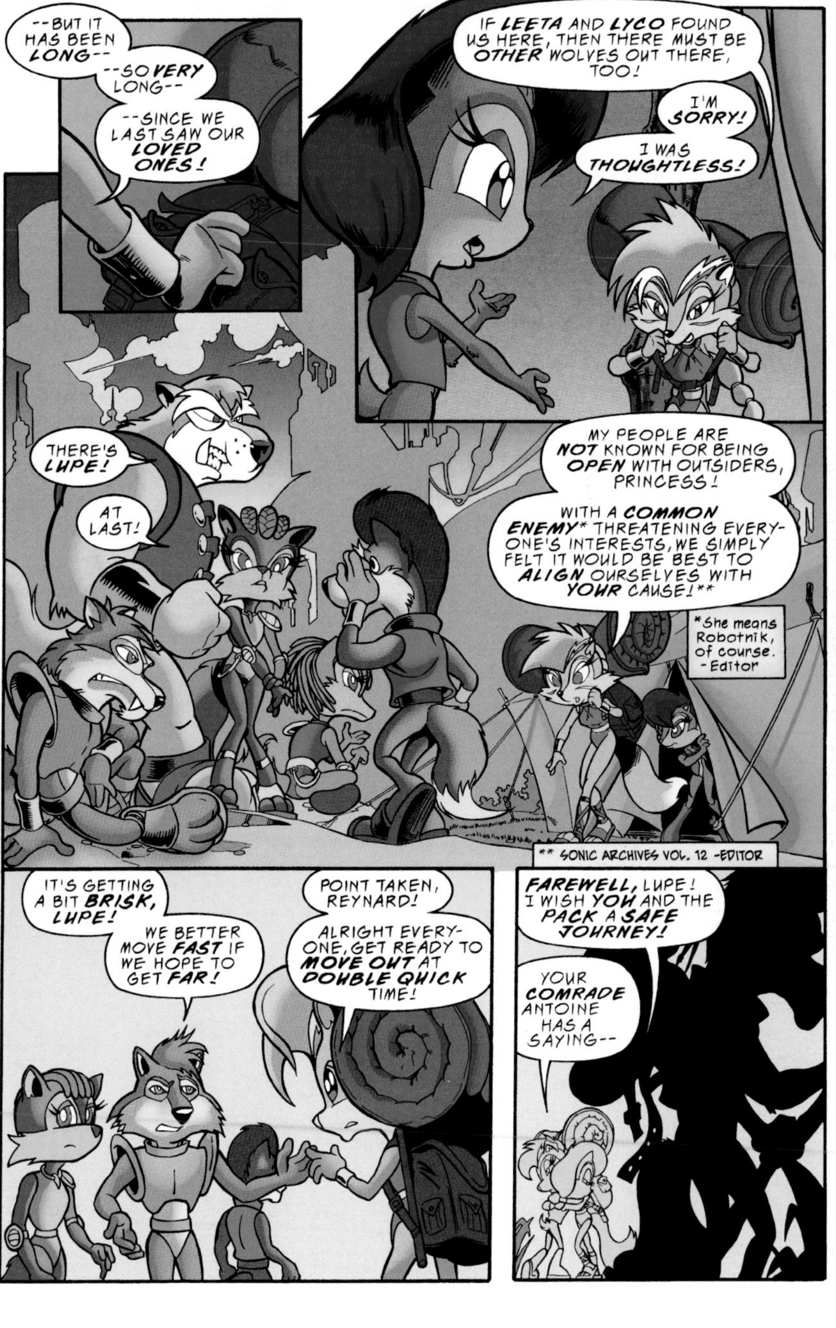
--BUT IT HAS BEEN LONG--
--SO VERY LONG--
--SINCE WE LAST SAW OUR LOVED ONES!
IF LEETA AND LYCO FOUND US HERE, THEN THERE MUST BE OTHER WOLVES OUT THERE, TOO!
I'M SORRY!
I WAS THOUGHTLESS!
THERE'S LUPE!
AT LAST!
MY PEOPLE ARE NOT KNOWN FOR BEING OPEN WITH OUTSIDERS, PRINCESS!
WITH A COMMON ENEMY* THREATENING EVERY-ONE'S INTERESTS, WE SIMPLY FELT IT WOULD BE BEST TO ALIGN OURSELVES WITH YOUR CAUSE!**
*She means Robotnik, of course. -Editor
** SONIC ARCHIVES VOL. 12 -EDITOR
IT'S GETTING A BIT BRISK, LUPE!
WE BETTER MOVE FAST IF WE HOPE TO GET FAR!
POINT TAKEN, REYNARD!
ALRIGHT EVERY-ONE, GET READY TO MOVE OUT AT DOUBLE QUICK TIME!
FAREWELL, LUPE! I WISH YOU AND THE PACK A SAFE JOURNEY!
YOUR COMRADE ANTOINE HAS A SAYING--

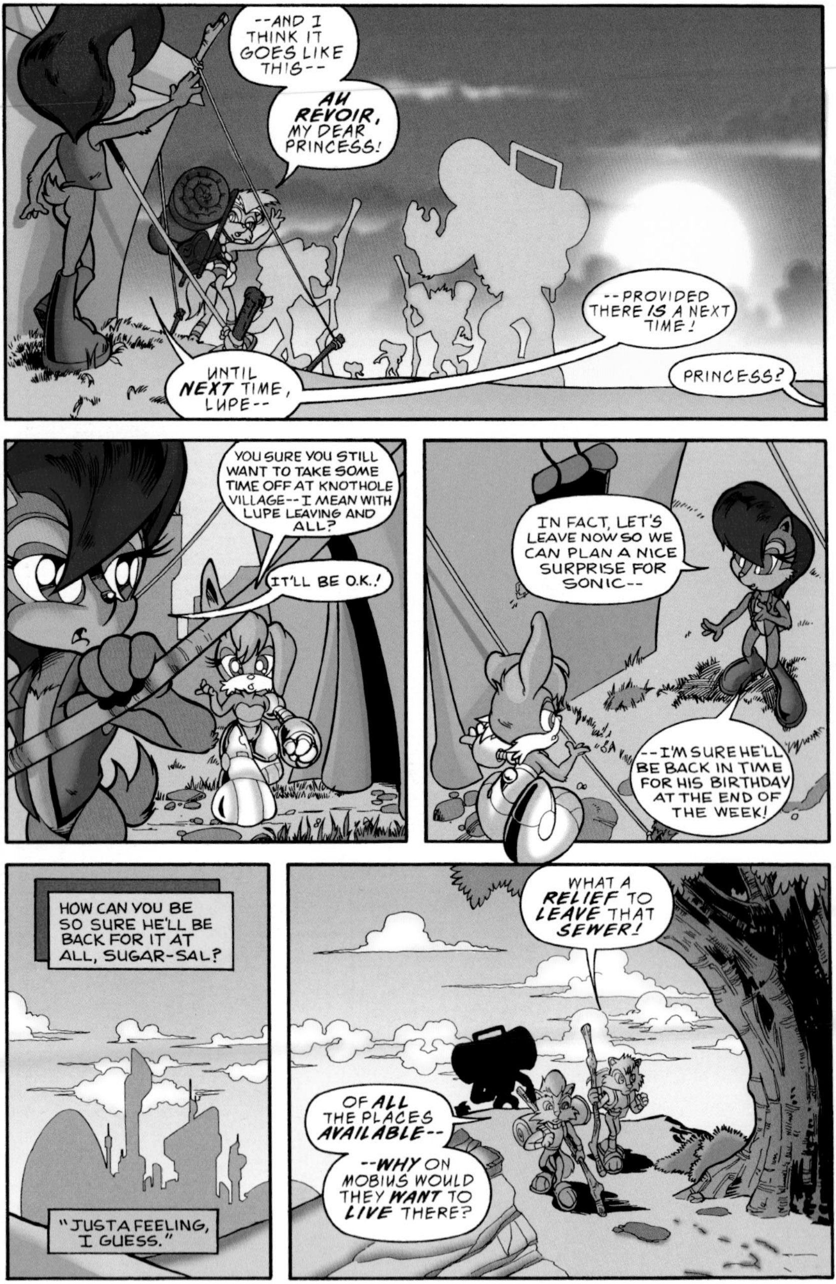
--AND I THINK IT GOES LIKE THIS--
AU REVOIR, MY DEAR PRINCESS!
UNTIL NEXT TIME, LUPE--
--PROVIDED THERE IS A NEXT TIME!
PRINCESS?
YOU SURE YOU STILL WANT TO TAKE SOME TIME OFF AT KNOTHOLE VILLAGE--I MEAN WITH LUPE LEAVING AND ALL?
IT'LL BE O.K.!
IN FACT, LET'S LEAVE NOW SO WE CAN PLAN A NICE SURPRISE FOR SONIC--
--I'M SURE HE'LL BE BACK IN TIME FOR HIS BIRTHDAY AT THE END OF THE WEEK!
HOW CAN YOU BE SO SURE HE'LL BE BACK FOR IT AT ALL, SUGAR-SAL?
"JUST A FEELING, I GUESS."
WHAT A RELIEF TO LEAVE THAT SEWER!
OF ALL THE PLACES AVAILABLE--
--WHY ON MOBIUS WOULD THEY WANT TO LIVE THERE?

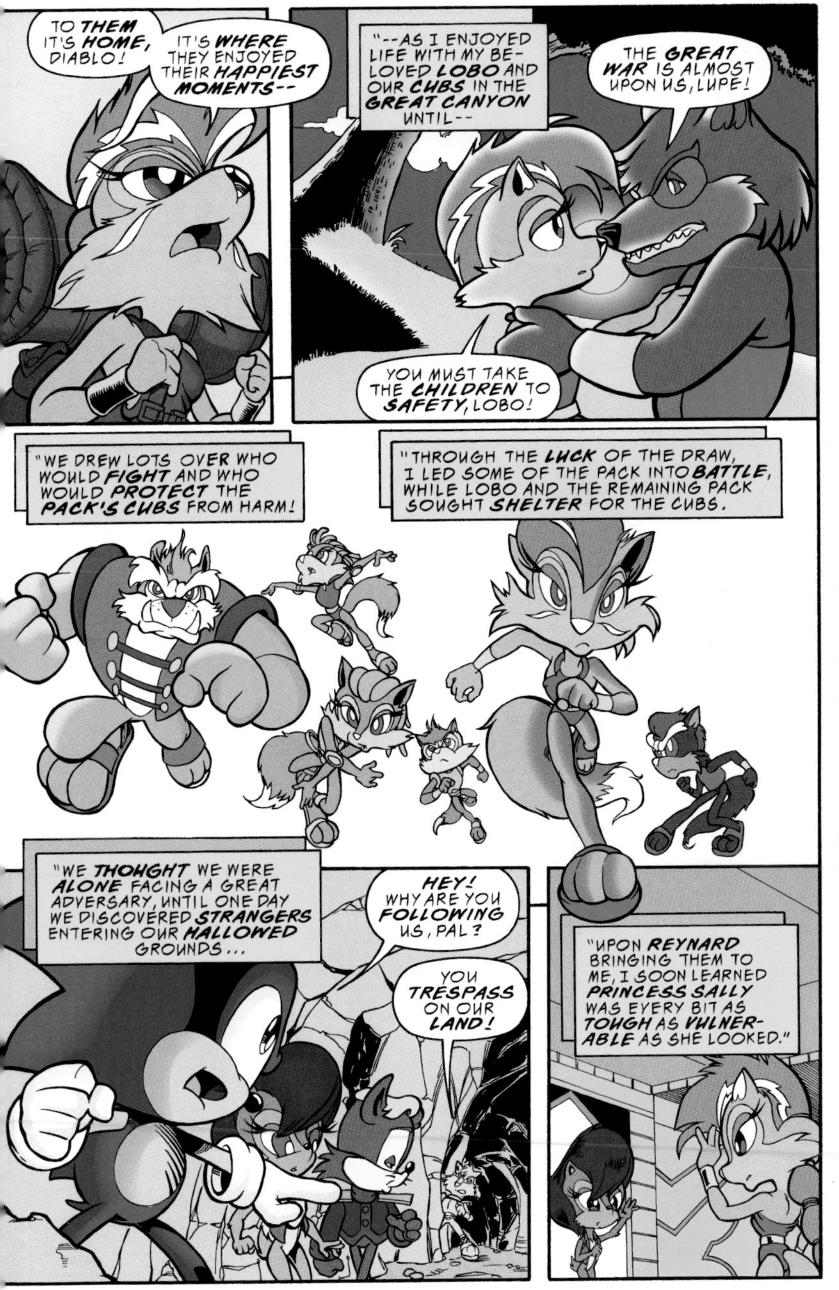
TO THEM IT'S HOME, DIABLO!
IT'S WHERE THEY ENJOYED THEIR HAPPIEST MOMENTS--
"--AS I ENJOYED LIFE WITH MY BE-LOVED LOBO AND OUR CUBS IN THE GREAT CANYON UNTIL--
THE GREAT WAR IS ALMOST UPON US, LUPE!
YOU MUST TAKE THE CHILDREN TO SAFETY, LOBO!
"WE DREW LOTS OVER WHO WOULD FIGHT AND WHO WOULD PROTECT THE PACK'S CUBS FROM HARM!
"THROUGH THE LUCK OF THE DRAW, I LED SOME OF THE PACK INTO BATTLE, WHILE LOBO AND THE REMAINING PACK SOUGHT SHELTER FOR THE CUBS.
"WE THOUGHT WE WERE ALONE FACING A GREAT ADVERSARY, UNTIL ONE DAY WE DISCOVERED STRANGERS ENTERING OUR HALLOWED GROUNDS...
HEY! WHY ARE YOU FOLLOWING US, PAL?
YOU TRESPASS ON OUR LAND!
"UPON REYNARD BRINGING THEM TO ME, I SOON LEARNED PRINCESS SALLY WAS EVERY BIT AS TOUGH AS VULNER-ABLE AS SHE LOOKED."

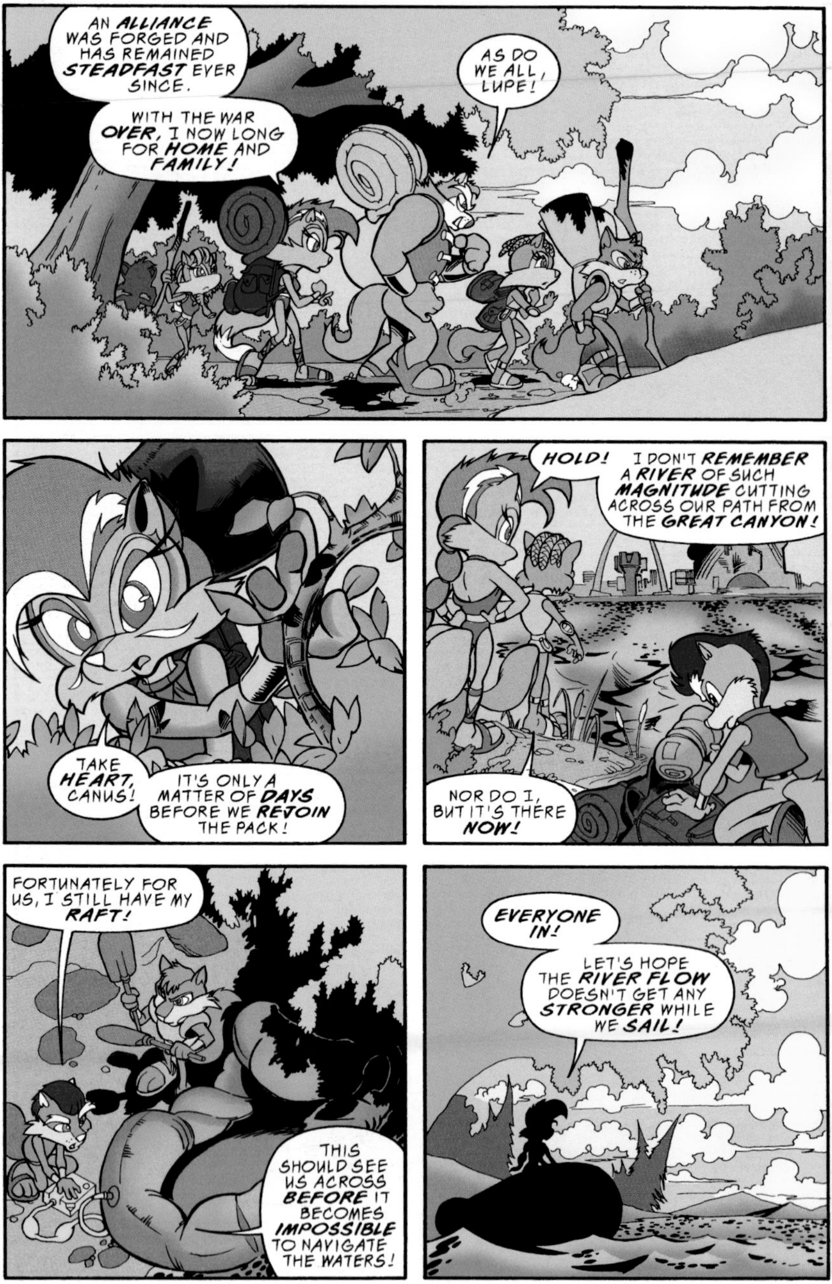

AN ALLIANCE WAS FORGED AND HAS REMAINED STEADFAST EVER SINCE.
WITH THE WAR OVER, I NOW LONG FOR HOME AND FAMILY!
AS DO WE ALL, LUPE!
TAKE HEART, CANUS!
IT'S ONLY A MATTER OF DAYS BEFORE WE REJOIN THE PACK!
HOLD! I DON'T REMEMBER A RIVER OF SUCH MAGNITUDE CUTTING ACROSS OUR PATH FROM THE GREAT CANYON!
NOR DO I, BUT IT'S THERE NOW!
FORTUNATELY FOR US, I STILL HAVE MY RAFT!
THIS SHOULD SEE US ACROSS BEFORE IT BECOMES IMPOSSIBLE TO NAVIGATE THE WATERS!
EVERYONE IN!
LET'S HOPE THE RIVER FLOW DOESN'T GET ANY STRONGER WHILE WE SAIL!

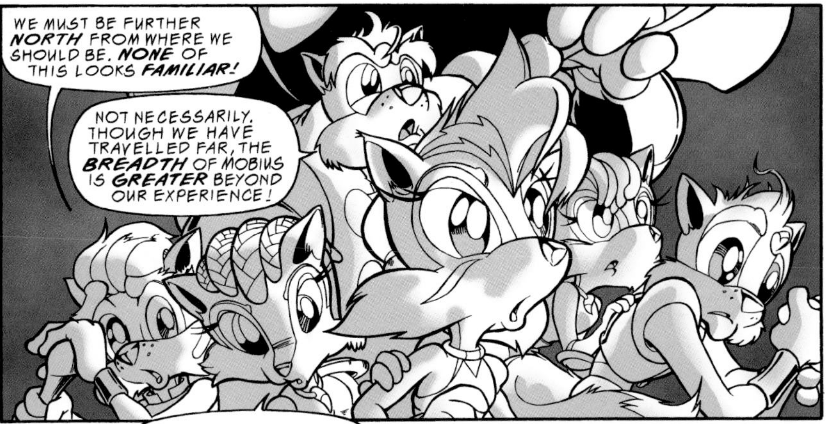
WE MUST BE FURTHER NORTH FROM WHERE WE SHOULD BE. NONE OF THIS LOOKS FAMILIAR!
NOT NECESSARILY. THOUGH WE HAVE TRAVELLED FAR, THE BREADTH OF MOBIUS IS GREATER BEYOND OUR EXPERIENCE!

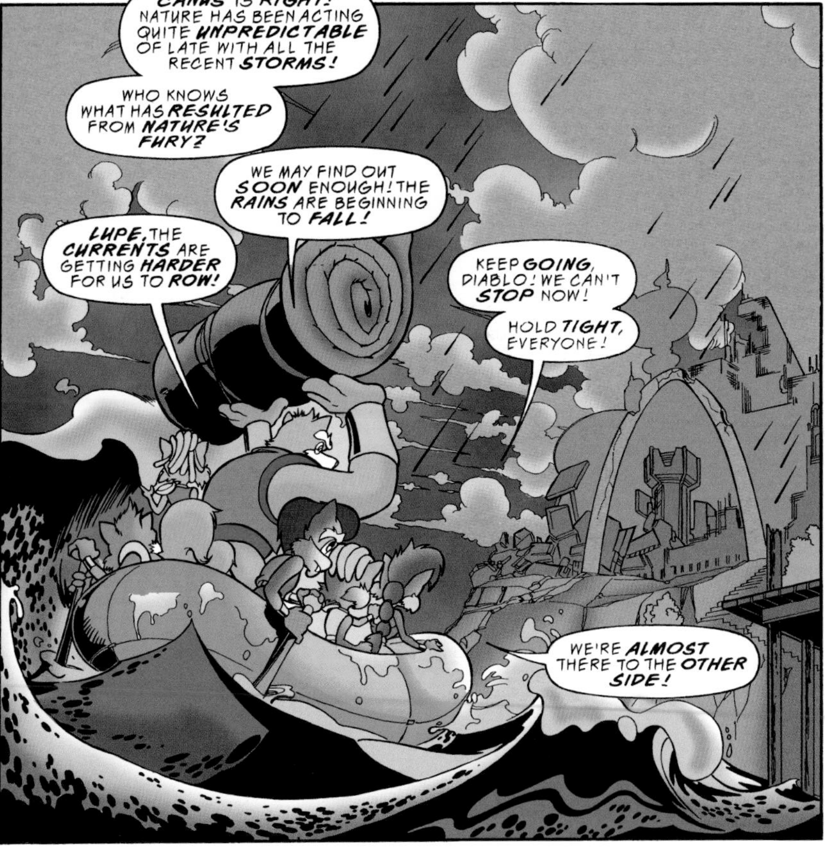
CANUS IS RIGHT! NATURE HAS BEEN ACTING QUITE UNPREDICTABLE OF LATE WITH ALL THE RECENT STORMS!
WHO KNOWS WHAT HAS RESULTED FROM NATURE'S FURY?
WE MAY FIND OUT SOON ENOUGH! THE RAINS ARE BEGINNING TO FALL!
LUPE, THE CURRENTS ARE GETTING HARDER FOR US TO ROW!
KEEP GOING, DIABLO! WE CAN'T STOP NOW!
HOLD TIGHT, EVERYONE!
WE'RE ALMOST THERE TO THE OTHER SIDE!

To be continued

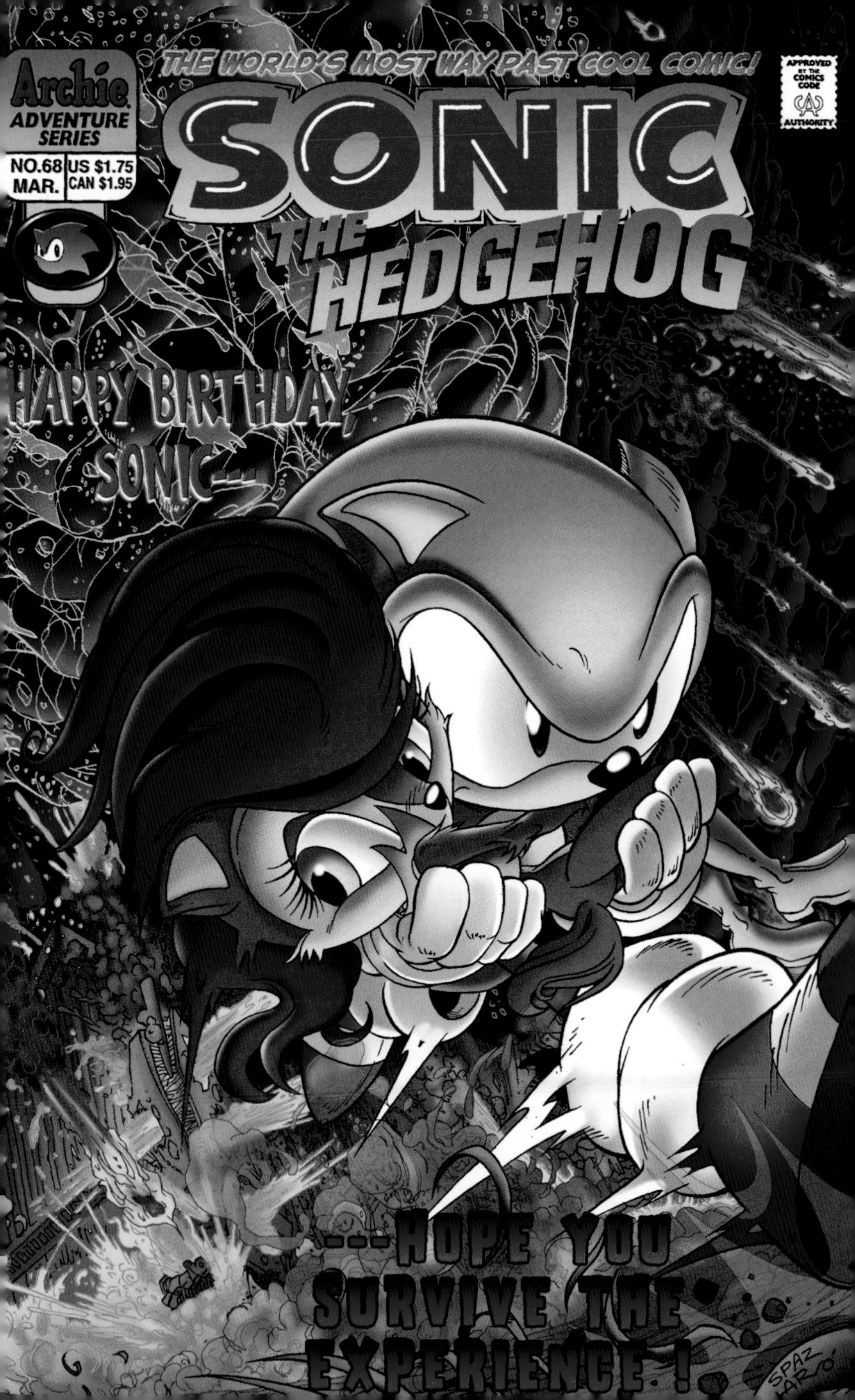
Archie
ADVENTURE SERIES
NO.68 MAR.
US $1.75
CAN $1.95
THE WORLD'S MOST WAY PAST COOL COMIC!
APPROVED BY THE COMICS CODE AUTHORITY
SONIC THE HEDGEHOG
HAPPY BIRTHDAY, SONIC...
...HOPE YOU SURVIVE THE EXPERIENCE!

HE PLANET MOBIUS WAS ONCE A VIRTUAL PARADISE UNTIL IT WAS CONQUERED BY THE EVIL DOCTOR ROBOTNIK! IS TECHNOLOGICAL TYRANNY WOULD HAVE CONTINUED IF NOT FOR A HEROIC GROUP OF FREEDOM FIGHTERS WHO ANDED TOGETHER AND RESTORED ORDER TO THE KINGDOM OF ACORN! THE BRAVEST AMONG THEM IS A BLUE STREAK LLED WITH THE MOST ATTITUDE GOING AROUND - - AND, WITHOUT A DOUBT, HE IS THE FASTEST THING ALIVE!

RCHIE COMICS AND SEGA PRESENT... SONIC THE HEDGEHOG!

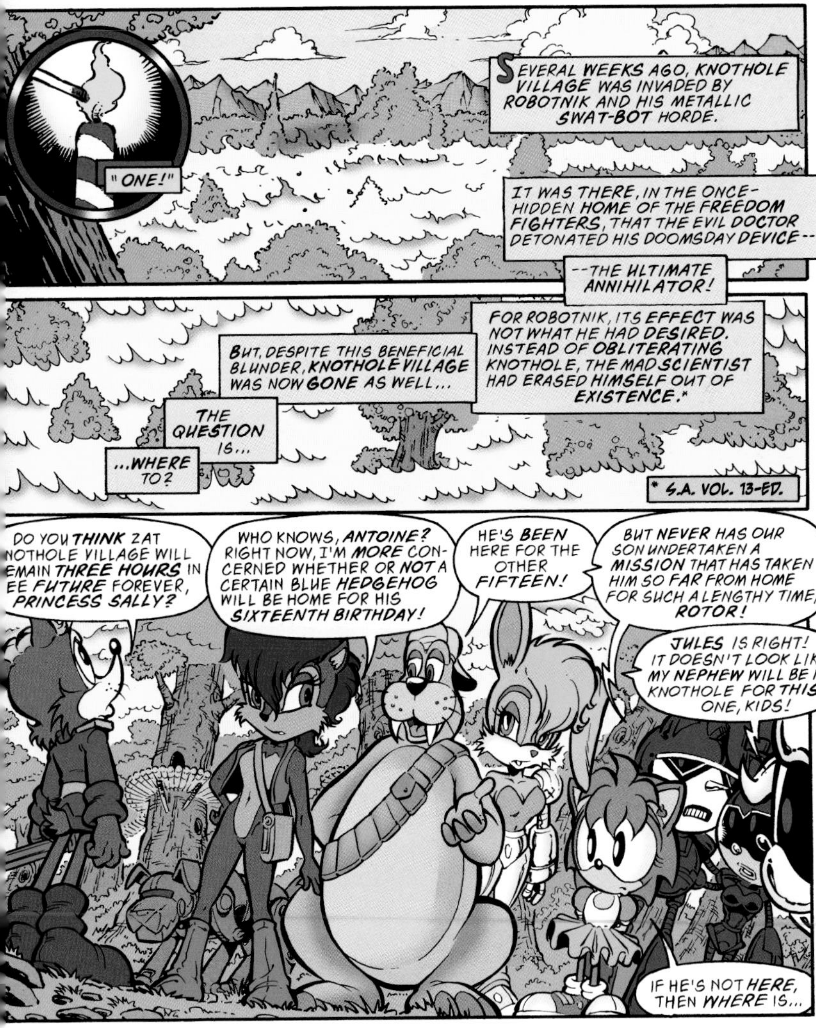

SEVERAL WEEKS AGO, KNOTHOLE VILLAGE WAS INVADED BY ROBOTNIK AND HIS METALLIC SWAT-BOT HORDE.
"ONE!"
IT WAS THERE, IN THE ONCE-HIDDEN HOME OF THE FREEDOM FIGHTERS, THAT THE EVIL DOCTOR DETONATED HIS DOOMSDAY DEVICE--
--THE ULTIMATE ANNIHILATOR!
FOR ROBOTNIK, ITS EFFECT WAS NOT WHAT HE HAD DESIRED. INSTEAD OF OBLITERATING KNOTHOLE, THE MAD SCIENTIST HAD ERASED HIMSELF OUT OF EXISTENCE.*
BUT, DESPITE THIS BENEFICIAL BLUNDER, KNOTHOLE VILLAGE WAS NOW GONE AS WELL...
THE QUESTION IS...
...WHERE TO?
* S.A. VOL. 13-ED.
DO YOU THINK ZAT NOTHOLE VILLAGE WILL EMAIN THREE HOURS IN EE FUTURE FOREVER, PRINCESS SALLY?
WHO KNOWS, ANTOINE? RIGHT NOW, I'M MORE CONCERNED WHETHER OR NOT A CERTAIN BLUE HEDGEHOG WILL BE HOME FOR HIS SIXTEENTH BIRTHDAY!
HE'S BEEN HERE FOR THE OTHER FIFTEEN!
BUT NEVER HAS OUR SON UNDERTAKEN A MISSION THAT HAS TAKEN HIM SO FAR FROM HOME FOR SUCH A LENGTHY TIME, ROTOR!
JULES IS RIGHT! IT DOESN'T LOOK LIKE MY NEPHEW WILL BE IN KNOTHOLE FOR THIS ONE, KIDS!
IF HE'S NOT HERE, THEN WHERE IS...

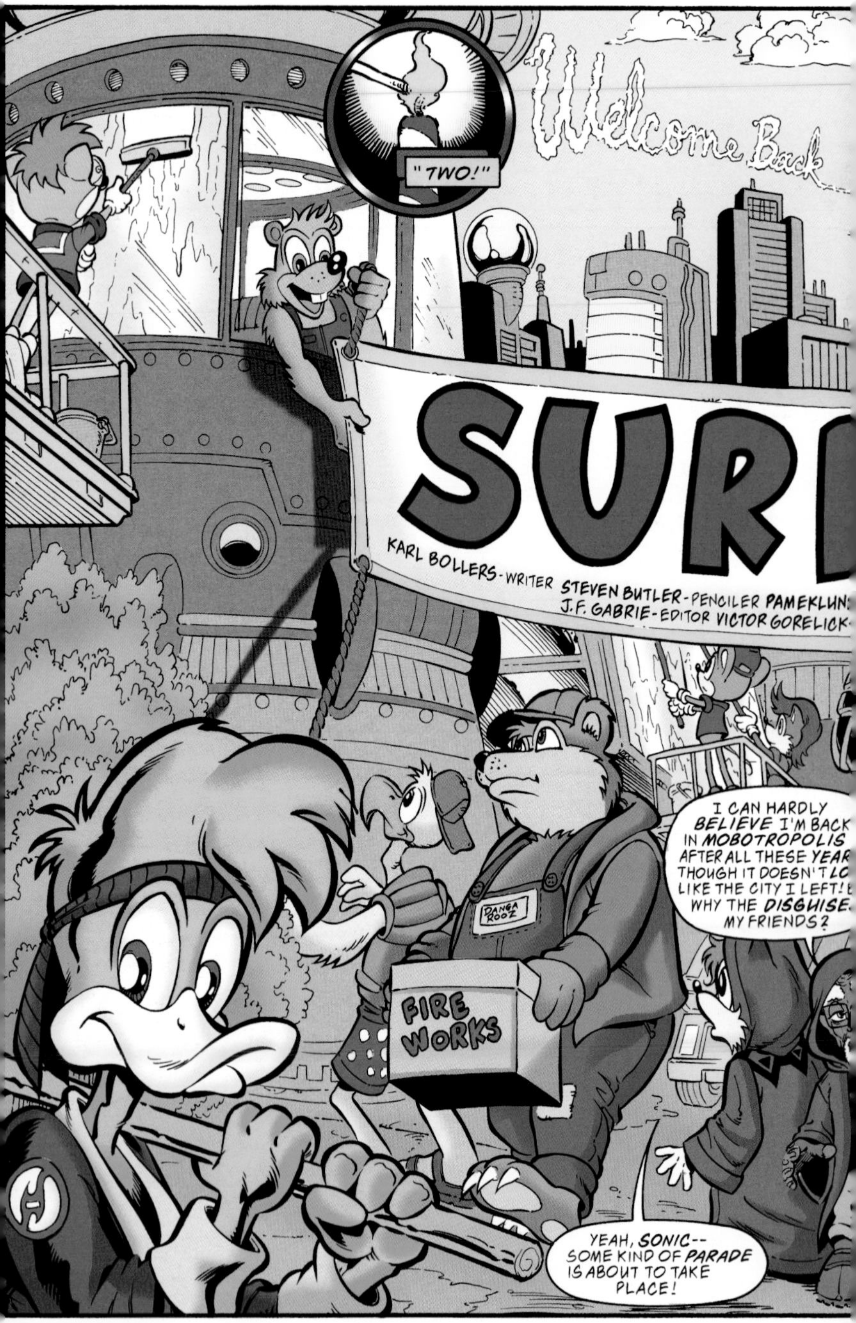
"TWO!"
Welcome Back
SUR
KARL BOLLERS-WRITER STEVEN BUTLER-PENCILER PAMEKLUN
J.F. GABRIE-EDITOR VICTOR GORELICK-
I CAN HARDLY BELIEVE I'M BACK IN MOBOTROPOLIS AFTER ALL THESE YEAR THOUGH IT DOESN'T LO LIKE THE CITY I LEFT! WHY THE DISGUISE MY FRIENDS?
DANGA ROOZ
FIRE WORKS
YEAH, SONIC-- SOME KIND OF PARADE IS ABOUT TO TAKE PLACE!

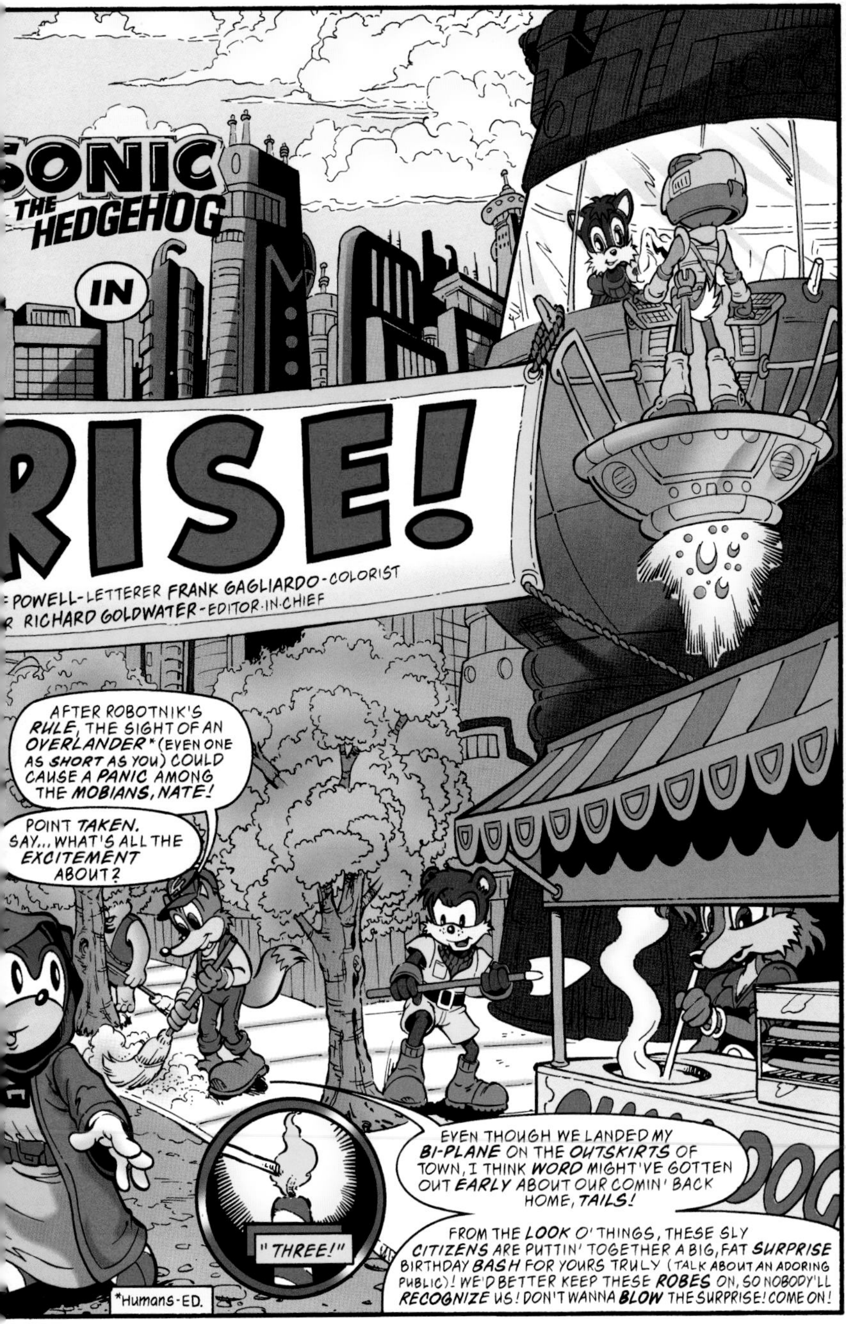
SONIC THE HEDGEHOG
IN
RISE!
F POWELL-LETTERER FRANK GAGLIARDO-COLORIST
R RICHARD GOLDWATER-EDITOR-IN-CHIEF
AFTER ROBOTNIK'S RULE, THE SIGHT OF AN OVERLANDER* (EVEN ONE AS SHORT AS YOU) COULD CAUSE A PANIC AMONG THE MOBIANS, NATE!
POINT TAKEN. SAY... WHAT'S ALL THE EXCITEMENT ABOUT?
"THREE!"
EVEN THOUGH WE LANDED MY BI-PLANE ON THE OUTSKIRTS OF TOWN, I THINK WORD MIGHT'VE GOTTEN OUT EARLY ABOUT OUR COMIN' BACK HOME, TAILS!
FROM THE LOOK O' THINGS, THESE SLY CITIZENS ARE PUTTIN' TOGETHER A BIG, FAT SURPRISE BIRTHDAY BASH FOR YOURS TRULY (TALK ABOUT AN ADORING PUBLIC)! WE'D BETTER KEEP THESE ROBES ON, SO NOBODY'LL RECOGNIZE US! DON'T WANNA BLOW THE SURPRISE! COME ON!
*Humans-ED.

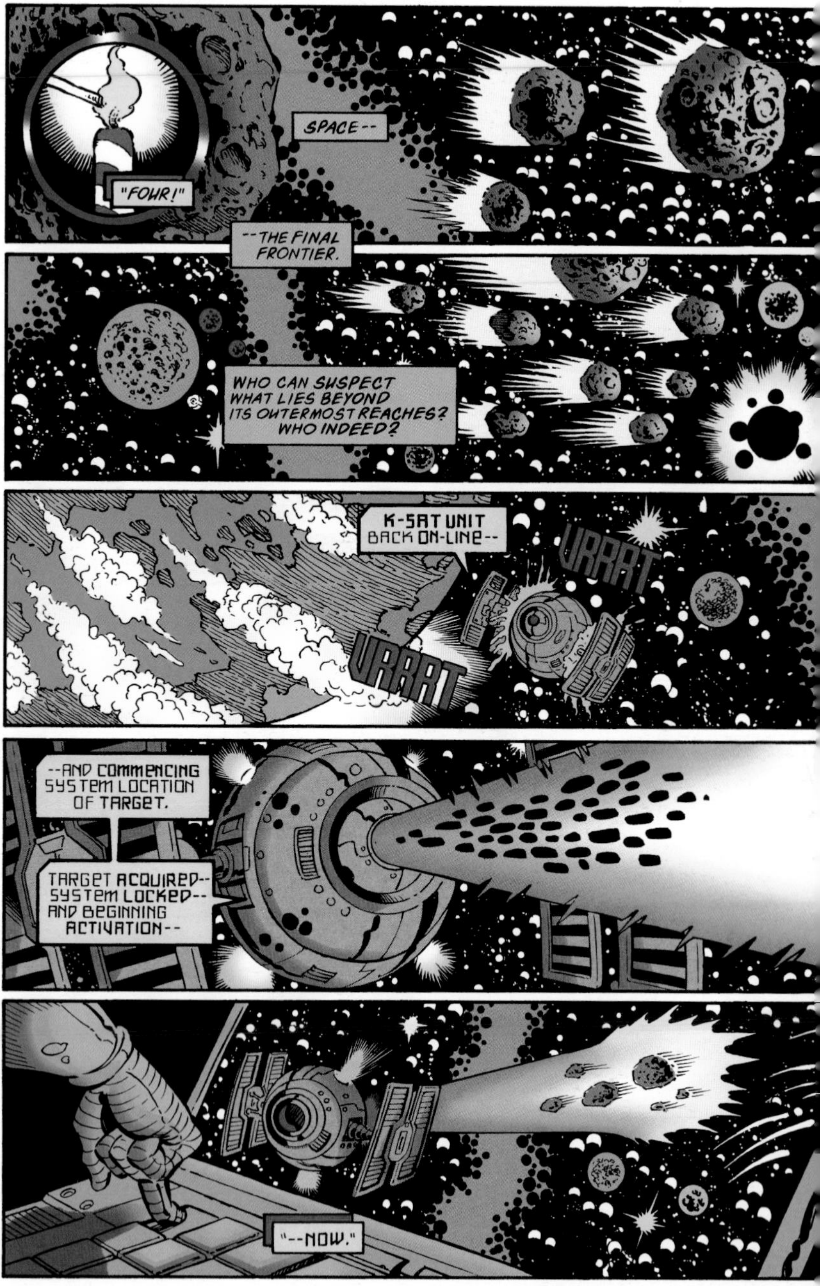
"FOUR!"
SPACE--
--THE FINAL FRONTIER.
WHO CAN SUSPECT WHAT LIES BEYOND ITS OUTERMOST REACHES? WHO INDEED?
K-SAT UNIT BACK ON-LINE--
VRRRT
VRRRT
--AND COMMENCING SYSTEM LOCATION OF TARGET.
TARGET ACQUIRED-- SYSTEM LOCKED-- AND BEGINNING ACTIVATION--
"--NOW."

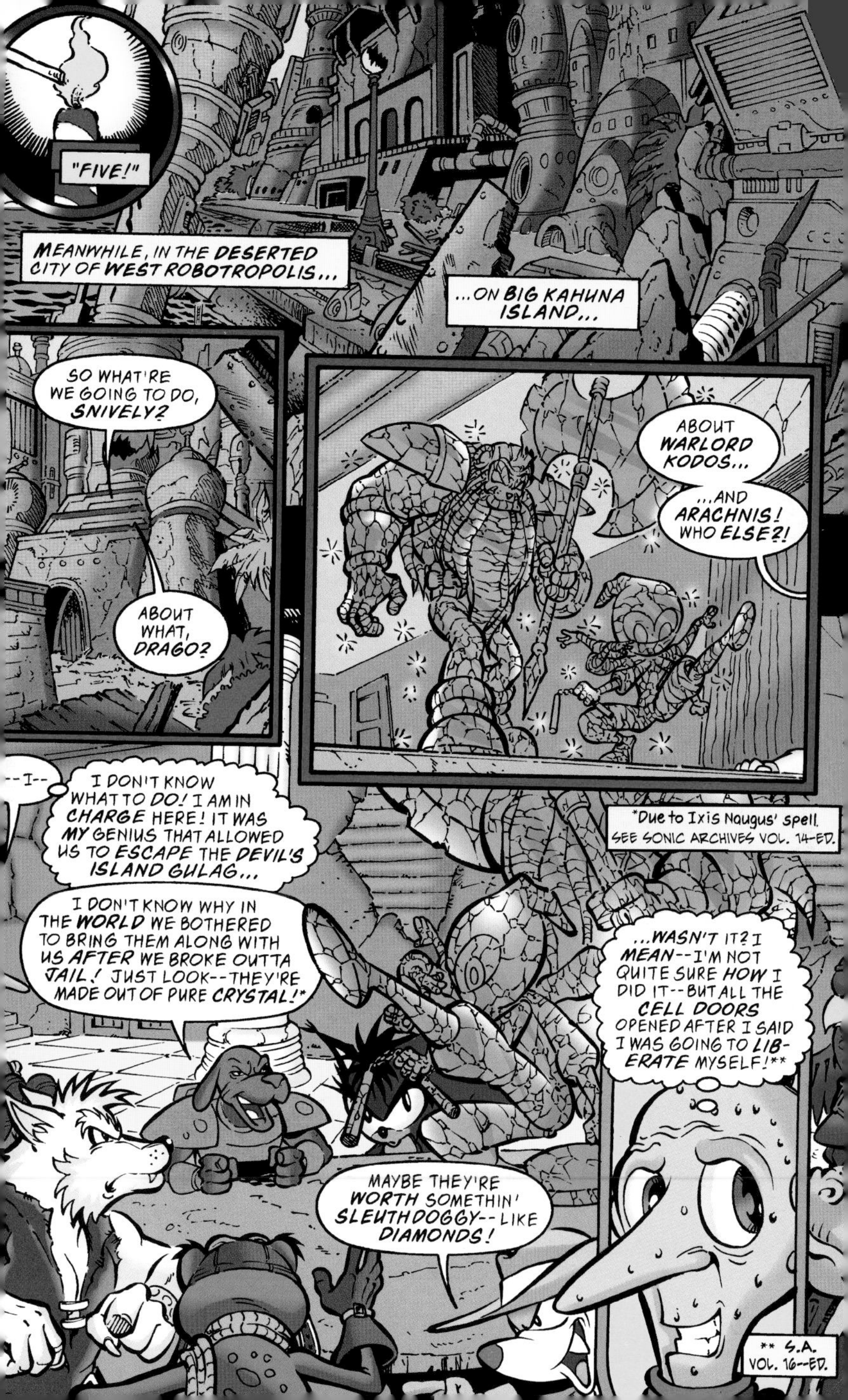
"FIVE!"
MEANWHILE, IN THE DESERTED CITY OF WEST ROBOTROPOLIS...
...ON BIG KAHUNA ISLAND...
SO WHAT'RE WE GOING TO DO, SNIVELY?
ABOUT WHAT, DRAGO?
ABOUT WARLORD KODOS...
...AND ARACHNIS! WHO ELSE?!
--I--
I DON'T KNOW WHAT TO DO! I AM IN CHARGE HERE! IT WAS MY GENIUS THAT ALLOWED US TO ESCAPE THE DEVIL'S ISLAND GULAG...
*Due to Ixis Naugus' spell. SEE SONIC ARCHIVES VOL. 14-ED.
I DON'T KNOW WHY IN THE WORLD WE BOTHERED TO BRING THEM ALONG WITH US AFTER WE BROKE OUTTA JAIL! JUST LOOK--THEY'RE MADE OUT OF PURE CRYSTAL!*
...WASN'T IT? I MEAN--I'M NOT QUITE SURE HOW I DID IT--BUT ALL THE CELL DOORS OPENED AFTER I SAID I WAS GOING TO LIBERATE MYSELF!**
MAYBE THEY'RE WORTH SOMETHIN' SLEUTHDOGGY--LIKE DIAMONDS!
** S.A. VOL. 16--ED.

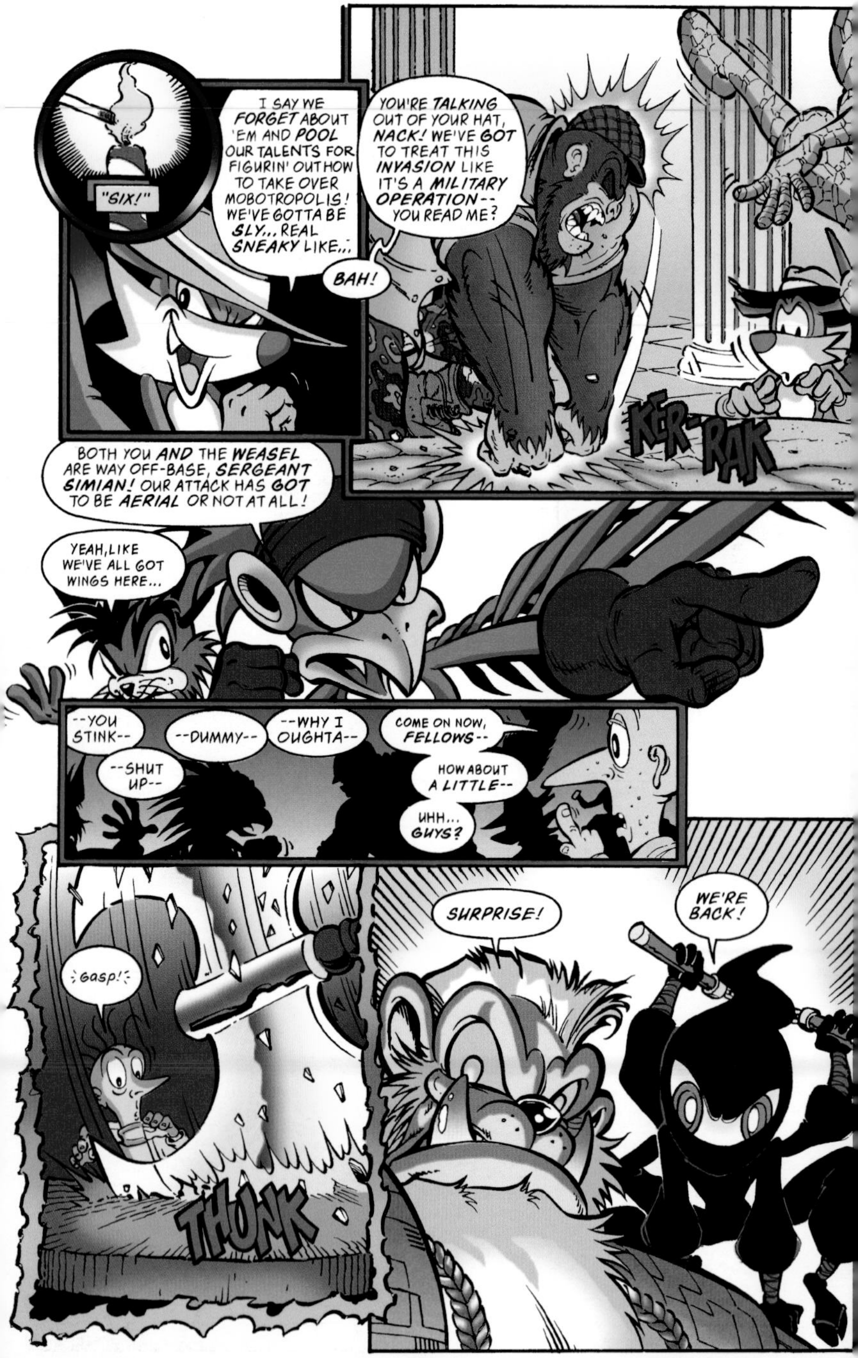
"SIX!"
I SAY WE FORGET ABOUT 'EM AND POOL OUR TALENTS FOR FIGURIN' OUT HOW TO TAKE OVER MOBOTROPOLIS! WE'VE GOTTA BE SLY... REAL SNEAKY LIKE...
YOU'RE TALKING OUT OF YOUR HAT, NACK! WE'VE GOT TO TREAT THIS INVASION LIKE IT'S A MILITARY OPERATION-- YOU READ ME?
BAH!
KER-RAK
BOTH YOU AND THE WEASEL ARE WAY OFF-BASE, SERGEANT SIMIAN! OUR ATTACK HAS GOT TO BE AERIAL OR NOT AT ALL!
YEAH, LIKE WE'VE ALL GOT WINGS HERE...
--YOU STINK--
--SHUT UP--
--DUMMY--
--WHY I OUGHTA--
COME ON NOW, FELLOWS--
HOW ABOUT A LITTLE--
UHH... GUYS?
Gasp!
THUNK
SURPRISE!
WE'RE BACK!

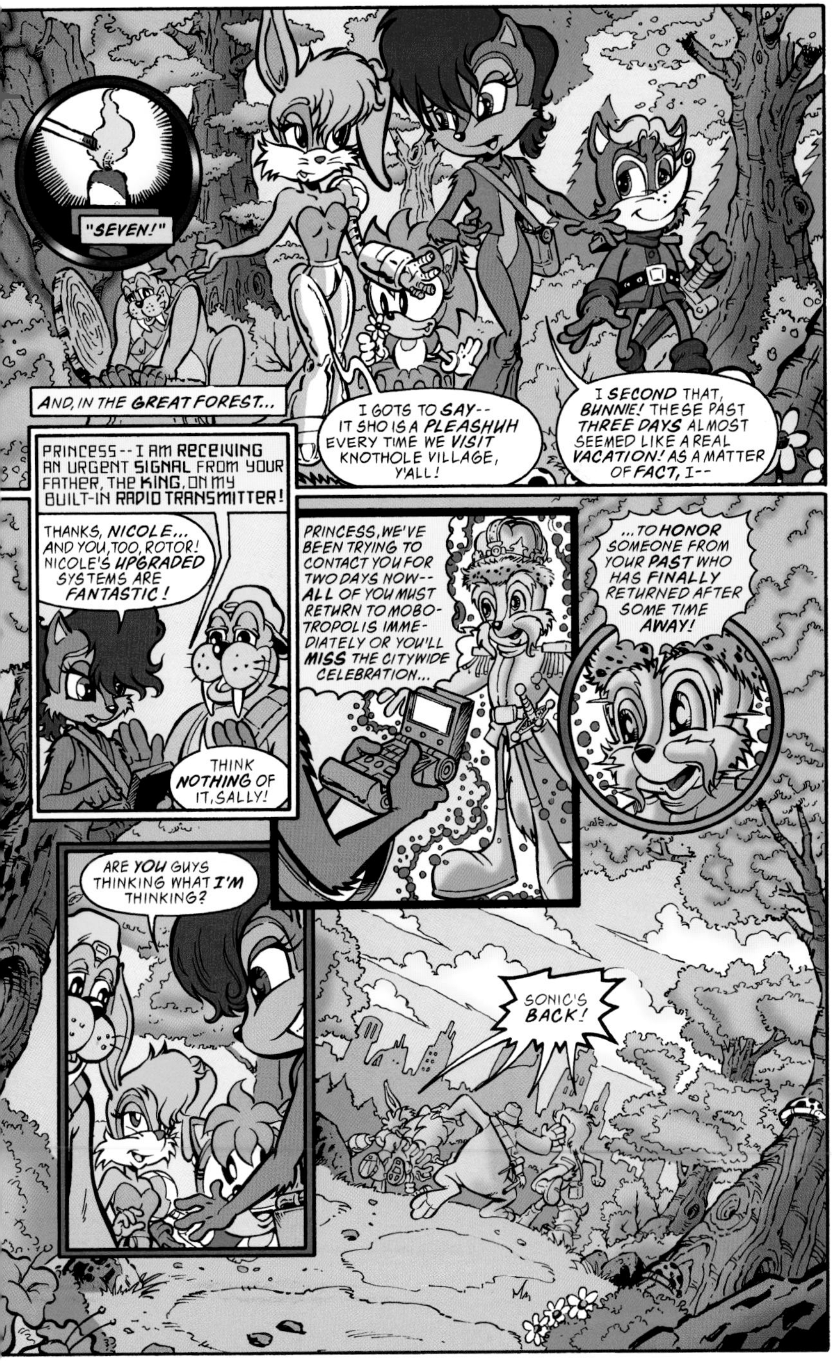
"SEVEN!"
AND, IN THE GREAT FOREST...
I GOTS TO SAY-- IT SHO IS A PLEASHUH EVERY TIME WE VISIT KNOTHOLE VILLAGE, Y'ALL!
I SECOND THAT, BUNNIE! THESE PAST THREE DAYS ALMOST SEEMED LIKE A REAL VACATION! AS A MATTER OF FACT, I--
PRINCESS--I AM RECEIVING AN URGENT SIGNAL FROM YOUR FATHER, THE KING, ON MY BUILT-IN RADIO TRANSMITTER!
THANKS, NICOLE... AND YOU, TOO, ROTOR! NICOLE'S UPGRADED SYSTEMS ARE FANTASTIC!
THINK NOTHING OF IT, SALLY!
PRINCESS, WE'VE BEEN TRYING TO CONTACT YOU FOR TWO DAYS NOW-- ALL OF YOU MUST RETURN TO MOBOTROPOLIS IMMEDIATELY OR YOU'LL MISS THE CITYWIDE CELEBRATION...
...TO HONOR SOMEONE FROM YOUR PAST WHO HAS FINALLY RETURNED AFTER SOME TIME AWAY!
ARE YOU GUYS THINKING WHAT I'M THINKING?
SONIC'S BACK!

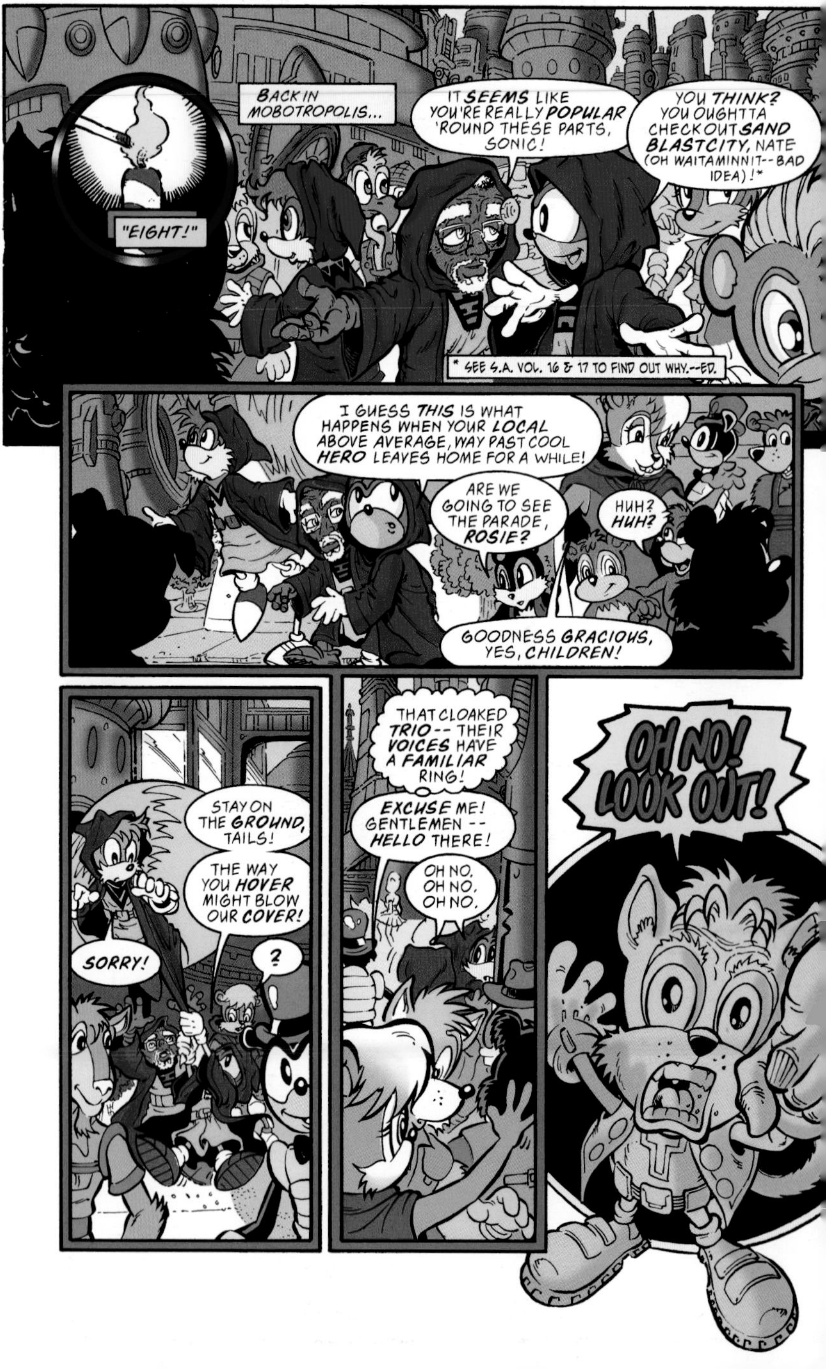
BACK IN MOBOTROPOLIS...
"EIGHT!"
IT SEEMS LIKE YOU'RE REALLY POPULAR 'ROUND THESE PARTS, SONIC!
YOU THINK? YOU OUGHTTA CHECK OUT SAND BLAST CITY, NATE (OH WAITAMINNIT-- BAD IDEA)!*
* SEE S.A. VOL. 16 & 17 TO FIND OUT WHY.--ED.
I GUESS THIS IS WHAT HAPPENS WHEN YOUR LOCAL ABOVE AVERAGE, WAY PAST COOL HERO LEAVES HOME FOR A WHILE!
ARE WE GOING TO SEE THE PARADE, ROSIE?
HUH? HUH?
GOODNESS GRACIOUS, YES, CHILDREN!
STAY ON THE GROUND, TAILS!
THE WAY YOU HOVER MIGHT BLOW OUR COVER!
SORRY!
?
THAT CLOAKED TRIO-- THEIR VOICES HAVE A FAMILIAR RING!
EXCUSE ME! GENTLEMEN -- HELLO THERE!
OH NO, OH NO, OH NO.
OH NO! LOOK OUT!

BONUS PIN-UP

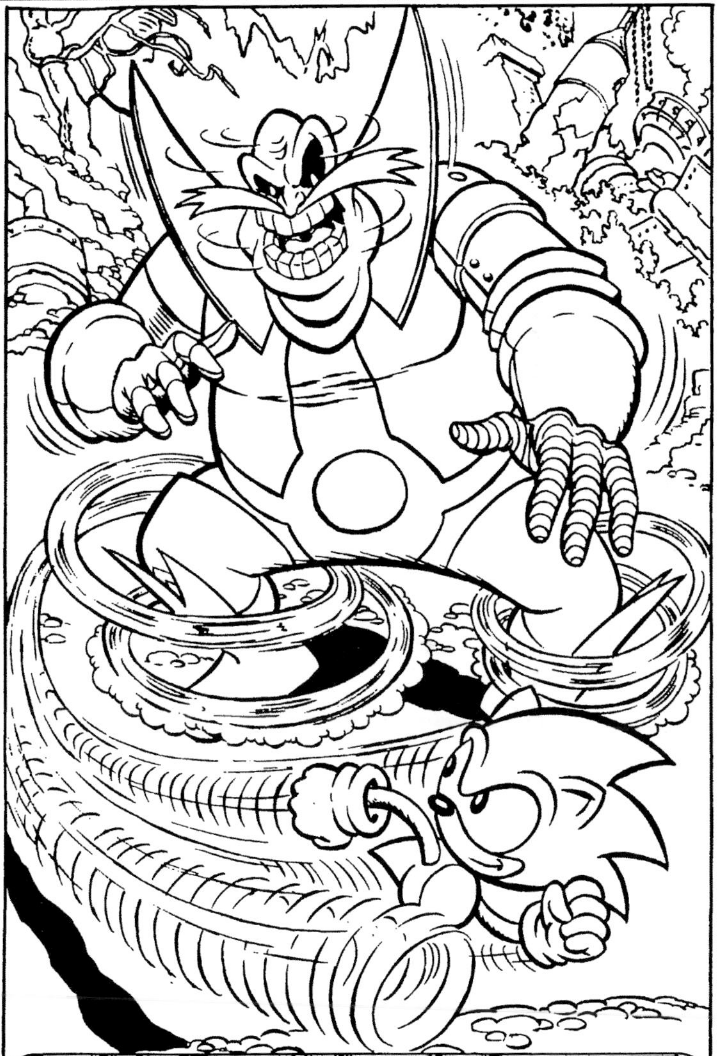

PRO ART BY

FORMER "BRENDA STARR" COMIC STRIP ARTIST

RAMONA FRADON.

COLOR & ENJOY!

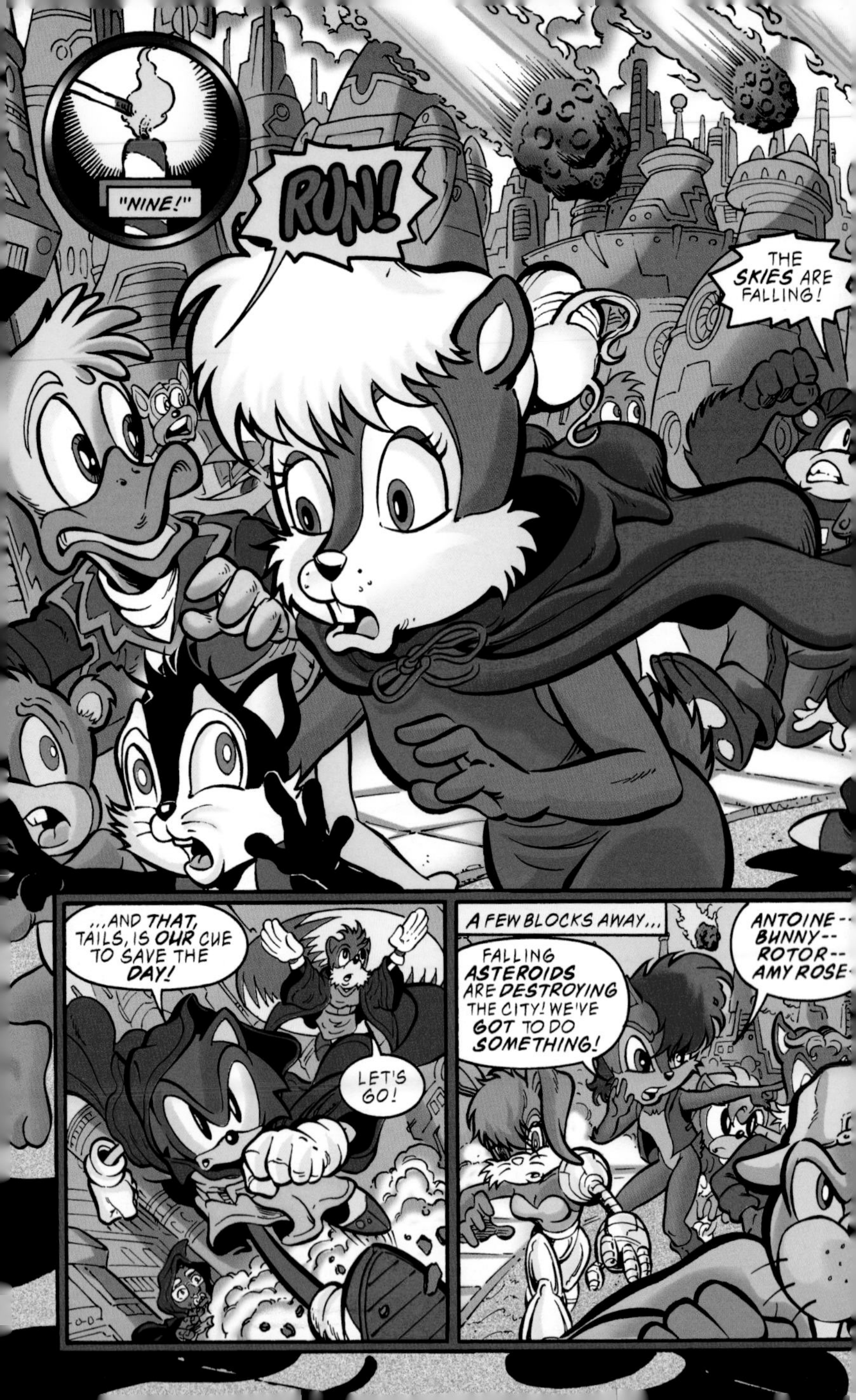
"NINE!"
RUN!
THE SKIES ARE FALLING!
...AND THAT, TAILS, IS OUR CUE TO SAVE THE DAY!
LET'S GO!
A FEW BLOCKS AWAY...
FALLING ASTEROIDS ARE DESTROYING THE CITY! WE'VE GOT TO DO SOMETHING!
ANTOINE-- BUNNY-- ROTOR-- AMY ROSE--

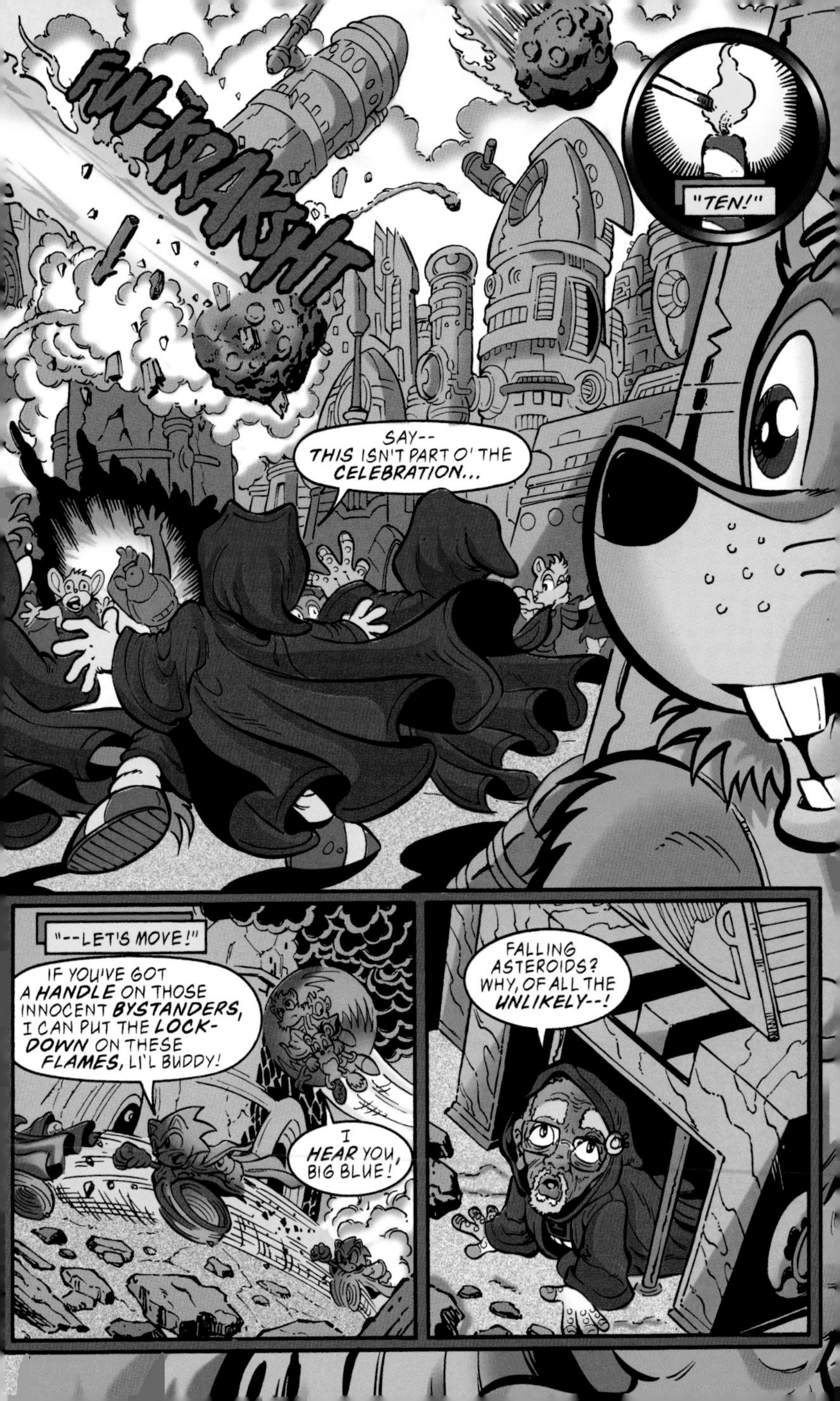
FWI-KRAKSHT!
"TEN!"
SAY-- THIS ISN'T PART O' THE CELEBRATION...
"--LET'S MOVE!"
IF YOU'VE GOT A HANDLE ON THOSE INNOCENT BYSTANDERS, I CAN PUT THE LOCK-DOWN ON THESE FLAMES, LI'L BUDDY!
I HEAR YOU, BIG BLUE!
FALLING ASTEROIDS? WHY, OF ALL THE UNLIKELY--!

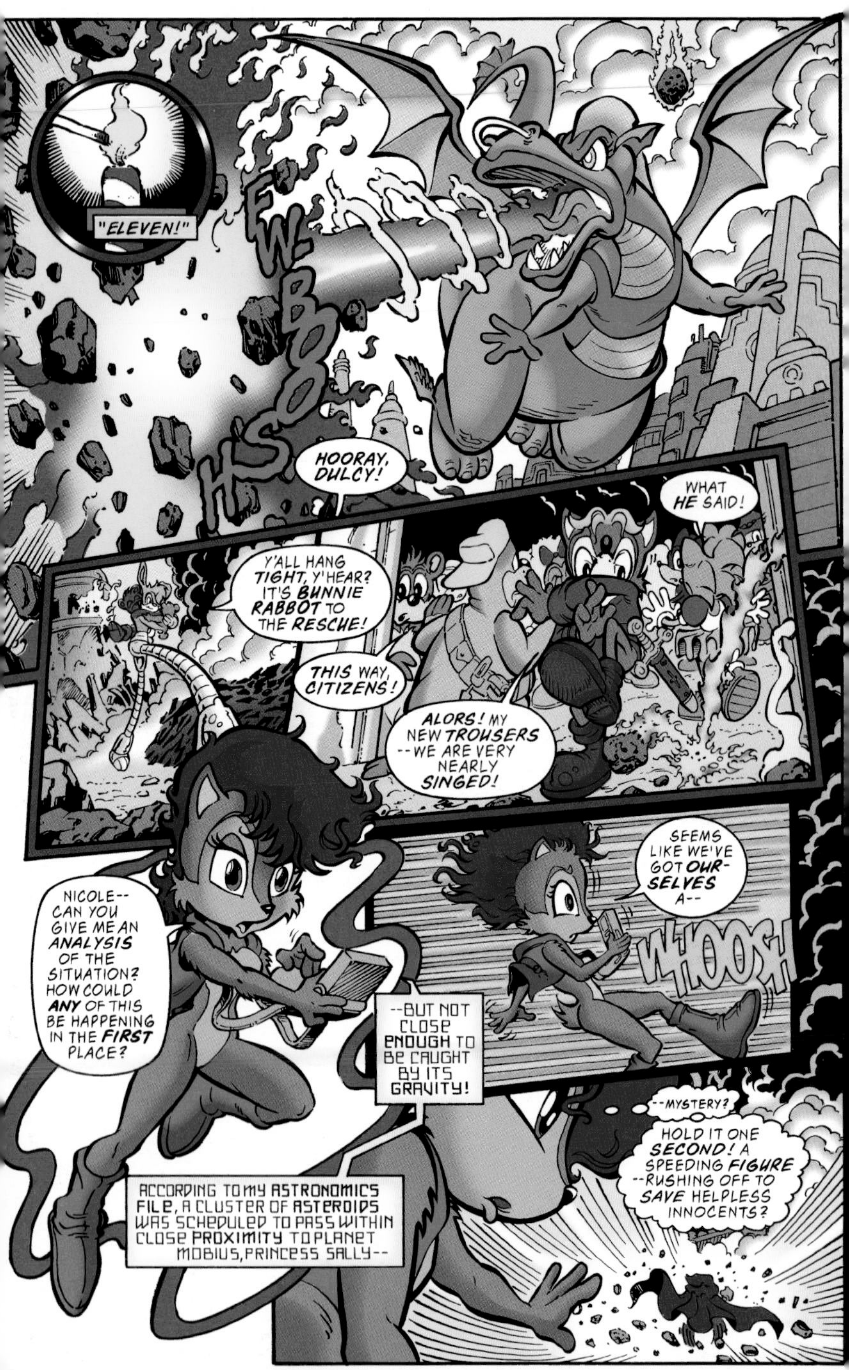
"ELEVEN!"
FWOOOSH
HOORAY, DULCY!
WHAT HE SAID!
Y'ALL HANG TIGHT, Y'HEAR? IT'S BUNNIE RABBOT TO THE RESCUE!
THIS WAY, CITIZENS!
ALORS! MY NEW TROUSERS --WE ARE VERY NEARLY SINGED!
NICOLE-- CAN YOU GIVE ME AN ANALYSIS OF THE SITUATION? HOW COULD ANY OF THIS BE HAPPENING IN THE FIRST PLACE?
ACCORDING TO MY ASTRONOMICS FILE, A CLUSTER OF ASTEROIDS WAS SCHEDULED TO PASS WITHIN CLOSE PROXIMITY TO PLANET MOBIUS, PRINCESS SALLY--
--BUT NOT CLOSE ENOUGH TO BE CAUGHT BY ITS GRAVITY!
SEEMS LIKE WE'VE GOT OURSELVES A--
WHOOSH
--MYSTERY?
HOLD IT ONE SECOND! A SPEEDING FIGURE --RUSHING OFF TO SAVE HELPLESS INNOCENTS?

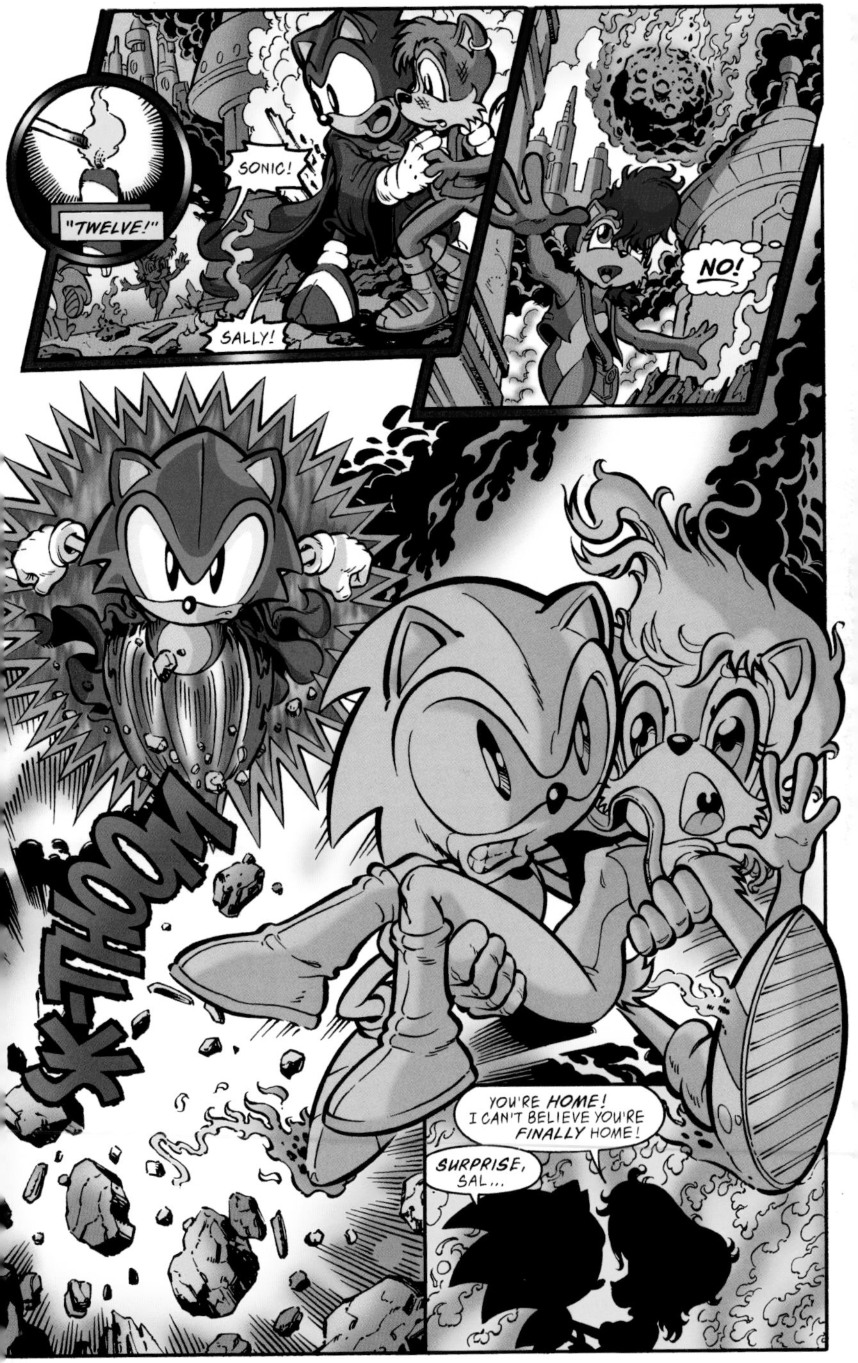
"TWELVE!"
SONIC!
SALLY!
NO!
SK-THOOM!
YOU'RE HOME! I CAN'T BELIEVE YOU'RE FINALLY HOME!
SURPRISE, SAL...

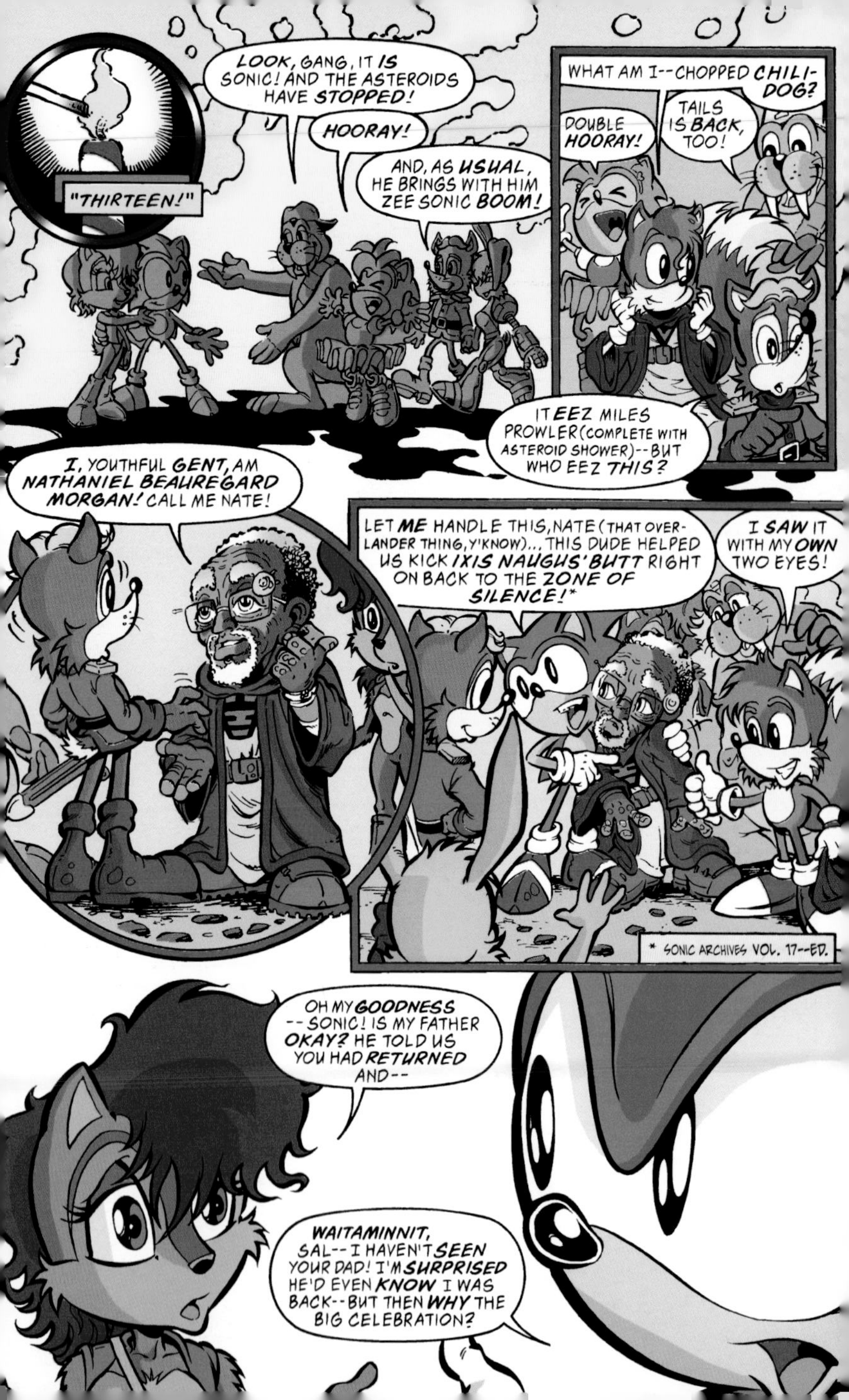

"THIRTEEN!"
LOOK, GANG, IT IS SONIC! AND THE ASTEROIDS HAVE STOPPED!
HOORAY!
AND, AS USUAL, HE BRINGS WITH HIM ZEE SONIC BOOM!
WHAT AM I--CHOPPED CHILI-DOG?
DOUBLE HOORAY!
TAILS IS BACK, TOO!
IT EEZ MILES PROWLER (COMPLETE WITH ASTEROID SHOWER)--BUT WHO EEZ THIS?
I, YOUTHFUL GENT, AM NATHANIEL BEAUREGARD MORGAN! CALL ME NATE!
LET ME HANDLE THIS, NATE (THAT OVER-LANDER THING, Y'KNOW)... THIS DUDE HELPED US KICK IXIS NAUGUS' BUTT RIGHT ON BACK TO THE ZONE OF SILENCE!*
I SAW IT WITH MY OWN TWO EYES!
* SONIC ARCHIVES VOL. 17--ED.
OH MY GOODNESS --SONIC! IS MY FATHER OKAY? HE TOLD US YOU HAD RETURNED AND--
WAITAMINNIT, SAL--I HAVEN'T SEEN YOUR DAD! I'M SURPRISED HE'D EVEN KNOW I WAS BACK--BUT THEN WHY THE BIG CELEBRATION?

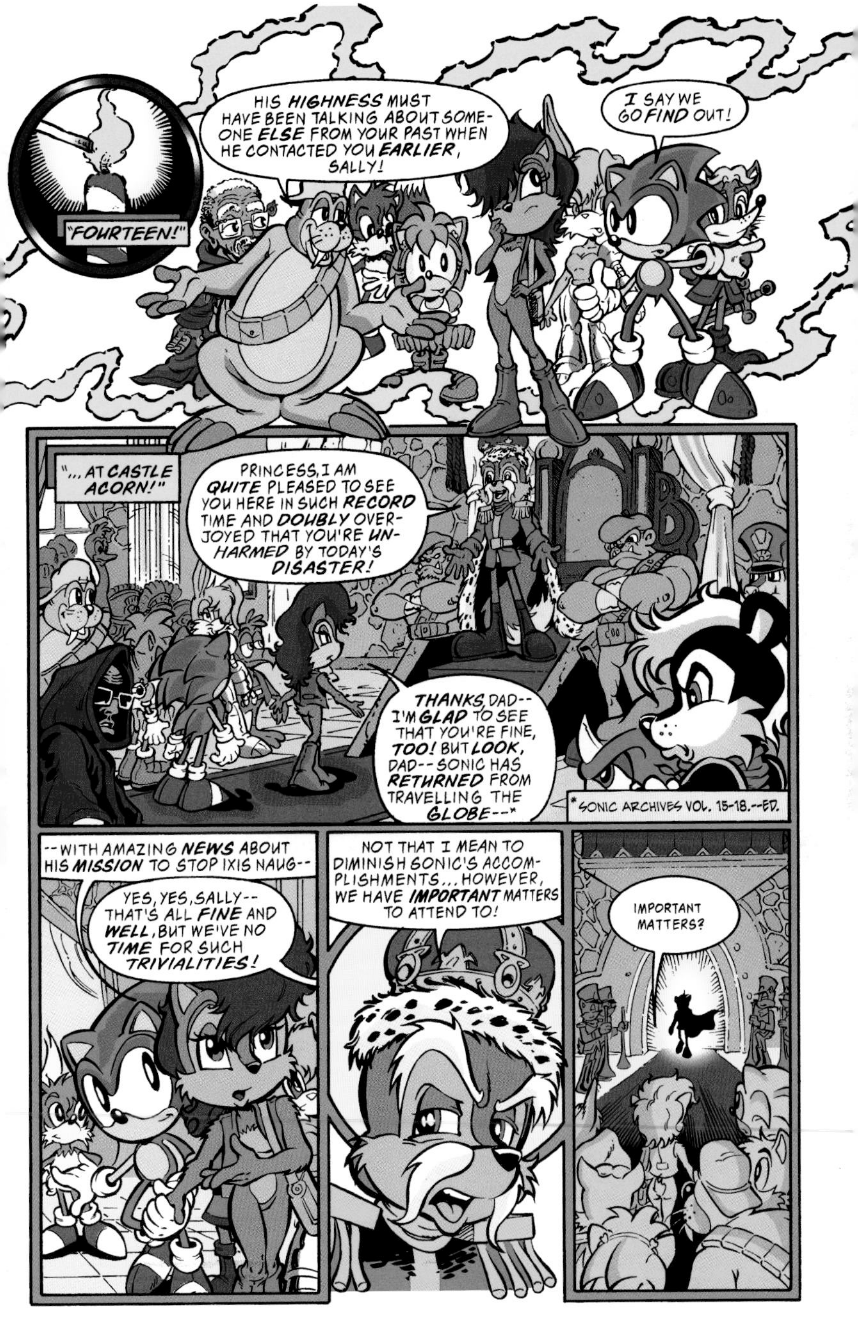
"FOURTEEN!"
HIS HIGHNESS MUST HAVE BEEN TALKING ABOUT SOME-ONE ELSE FROM YOUR PAST WHEN HE CONTACTED YOU EARLIER, SALLY!
I SAY WE GO FIND OUT!
"... AT CASTLE ACORN!"
PRINCESS, I AM QUITE PLEASED TO SEE YOU HERE IN SUCH RECORD TIME AND DOUBLY OVER-JOYED THAT YOU'RE UN-HARMED BY TODAY'S DISASTER!
THANKS, DAD-- I'M GLAD TO SEE THAT YOU'RE FINE, TOO! BUT LOOK, DAD-- SONIC HAS RETURNED FROM TRAVELLING THE GLOBE--*
*SONIC ARCHIVES VOL. 15-18.--ED.
--WITH AMAZING NEWS ABOUT HIS MISSION TO STOP IXIS NAUG--
YES, YES, SALLY-- THAT'S ALL FINE AND WELL, BUT WE'VE NO TIME FOR SUCH TRIVIALITIES!
NOT THAT I MEAN TO DIMINISH SONIC'S ACCOM-PLISHMENTS... HOWEVER, WE HAVE IMPORTANT MATTERS TO ATTEND TO!
IMPORTANT MATTERS?

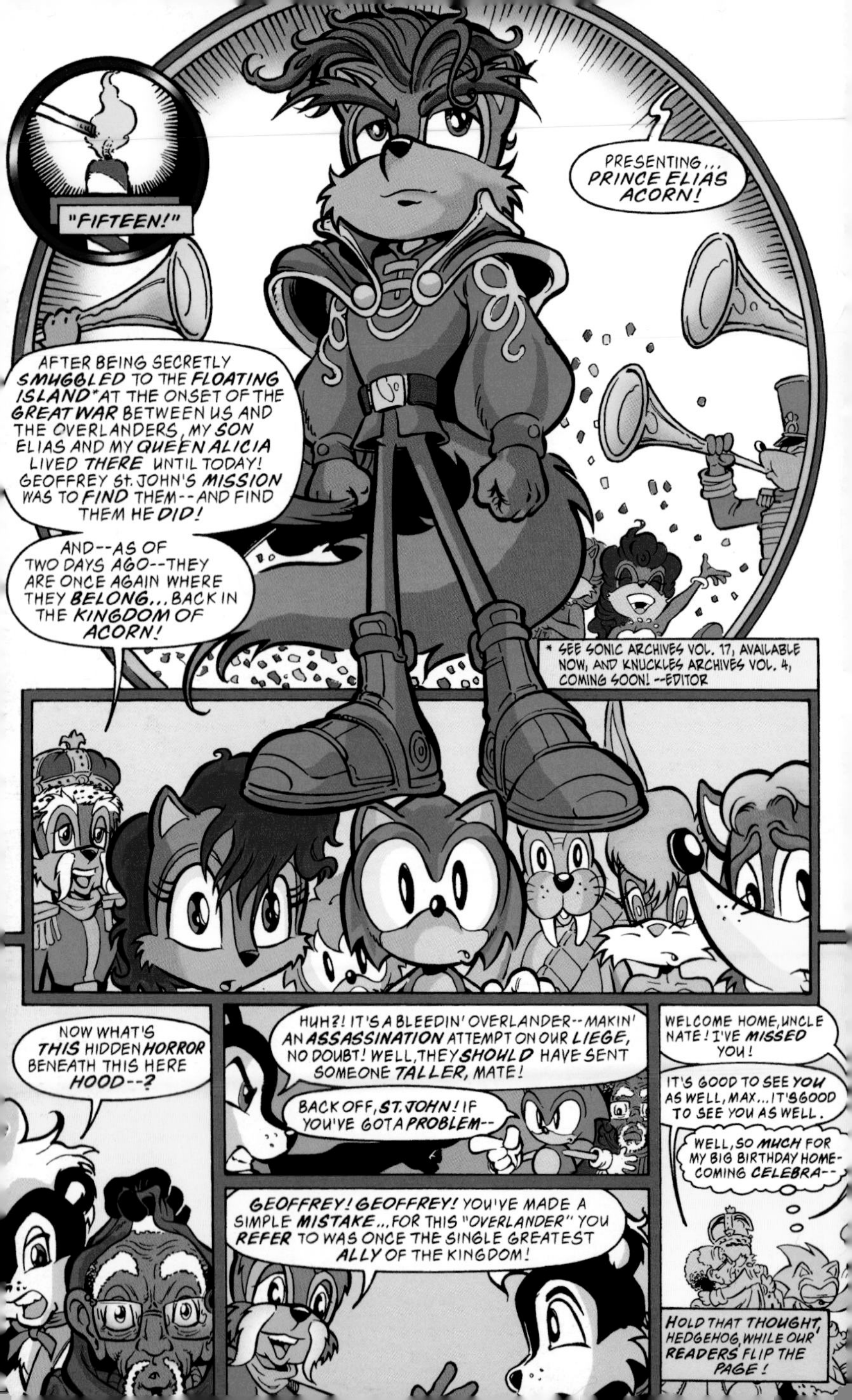
"FIFTEEN!"
PRESENTING... PRINCE ELIAS ACORN!
AFTER BEING SECRETLY SMUGGLED TO THE FLOATING ISLAND* AT THE ONSET OF THE GREAT WAR BETWEEN US AND THE OVERLANDERS, MY SON ELIAS AND MY QUEEN ALICIA LIVED THERE UNTIL TODAY! GEOFFREY St. JOHN'S MISSION WAS TO FIND THEM--AND FIND THEM HE DID!
AND--AS OF TWO DAYS AGO--THEY ARE ONCE AGAIN WHERE THEY BELONG... BACK IN THE KINGDOM OF ACORN!
* SEE SONIC ARCHIVES VOL. 17, AVAILABLE NOW, AND KNUCKLES ARCHIVES VOL. 4, COMING SOON! --EDITOR
NOW WHAT'S THIS HIDDEN HORROR BENEATH THIS HERE HOOD--?
HUH?! IT'S A BLEEDIN' OVERLANDER--MAKIN' AN ASSASSINATION ATTEMPT ON OUR LIEGE, NO DOUBT! WELL, THEY SHOULD HAVE SENT SOMEONE TALLER, MATE!
BACK OFF, ST. JOHN! IF YOU'VE GOT A PROBLEM--
WELCOME HOME, UNCLE NATE! I'VE MISSED YOU!
IT'S GOOD TO SEE YOU AS WELL, MAX... IT'S GOOD TO SEE YOU AS WELL.
WELL, SO MUCH FOR MY BIG BIRTHDAY HOME-COMING CELEBRA--
GEOFFREY! GEOFFREY! YOU'VE MADE A SIMPLE MISTAKE... FOR THIS "OVERLANDER" YOU REFER TO WAS ONCE THE SINGLE GREATEST ALLY OF THE KINGDOM!
HOLD THAT THOUGHT, HEDGEHOG, WHILE OUR READERS FLIP THE PAGE!

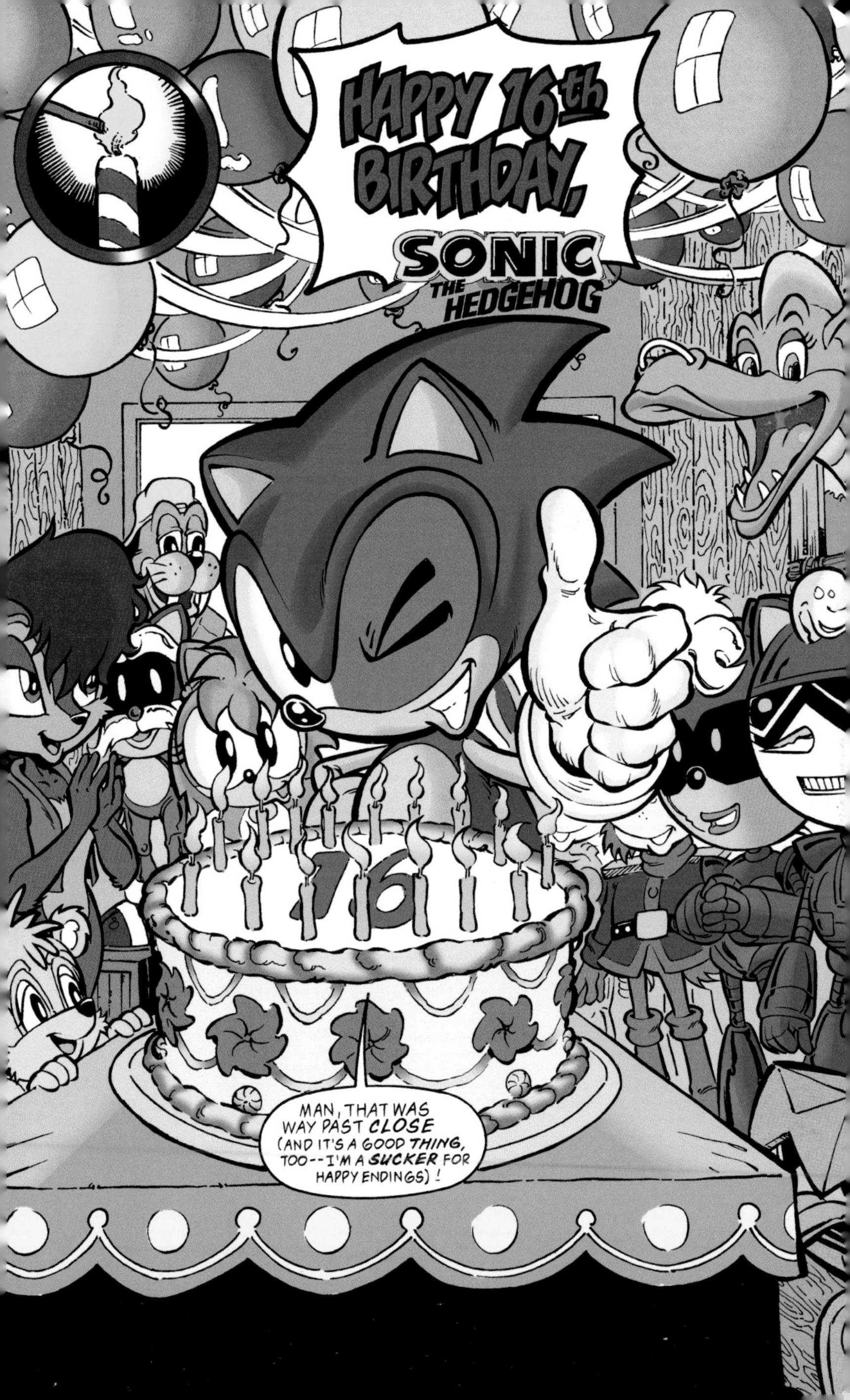
HAPPY 16th BIRTHDAY,
SONIC THE HEDGEHOG
MAN, THAT WAS WAY PAST CLOSE (AND IT'S A GOOD THING, TOO--I'M A SUCKER FOR HAPPY ENDINGS)!

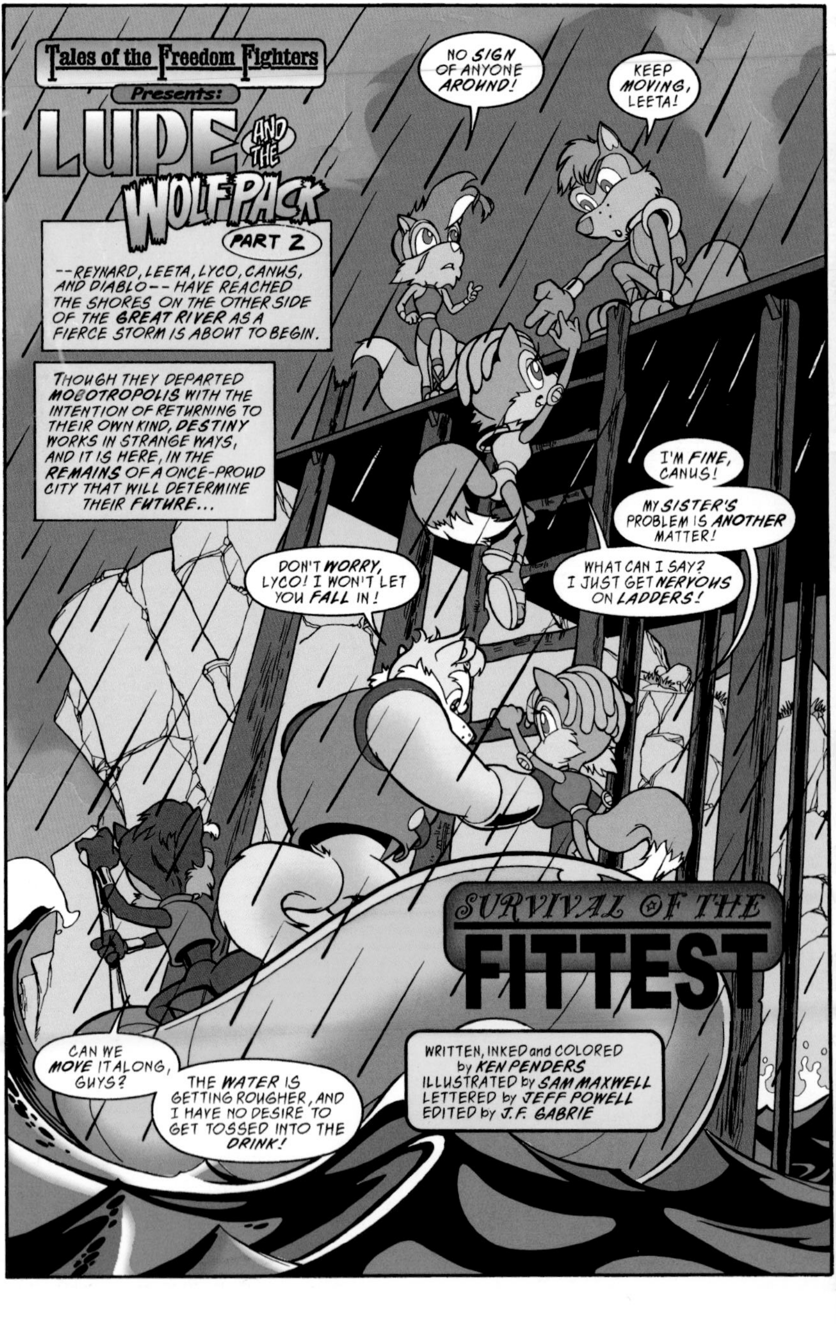
Tales of the Freedom Fighters
Presents:
LUPE AND THE WOLF PACK
PART 2
--REYNARD, LEETA, LYCO, CANUS, AND DIABLO-- HAVE REACHED THE SHORES ON THE OTHER SIDE OF THE GREAT RIVER AS A FIERCE STORM IS ABOUT TO BEGIN.
THOUGH THEY DEPARTED MOBOTROPOLIS WITH THE INTENTION OF RETURNING TO THEIR OWN KIND, DESTINY WORKS IN STRANGE WAYS, AND IT IS HERE, IN THE REMAINS OF A ONCE-PROUD CITY THAT WILL DETERMINE THEIR FUTURE...
NO SIGN OF ANYONE AROUND!
KEEP MOVING, LEETA!
I'M FINE, CANUS!
MY SISTER'S PROBLEM IS ANOTHER MATTER!
DON'T WORRY, LYCO! I WON'T LET YOU FALL IN!
WHAT CAN I SAY? I JUST GET NERVOUS ON LADDERS!
SURVIVAL OF THE FITTEST
CAN WE MOVE IT ALONG, GUYS?
THE WATER IS GETTING ROUGHER, AND I HAVE NO DESIRE TO GET TOSSED INTO THE DRINK!
WRITTEN, INKED and COLORED by KEN PENDERS
ILLUSTRATED by SAM MAXWELL
LETTERED by JEFF POWELL
EDITED by J.F. GABRIE

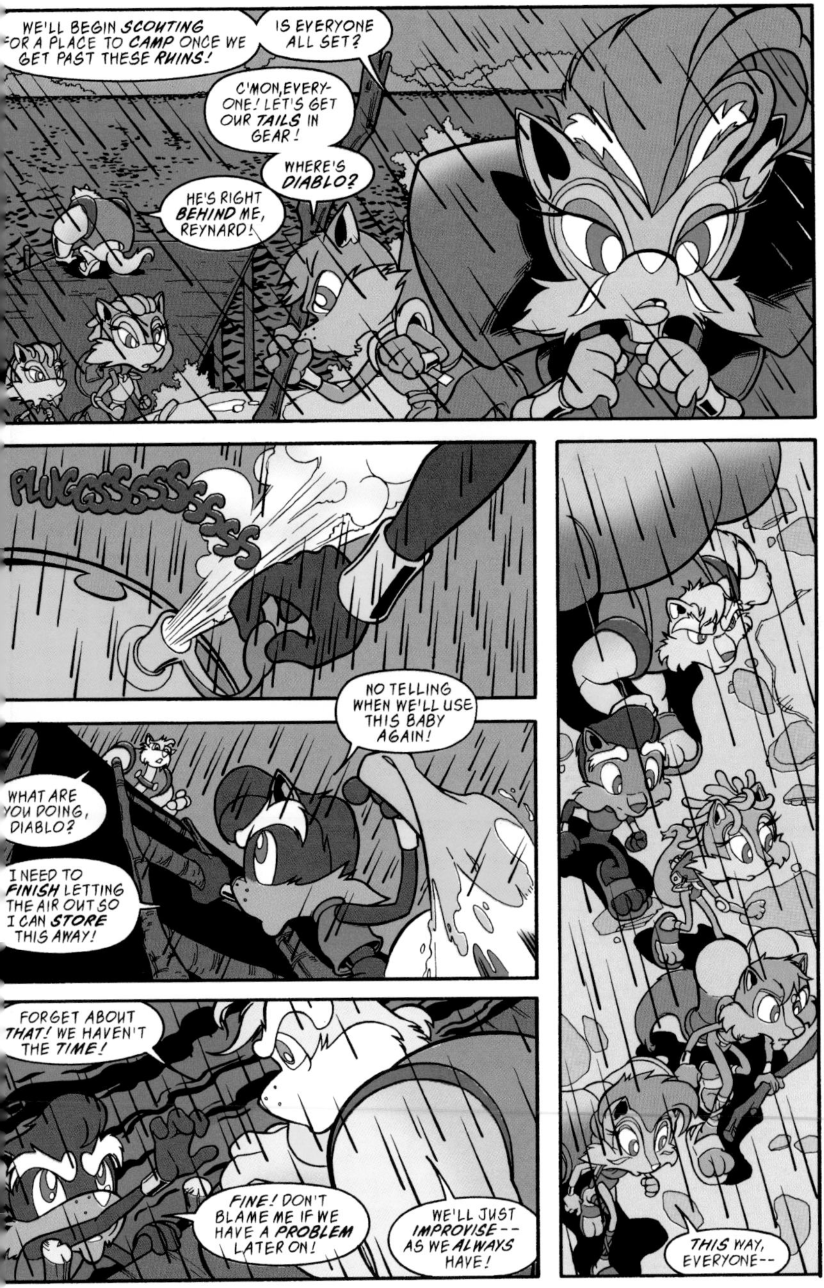

WE'LL BEGIN SCOUTING FOR A PLACE TO CAMP ONCE WE GET PAST THESE RUINS!
IS EVERYONE ALL SET?
C'MON, EVERYONE! LET'S GET OUR TAILS IN GEAR!
WHERE'S DIABLO?
HE'S RIGHT BEHIND ME, REYNARD!
PLUGGSSSSSSSSSS
NO TELLING WHEN WE'LL USE THIS BABY AGAIN!
WHAT ARE YOU DOING, DIABLO?
I NEED TO FINISH LETTING THE AIR OUT SO I CAN STORE THIS AWAY!
FORGET ABOUT THAT! WE HAVEN'T THE TIME!
FINE! DON'T BLAME ME IF WE HAVE A PROBLEM LATER ON!
WE'LL JUST IMPROVISE-- AS WE ALWAYS HAVE!
THIS WAY, EVERYONE--

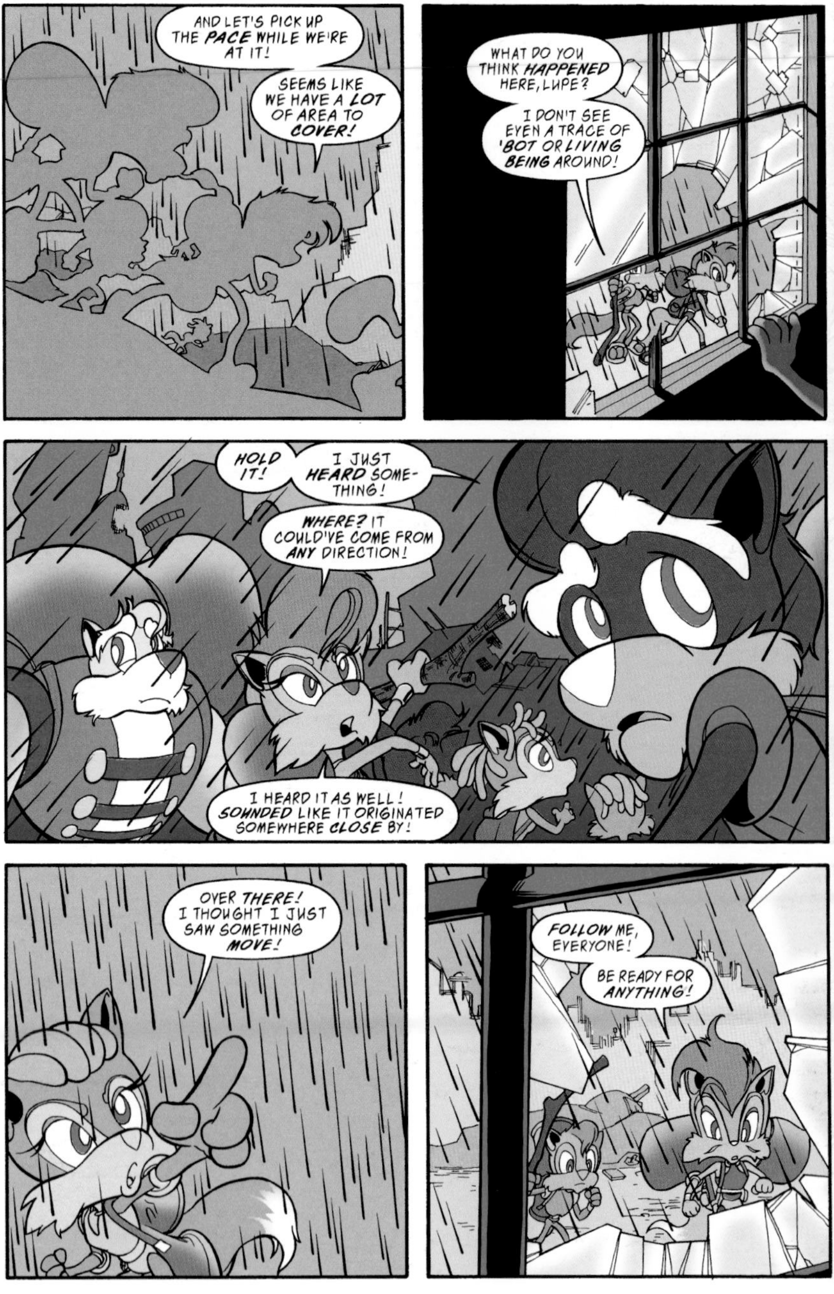
AND LET'S PICK UP THE PACE WHILE WE'RE AT IT!
SEEMS LIKE WE HAVE A LOT OF AREA TO COVER!
WHAT DO YOU THINK HAPPENED HERE, LUPE?
I DON'T SEE EVEN A TRACE OF 'BOT OR LIVING BEING AROUND!
HOLD IT!
I JUST HEARD SOME-THING!
WHERE? IT COULD'VE COME FROM ANY DIRECTION!
I HEARD IT AS WELL! SOUNDED LIKE IT ORIGINATED SOMEWHERE CLOSE BY!
OVER THERE! I THOUGHT I JUST SAW SOMETHING MOVE!
FOLLOW ME, EVERYONE!
BE READY FOR ANYTHING!

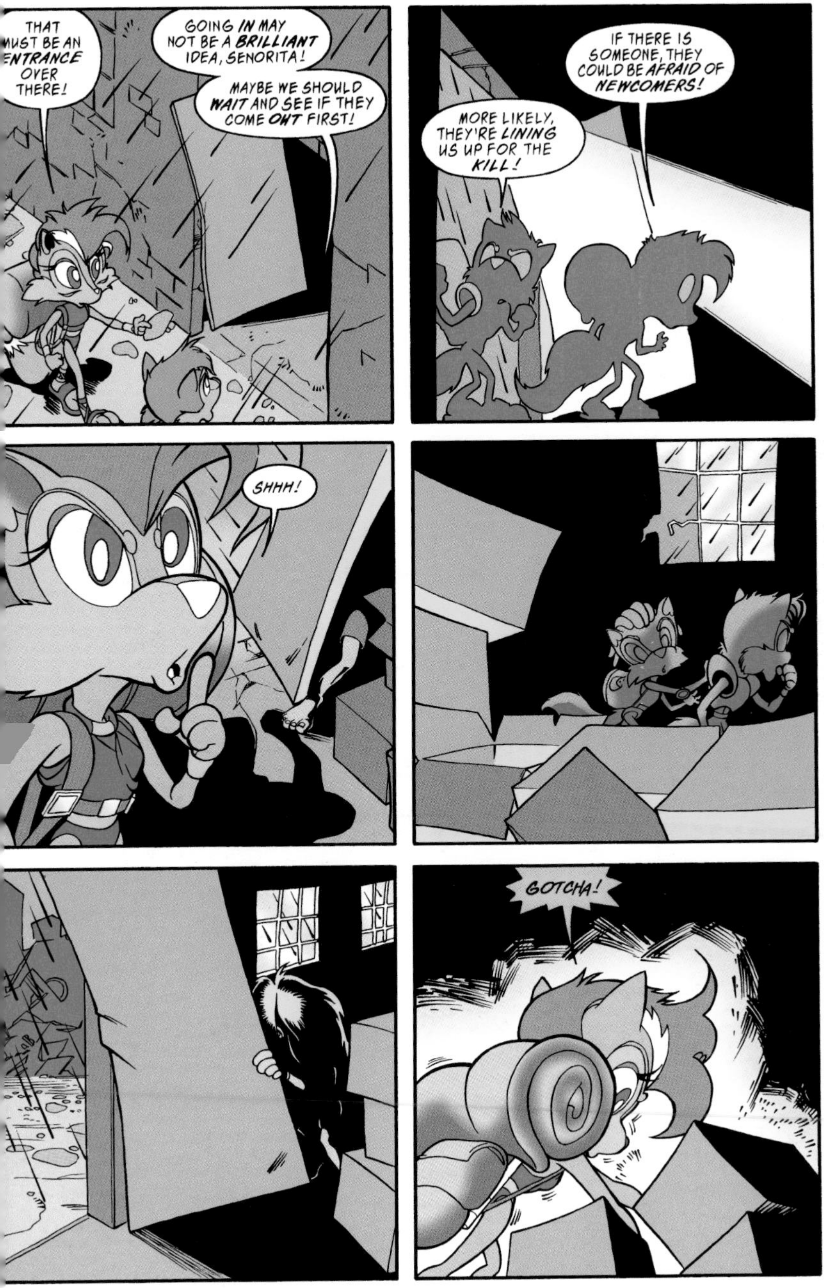
THAT MUST BE AN ENTRANCE OVER THERE!
GOING IN MAY NOT BE A BRILLIANT IDEA, SENORITA!
MAYBE WE SHOULD WAIT AND SEE IF THEY COME OUT FIRST!
IF THERE IS SOMEONE, THEY COULD BE AFRAID OF NEWCOMERS!
MORE LIKELY, THEY'RE LINING US UP FOR THE KILL!
SHHH!
GOTCHA!

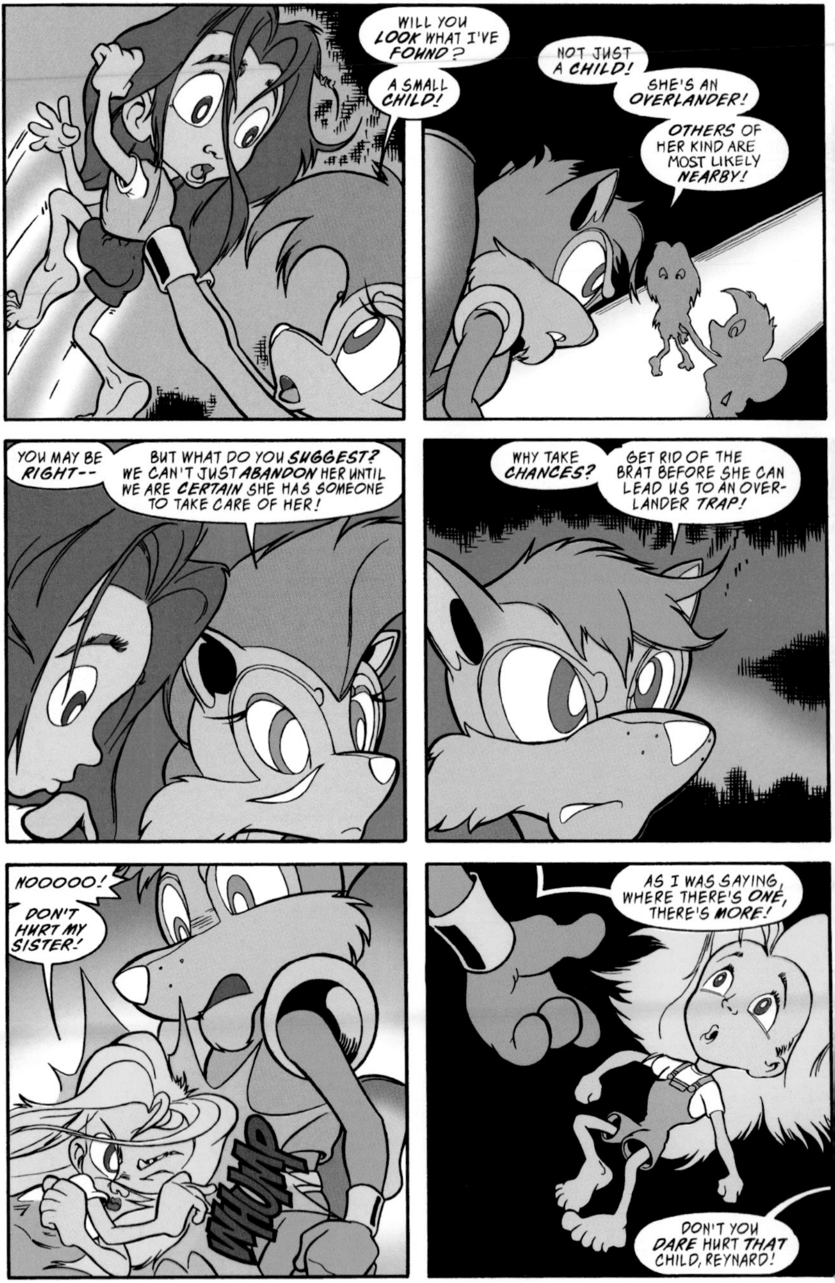
WILL YOU LOOK WHAT I'VE FOUND?
A SMALL CHILD!
NOT JUST A CHILD!
SHE'S AN OVERLANDER!
OTHERS OF HER KIND ARE MOST LIKELY NEARBY!
YOU MAY BE RIGHT--
BUT WHAT DO YOU SUGGEST? WE CAN'T JUST ABANDON HER UNTIL WE ARE CERTAIN SHE HAS SOMEONE TO TAKE CARE OF HER!
WHY TAKE CHANCES?
GET RID OF THE BRAT BEFORE SHE CAN LEAD US TO AN OVER-LANDER TRAP!
NOOOOO!
DON'T HURT MY SISTER!
WHUMP
AS I WAS SAYING, WHERE THERE'S ONE, THERE'S MORE!
DON'T YOU DARE HURT THAT CHILD, REYNARD!

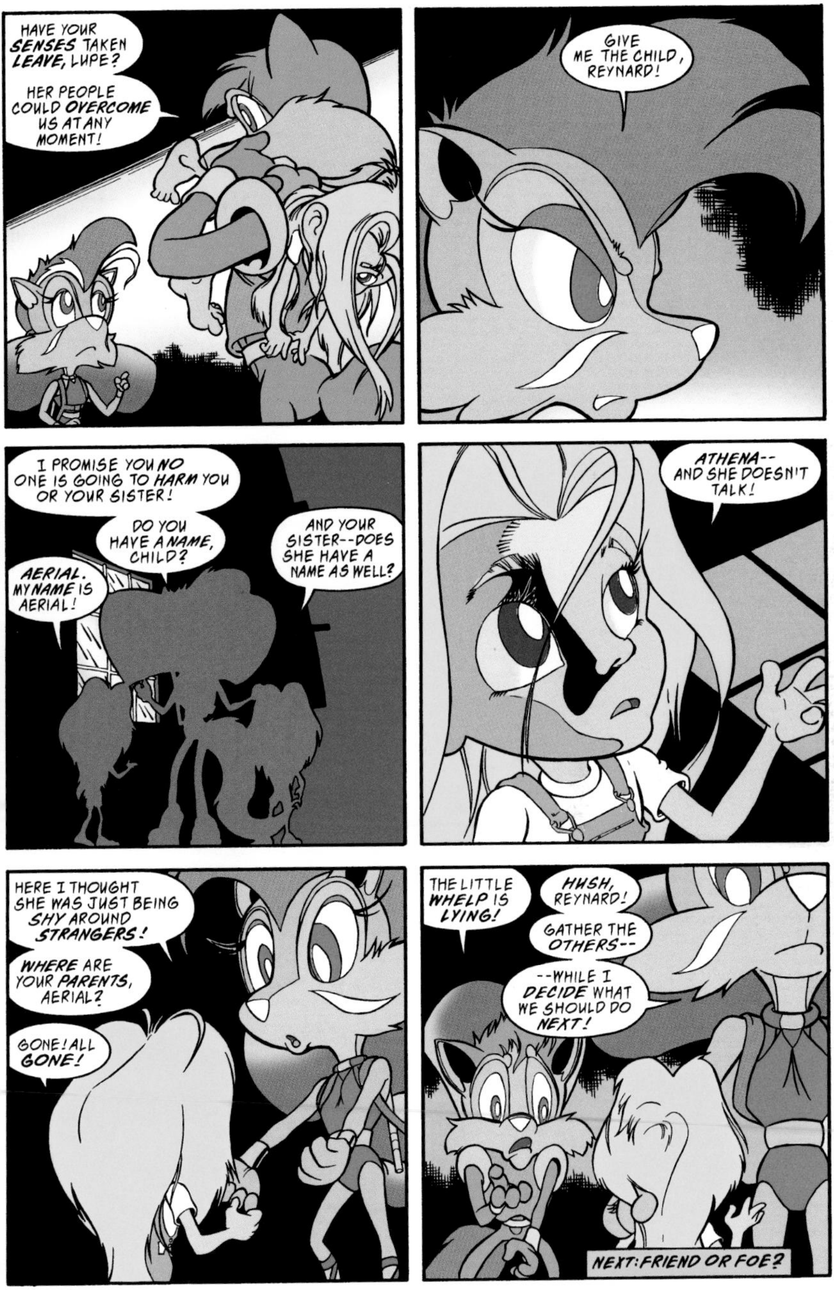
HAVE YOUR SENSES TAKEN LEAVE, LUPE?
HER PEOPLE COULD OVERCOME US AT ANY MOMENT!
GIVE ME THE CHILD, REYNARD!
I PROMISE YOU NO ONE IS GOING TO HARM YOU OR YOUR SISTER!
DO YOU HAVE A NAME, CHILD?
AERIAL. MY NAME IS AERIAL!
AND YOUR SISTER--DOES SHE HAVE A NAME AS WELL?
ATHENA-- AND SHE DOESN'T TALK!
HERE I THOUGHT SHE WAS JUST BEING SHY AROUND STRANGERS!
WHERE ARE YOUR PARENTS, AERIAL?
GONE! ALL GONE!
THE LITTLE WHELP IS LYING!
HUSH, REYNARD!
GATHER THE OTHERS--
--WHILE I DECIDE WHAT WE SHOULD DO NEXT!
NEXT: FRIEND OR FOE?

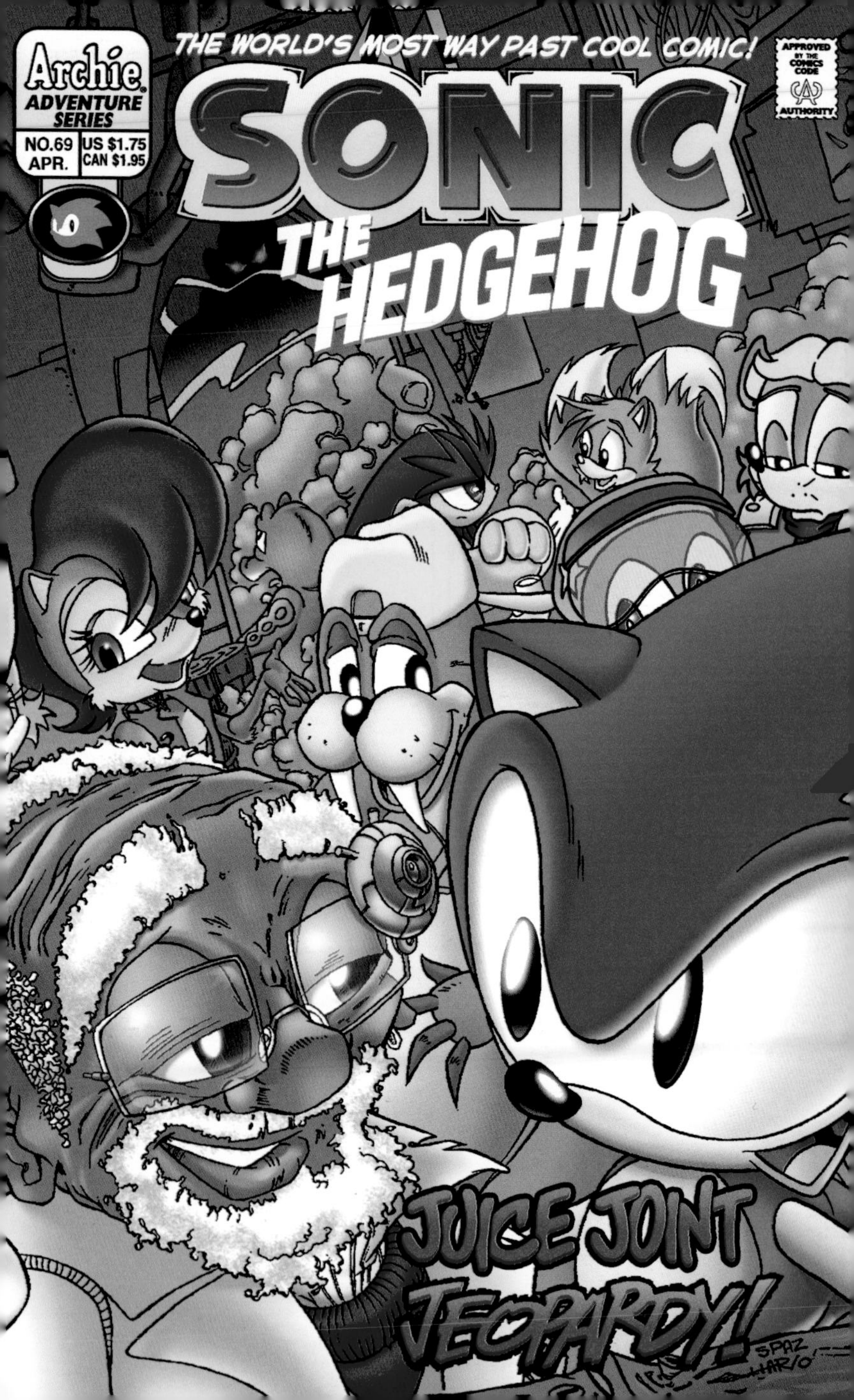
Archie
ADVENTURE SERIES
NO.69
APR.
US $1.75
CAN $1.95
THE WORLD'S MOST WAY PAST COOL COMIC!
APPROVED BY THE COMICS CODE AUTHORITY
SONIC THE HEDGEHOG
JUICE JOINT JEOPARDY!

THE PLANET MOBIUS WAS ONCE A VIRTUAL PARADISE UNTIL IT WAS CONQUERED BY THE EVIL DOCTOR ROBOTNIK! HIS TECHNOLOGICAL TYRANNY WOULD HAVE CONTINUED IF NOT FOR A HEROIC GROUP OF FREEDOM FIGHTERS WHO BANDED TOGETHER AND RESTORED ORDER TO THE KINGDOM OF ACORN! THE BRAVEST AMONG THEM IS A BLUE STREAK FILLED WITH THE MOST ATTITUDE GOING AROUND - - AND, WITHOUT A DOUBT, HE IS THE FASTEST THING ALIVE! ARCHIE COMICS AND SEGA PRESENT... SONIC THE HEDGEHOG!

THIS IS MOBOTROPOLIS--

--THE LARGEST CITY ON THE EARTH-LIKE WORLD OF MOBIUS.

WHEN JULIAN KINTOBOR, OF THE HOUSE OF IVO, CAME HERE SEEKING SANCTUARY OVER A DECADE AGO, ITS CITIZENS COULD NEVER SUSPECT HIS TRUE INTENTIONS--

--OR THAT HE WOULD BECOME THE EVIL DOCTOR ROBOTNIK, A MAN WHO WOULD CHANGE THE FACE OF MOBOTROPOLIS AND THE VERY PLANET--

--FOR THE WORSE!

NOW AFTER THE VILLAIN'S OVER-THROW ALL THESE YEARS LATER, THE POPULACE KNOWS BETTER. KING MAXIMILLIAN ACORN HAS RECLAIMED HIS CROWN AND HIS CASTLE, AND LIFE HAS RETURNED TO--

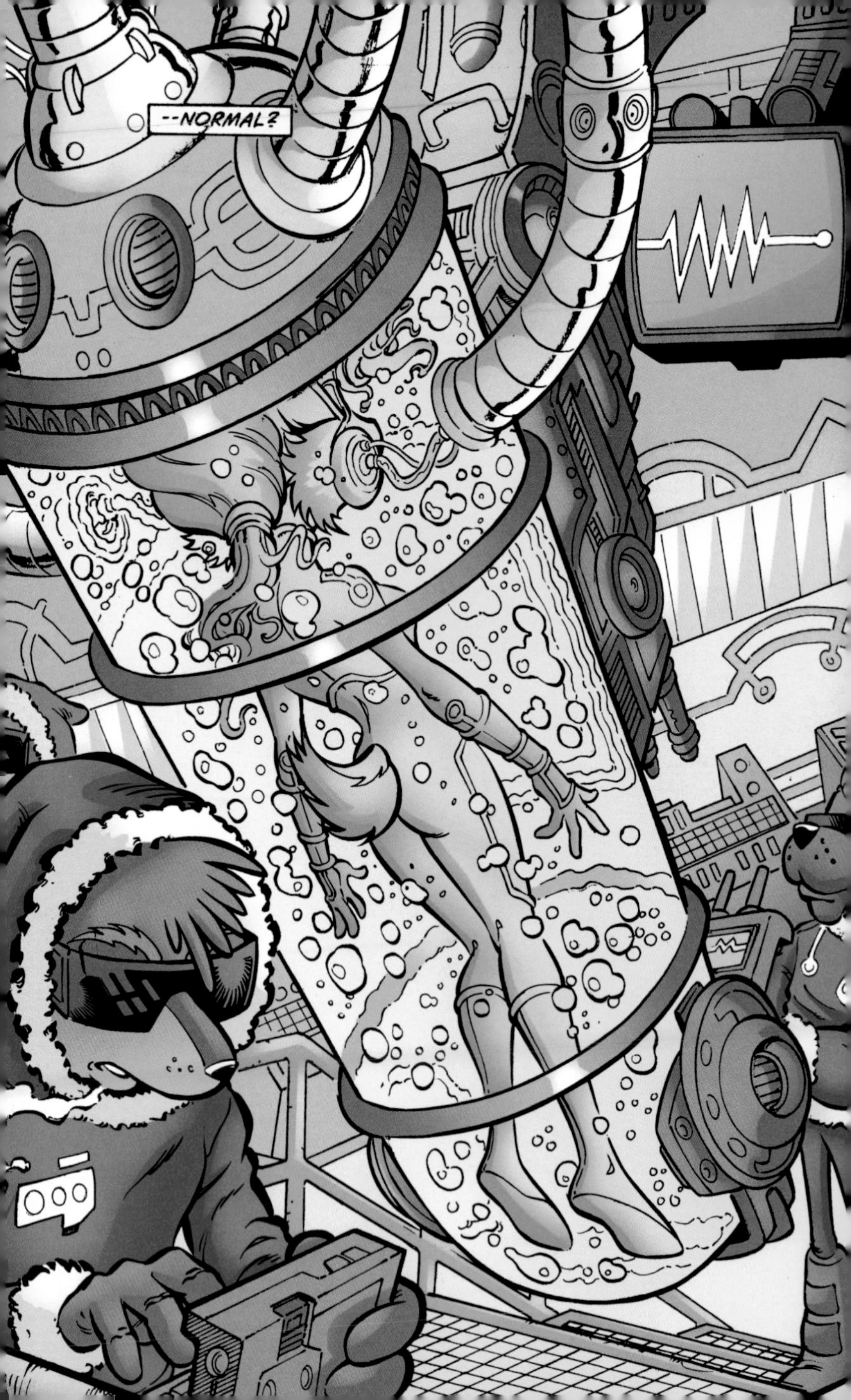
--NORMAL?

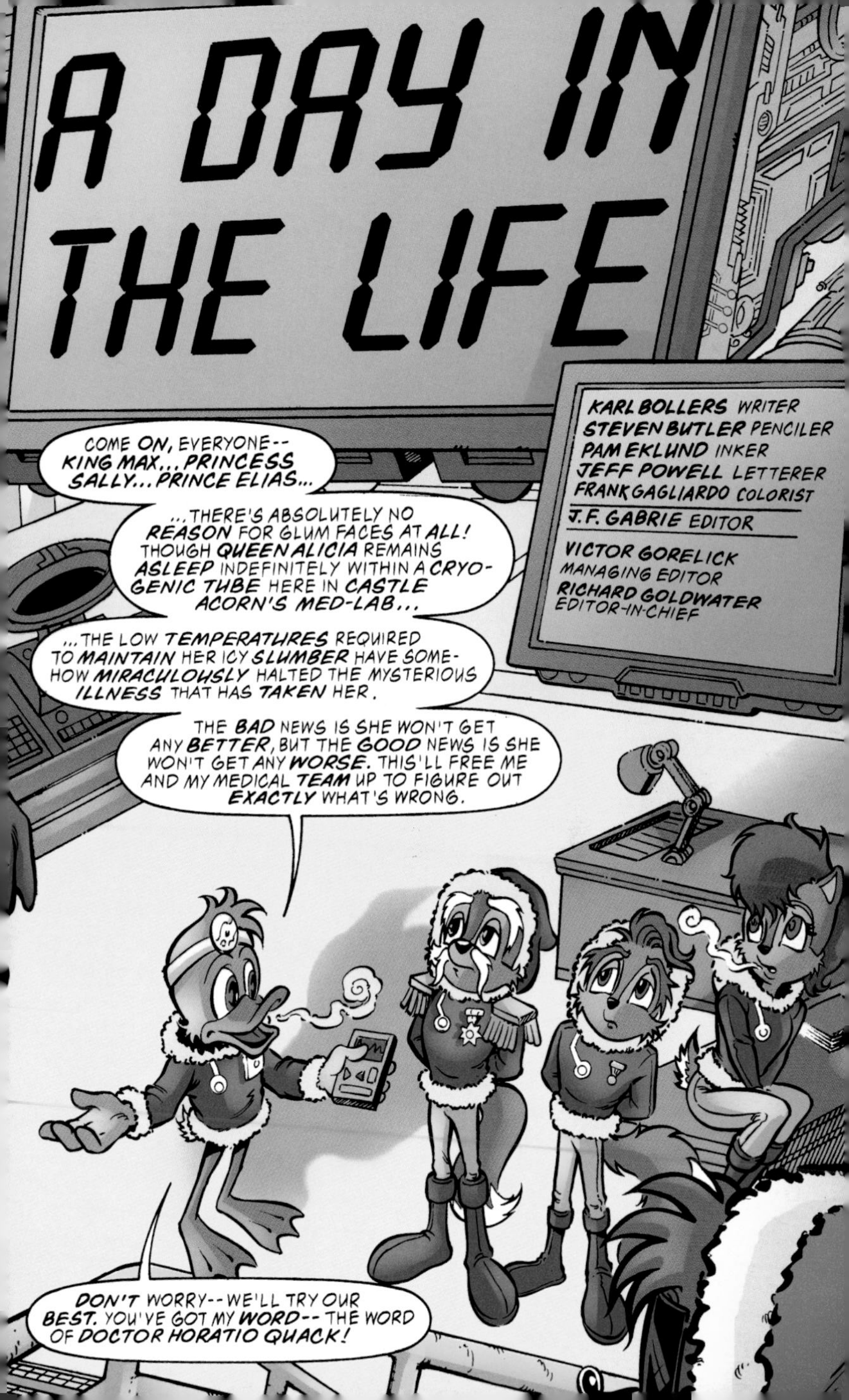
A DAY IN THE LIFE
KARL BOLLERS WRITER
STEVEN BUTLER PENCILER
PAM EKLUND INKER
JEFF POWELL LETTERER
FRANK GAGLIARDO COLORIST
J.F. GABRIE EDITOR
VICTOR GORELICK MANAGING EDITOR
RICHARD GOLDWATER EDITOR-IN-CHIEF
COME ON, EVERYONE-- KING MAX... PRINCESS SALLY... PRINCE ELIAS...
...THERE'S ABSOLUTELY NO REASON FOR GLUM FACES AT ALL! THOUGH QUEEN ALICIA REMAINS ASLEEP INDEFINITELY WITHIN A CRYO-GENIC TUBE HERE IN CASTLE ACORN'S MED-LAB...
...THE LOW TEMPERATURES REQUIRED TO MAINTAIN HER ICY SLUMBER HAVE SOME-HOW MIRACULOUSLY HALTED THE MYSTERIOUS ILLNESS THAT HAS TAKEN HER.
THE BAD NEWS IS SHE WON'T GET ANY BETTER, BUT THE GOOD NEWS IS SHE WON'T GET ANY WORSE. THIS'LL FREE ME AND MY MEDICAL TEAM UP TO FIGURE OUT EXACTLY WHAT'S WRONG.
DON'T WORRY--WE'LL TRY OUR BEST. YOU'VE GOT MY WORD-- THE WORD OF DOCTOR HORATIO QUACK!

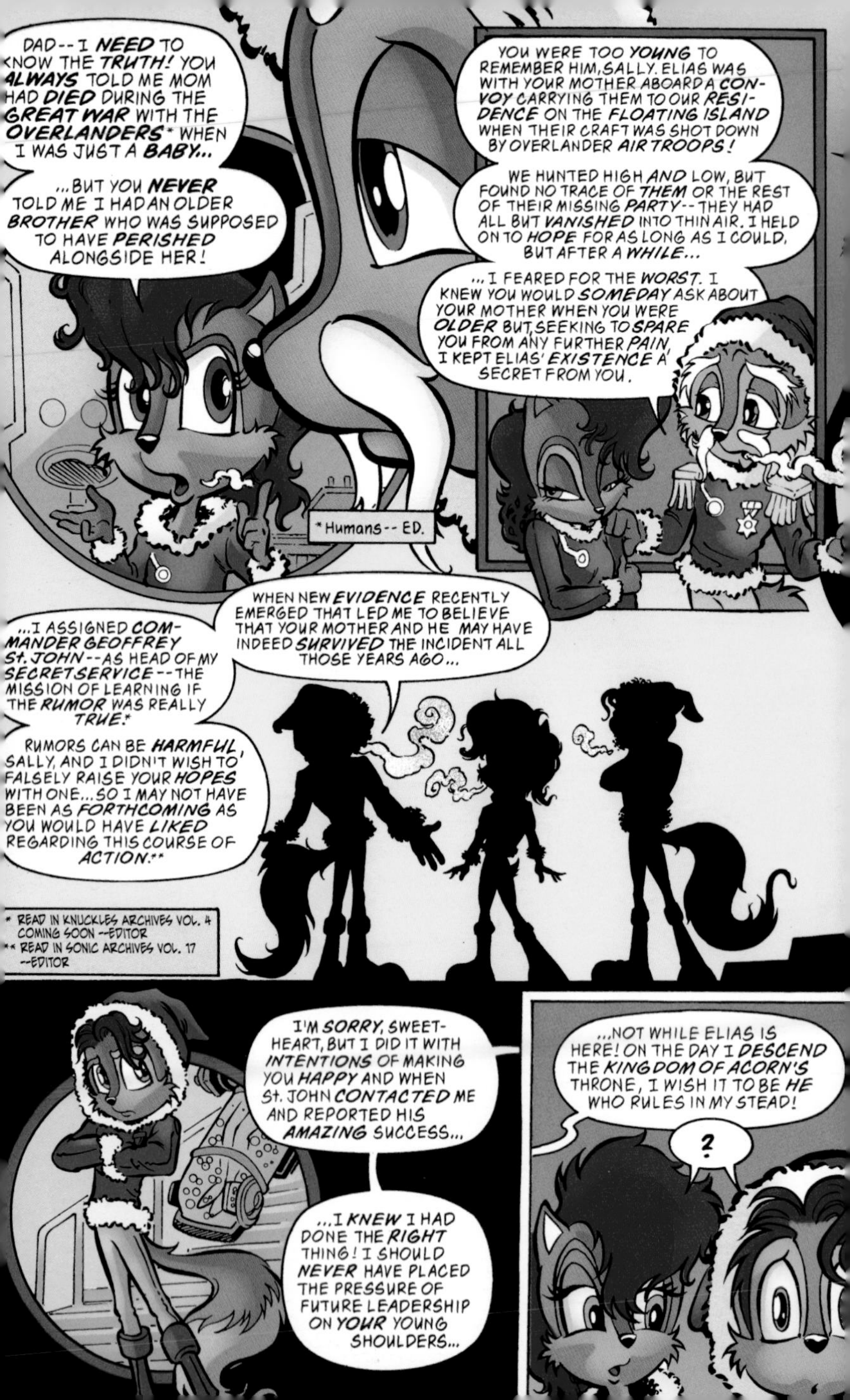
DAD--I NEED TO KNOW THE TRUTH! YOU ALWAYS TOLD ME MOM HAD DIED DURING THE GREAT WAR WITH THE OVERLANDERS* WHEN I WAS JUST A BABY...
...BUT YOU NEVER TOLD ME I HAD AN OLDER BROTHER WHO WAS SUPPOSED TO HAVE PERISHED ALONGSIDE HER!
*Humans--ED.
YOU WERE TOO YOUNG TO REMEMBER HIM, SALLY. ELIAS WAS WITH YOUR MOTHER ABOARD A CONVOY CARRYING THEM TO OUR RESIDENCE ON THE FLOATING ISLAND WHEN THEIR CRAFT WAS SHOT DOWN BY OVERLANDER AIR TROOPS!
WE HUNTED HIGH AND LOW, BUT FOUND NO TRACE OF THEM OR THE REST OF THEIR MISSING PARTY--THEY HAD ALL BUT VANISHED INTO THIN AIR. I HELD ON TO HOPE FOR AS LONG AS I COULD, BUT AFTER A WHILE...
...I FEARED FOR THE WORST. I KNEW YOU WOULD SOMEDAY ASK ABOUT YOUR MOTHER WHEN YOU WERE OLDER BUT, SEEKING TO SPARE YOU FROM ANY FURTHER PAIN, I KEPT ELIAS' EXISTENCE A SECRET FROM YOU.
WHEN NEW EVIDENCE RECENTLY EMERGED THAT LED ME TO BELIEVE THAT YOUR MOTHER AND HE MAY HAVE INDEED SURVIVED THE INCIDENT ALL THOSE YEARS AGO...
...I ASSIGNED COMMANDER GEOFFREY St. JOHN--AS HEAD OF MY SECRET SERVICE--THE MISSION OF LEARNING IF THE RUMOR WAS REALLY TRUE.*
RUMORS CAN BE HARMFUL, SALLY, AND I DIDN'T WISH TO FALSELY RAISE YOUR HOPES WITH ONE...SO I MAY NOT HAVE BEEN AS FORTHCOMING AS YOU WOULD HAVE LIKED REGARDING THIS COURSE OF ACTION.**
* READ IN KNUCKLES ARCHIVES VOL. 4 COMING SOON --EDITOR
** READ IN SONIC ARCHIVES VOL. 17 --EDITOR
I'M SORRY, SWEETHEART, BUT I DID IT WITH INTENTIONS OF MAKING YOU HAPPY AND WHEN St. JOHN CONTACTED ME AND REPORTED HIS AMAZING SUCCESS...
...I KNEW I HAD DONE THE RIGHT THING! I SHOULD NEVER HAVE PLACED THE PRESSURE OF FUTURE LEADERSHIP ON YOUR YOUNG SHOULDERS...
...NOT WHILE ELIAS IS HERE! ON THE DAY I DESCEND THE KINGDOM OF ACORN'S THRONE, I WISH IT TO BE HE WHO RULES IN MY STEAD!
?

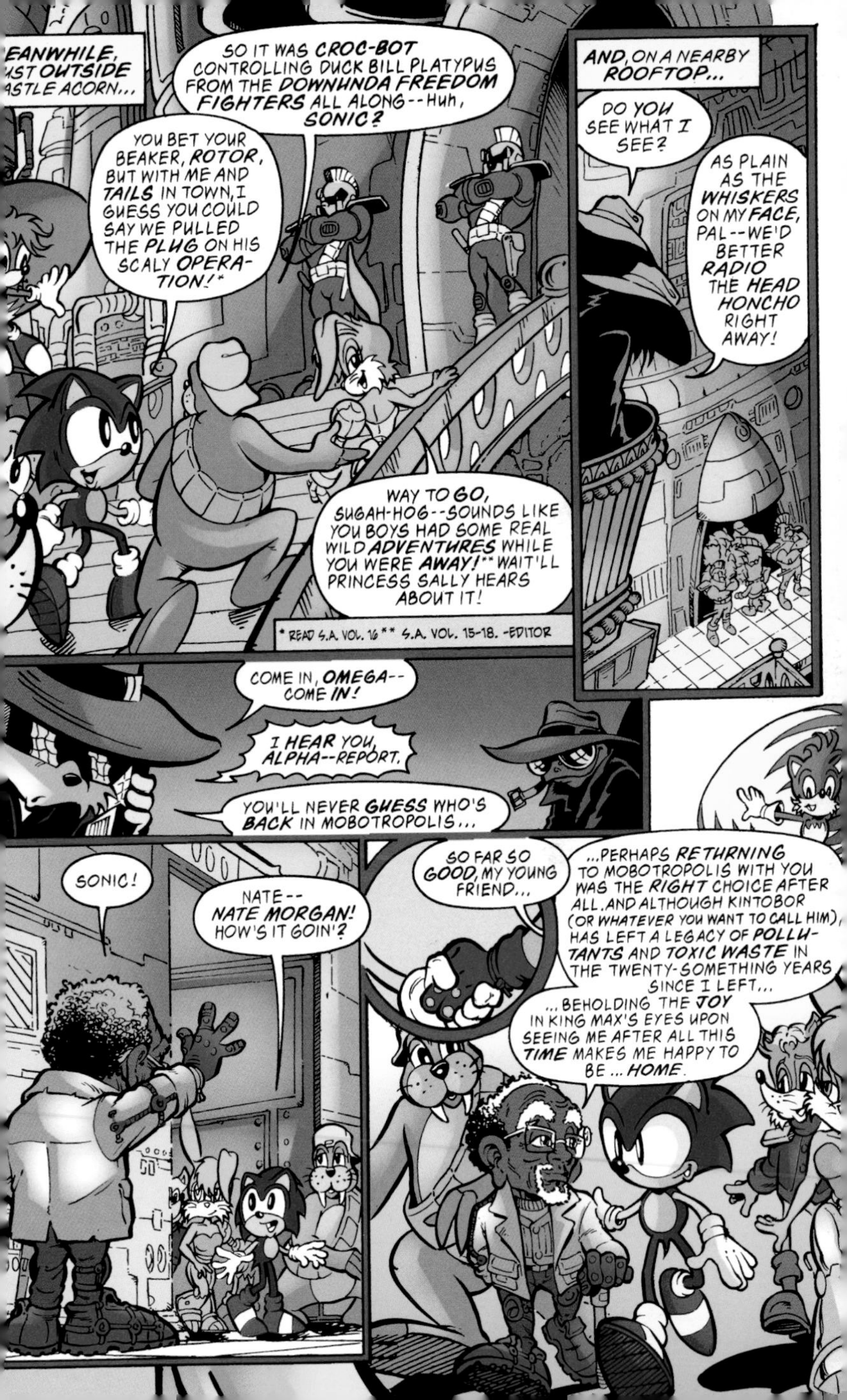
EANWHILE, UST OUTSIDE ASTLE ACORN...
SO IT WAS CROC-BOT CONTROLLING DUCK BILL PLATYPUS FROM THE DOWNUNDA FREEDOM FIGHTERS ALL ALONG--Huh, SONIC?
YOU BET YOUR BEAKER, ROTOR, BUT WITH ME AND TAILS IN TOWN, I GUESS YOU COULD SAY WE PULLED THE PLUG ON HIS SCALY OPERATION!*
WAY TO GO, SUGAH-HOG--SOUNDS LIKE YOU BOYS HAD SOME REAL WILD ADVENTURES WHILE YOU WERE AWAY!** WAIT'LL PRINCESS SALLY HEARS ABOUT IT!
* READ S.A. VOL. 16 ** S.A. VOL. 15-18. -EDITOR
AND, ON A NEARBY ROOFTOP...
DO YOU SEE WHAT I SEE?
AS PLAIN AS THE WHISKERS ON MY FACE, PAL--WE'D BETTER RADIO THE HEAD HONCHO RIGHT AWAY!
COME IN, OMEGA--COME IN!
I HEAR YOU, ALPHA--REPORT.
YOU'LL NEVER GUESS WHO'S BACK IN MOBOTROPOLIS...
SONIC!
NATE--NATE MORGAN! HOW'S IT GOIN'?
SO FAR SO GOOD, MY YOUNG FRIEND...
...PERHAPS RETURNING TO MOBOTROPOLIS WITH YOU WAS THE RIGHT CHOICE AFTER ALL. AND ALTHOUGH KINTOBOR (OR WHATEVER YOU WANT TO CALL HIM), HAS LEFT A LEGACY OF POLLUTANTS AND TOXIC WASTE IN THE TWENTY-SOMETHING YEARS SINCE I LEFT...
...BEHOLDING THE JOY IN KING MAX'S EYES UPON SEEING ME AFTER ALL THIS TIME MAKES ME HAPPY TO BE ... HOME.

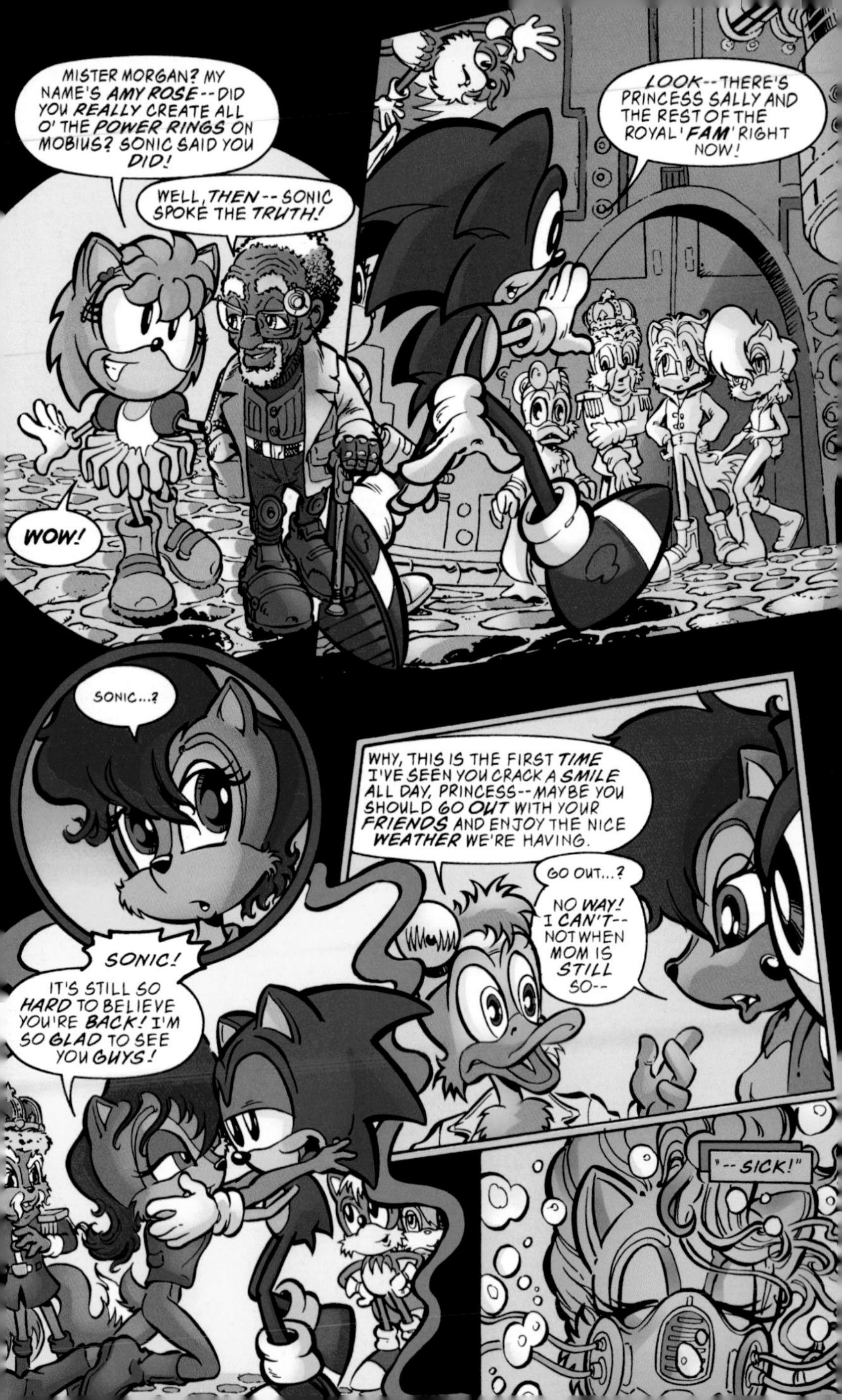

MISTER MORGAN? MY NAME'S AMY ROSE--DID YOU REALLY CREATE ALL O' THE POWER RINGS ON MOBIUS? SONIC SAID YOU DID!
WELL, THEN--SONIC SPOKE THE TRUTH!
WOW!
LOOK--THERE'S PRINCESS SALLY AND THE REST OF THE ROYAL 'FAM' RIGHT NOW!
SONIC...?
SONIC!
IT'S STILL SO HARD TO BELIEVE YOU'RE BACK! I'M SO GLAD TO SEE YOU GUYS!
WHY, THIS IS THE FIRST TIME I'VE SEEN YOU CRACK A SMILE ALL DAY, PRINCESS--MAYBE YOU SHOULD GO OUT WITH YOUR FRIENDS AND ENJOY THE NICE WEATHER WE'RE HAVING.
GO OUT...?
NO WAY! I CAN'T--NOT WHEN MOM IS STILL SO--
"--SICK!"

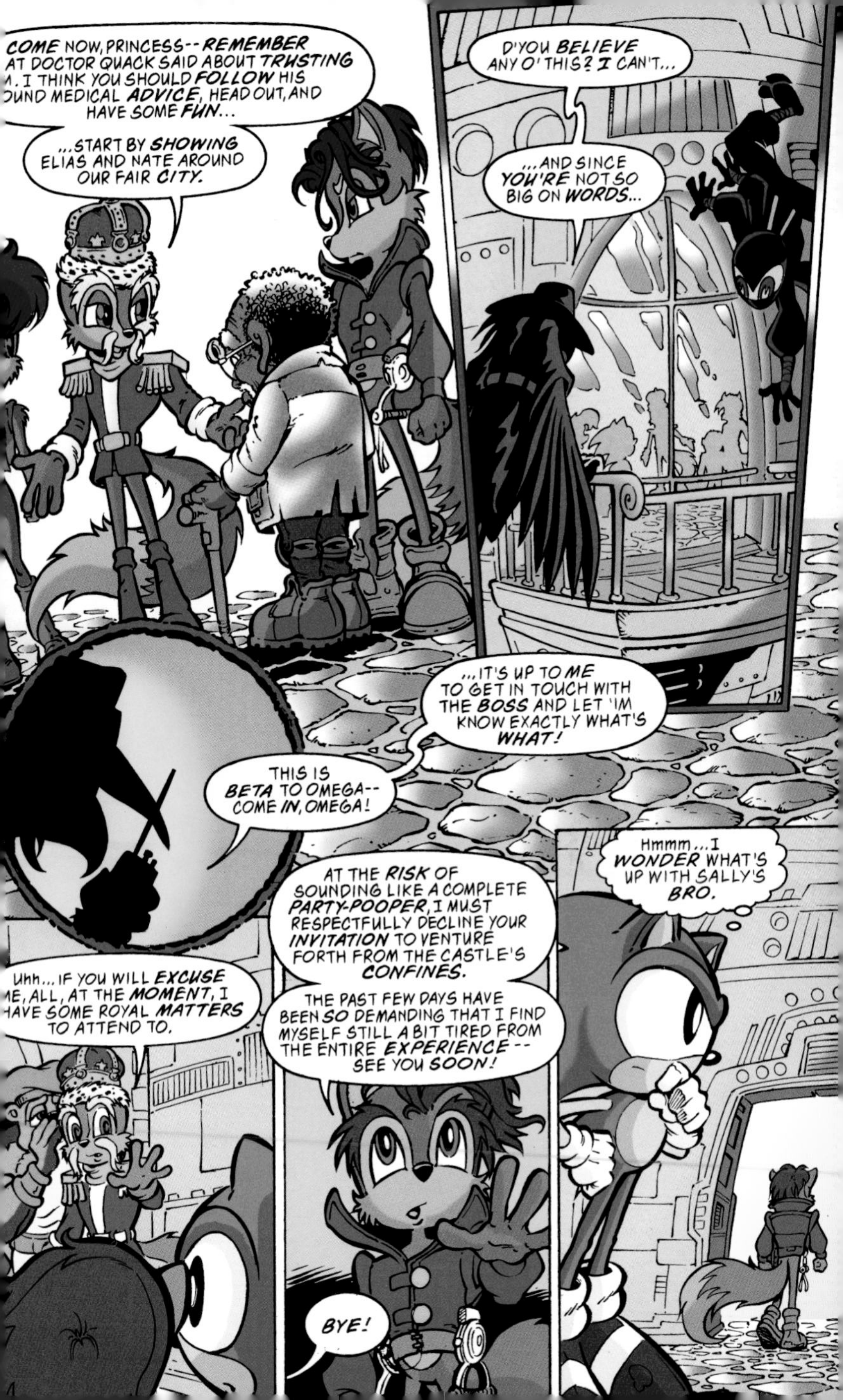
COME NOW, PRINCESS-- REMEMBER AT DOCTOR QUACK SAID ABOUT TRUSTING M. I THINK YOU SHOULD FOLLOW HIS OUND MEDICAL ADVICE, HEAD OUT, AND HAVE SOME FUN...
...START BY SHOWING ELIAS AND NATE AROUND OUR FAIR CITY.
D'YOU BELIEVE ANY O' THIS? I CAN'T...
...AND SINCE YOU'RE NOT SO BIG ON WORDS...
...IT'S UP TO ME TO GET IN TOUCH WITH THE BOSS AND LET 'IM KNOW EXACTLY WHAT'S WHAT!
THIS IS BETA TO OMEGA-- COME IN, OMEGA!
UHH... IF YOU WILL EXCUSE ME, ALL, AT THE MOMENT, I HAVE SOME ROYAL MATTERS TO ATTEND TO.
AT THE RISK OF SOUNDING LIKE A COMPLETE PARTY-POOPER, I MUST RESPECTFULLY DECLINE YOUR INVITATION TO VENTURE FORTH FROM THE CASTLE'S CONFINES.
THE PAST FEW DAYS HAVE BEEN SO DEMANDING THAT I FIND MYSELF STILL A BIT TIRED FROM THE ENTIRE EXPERIENCE -- SEE YOU SOON!
BYE!
Hmmm... I WONDER WHAT'S UP WITH SALLY'S BRO.

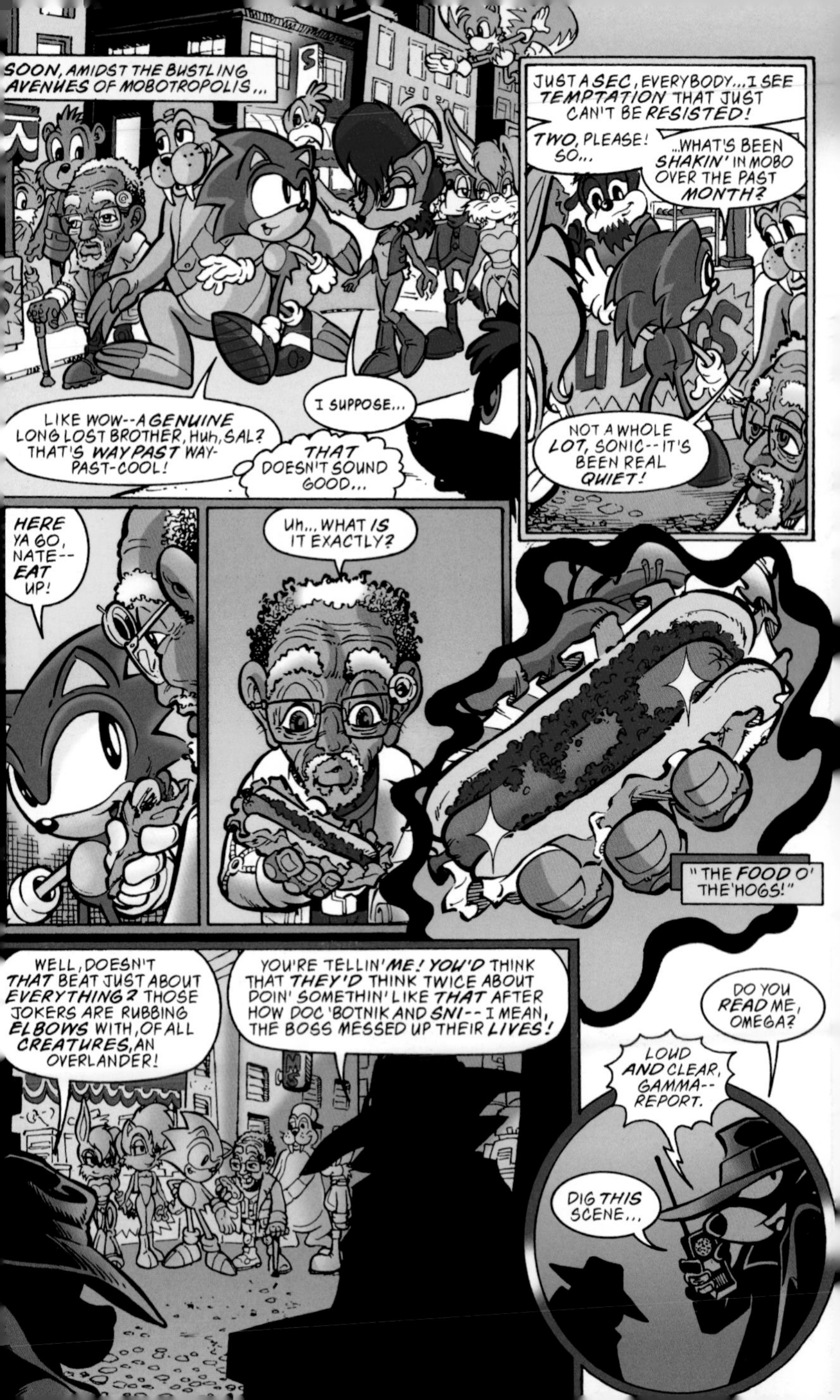
SOON, AMIDST THE BUSTLING AVENUES OF MOBOTROPOLIS...
LIKE WOW--A GENUINE LONG LOST BROTHER, Huh, SAL? THAT'S WAY PAST WAY-PAST-COOL!
I SUPPOSE...
THAT DOESN'T SOUND GOOD...
JUST A SEC, EVERYBODY...I SEE TEMPTATION THAT JUST CAN'T BE RESISTED!
TWO, PLEASE! SO...
...WHAT'S BEEN SHAKIN' IN MOBO OVER THE PAST MONTH?
NOT A WHOLE LOT, SONIC--IT'S BEEN REAL QUIET!
HERE YA GO, NATE--EAT UP!
Uh... WHAT IS IT EXACTLY?
"THE FOOD O' THE 'HOGS!"
WELL, DOESN'T THAT BEAT JUST ABOUT EVERYTHING? THOSE JOKERS ARE RUBBING ELBOWS WITH, OF ALL CREATURES, AN OVERLANDER!
YOU'RE TELLIN' ME! YOU'D THINK THAT THEY'D THINK TWICE ABOUT DOIN' SOMETHIN' LIKE THAT AFTER HOW DOC 'BOTNIK AND SNI-- I MEAN, THE BOSS MESSED UP THEIR LIVES!
DO YOU READ ME, OMEGA?
LOUD AND CLEAR, GAMMA-- REPORT.
DIG THIS SCENE...

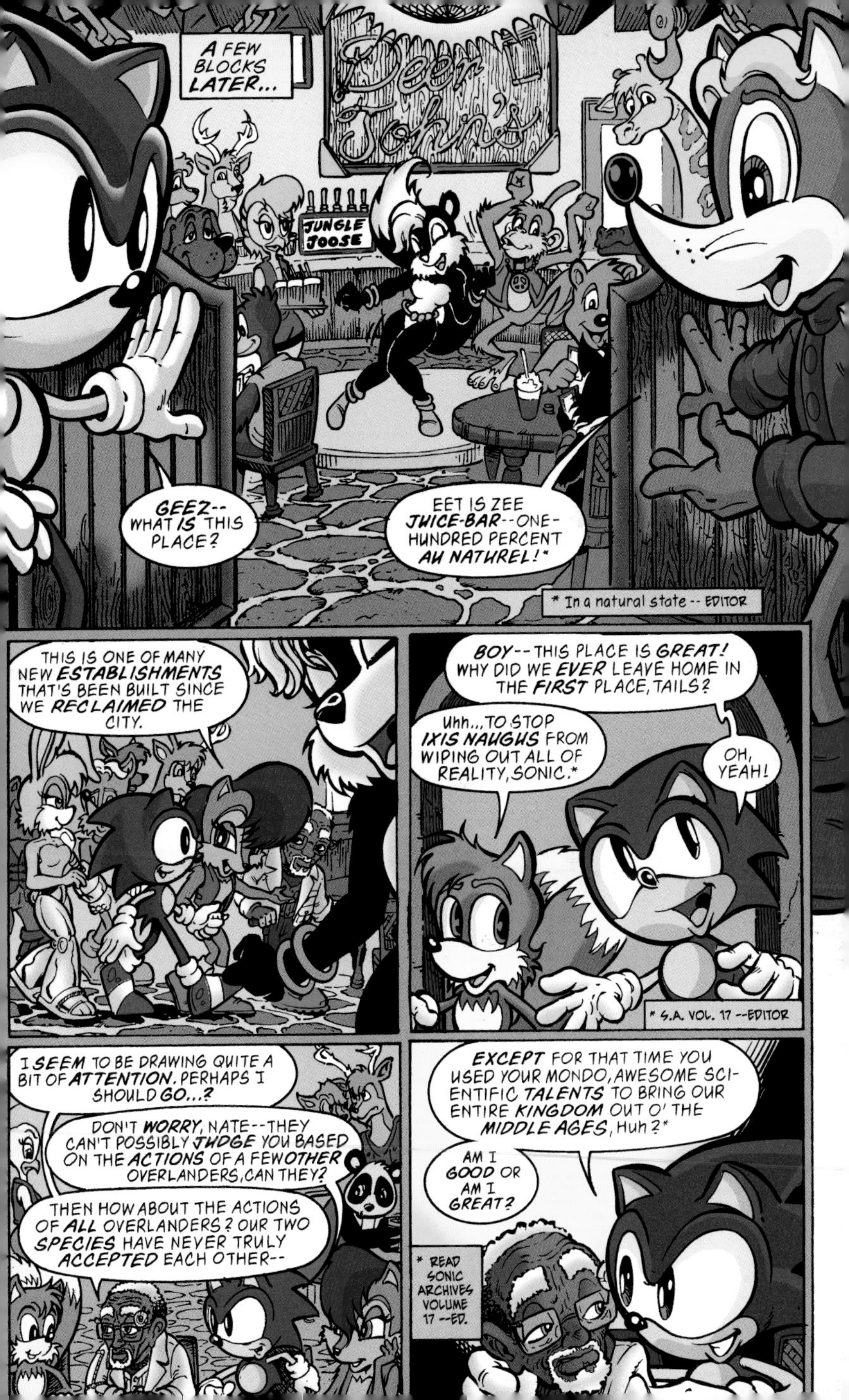
A FEW BLOCKS LATER...
Deer John's
JUNGLE JOOSE
GEEZ-- WHAT IS THIS PLACE?
EET IS ZEE JUICE-BAR--ONE-HUNDRED PERCENT AU NATUREL!*
* In a natural state -- EDITOR
THIS IS ONE OF MANY NEW ESTABLISHMENTS THAT'S BEEN BUILT SINCE WE RECLAIMED THE CITY.
BOY--THIS PLACE IS GREAT! WHY DID WE EVER LEAVE HOME IN THE FIRST PLACE, TAILS?
Uhh..., TO STOP IXIS NAUGUS FROM WIPING OUT ALL OF REALITY, SONIC.*
OH, YEAH!
* S.A. VOL. 17 --EDITOR
I SEEM TO BE DRAWING QUITE A BIT OF ATTENTION. PERHAPS I SHOULD GO...?
DON'T WORRY, NATE--THEY CAN'T POSSIBLY JUDGE YOU BASED ON THE ACTIONS OF A FEW OTHER OVERLANDERS, CAN THEY?
THEN HOW ABOUT THE ACTIONS OF ALL OVERLANDERS? OUR TWO SPECIES HAVE NEVER TRULY ACCEPTED EACH OTHER--
EXCEPT FOR THAT TIME YOU USED YOUR MONDO, AWESOME SCI-ENTIFIC TALENTS TO BRING OUR ENTIRE KINGDOM OUT O' THE MIDDLE AGES, Huh?*
AM I GOOD OR AM I GREAT?
* READ SONIC ARCHIVES VOLUME 17 --ED.

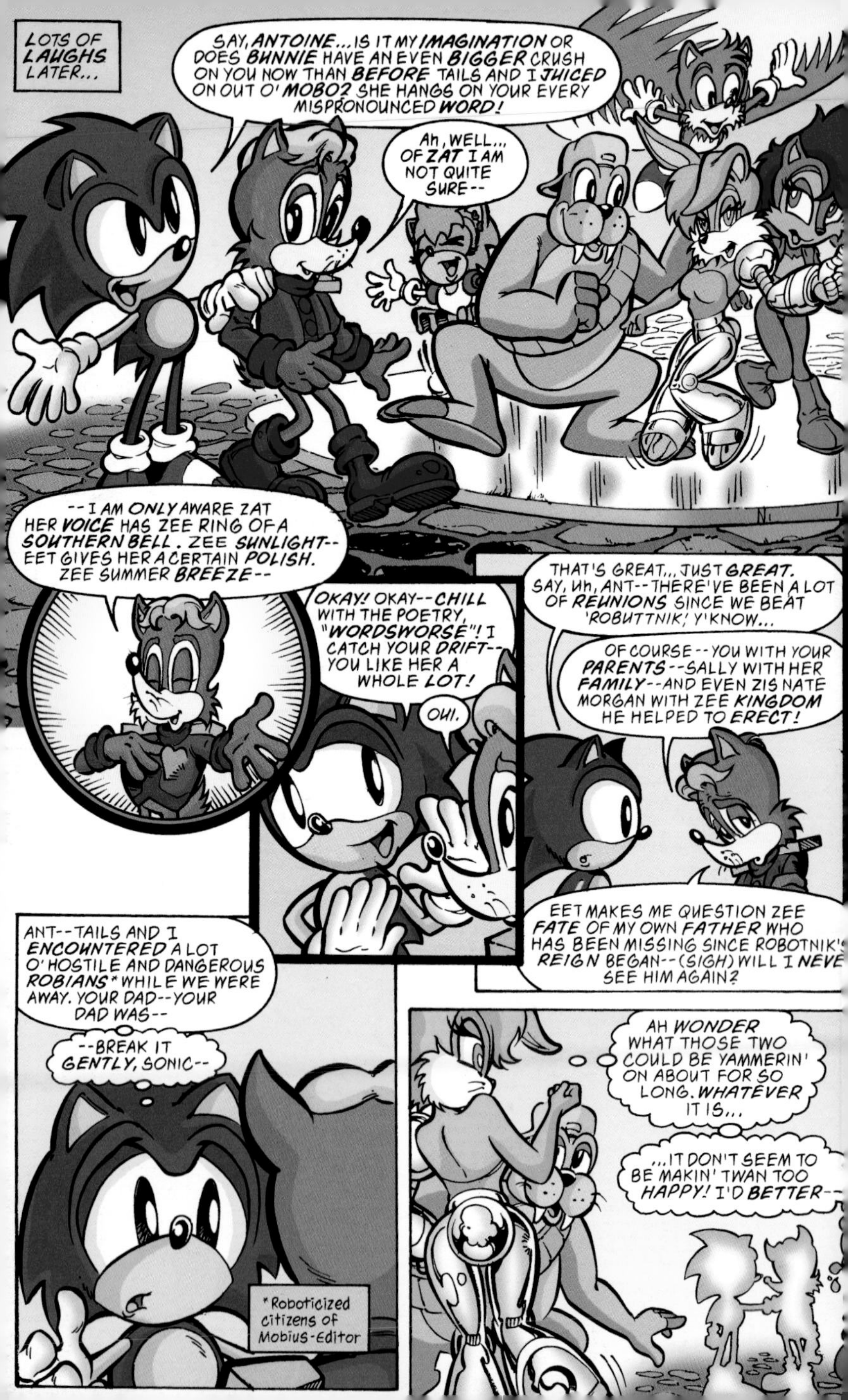
LOTS OF LAUGHS LATER...
SAY, ANTOINE... IS IT MY IMAGINATION OR DOES BUNNIE HAVE AN EVEN BIGGER CRUSH ON YOU NOW THAN BEFORE TAILS AND I JUICED ON OUT O' MOBO? SHE HANGS ON YOUR EVERY MISPRONOUNCED WORD!
AH, WELL... OF ZAT I AM NOT QUITE SURE--
--I AM ONLY AWARE ZAT HER VOICE HAS ZEE RING OF A SOUTHERN BELL. ZEE SUNLIGHT-- EET GIVES HER A CERTAIN POLISH. ZEE SUMMER BREEZE--
OKAY! OKAY--CHILL WITH THE POETRY, "WORDSWORSE"! I CATCH YOUR DRIFT-- YOU LIKE HER A WHOLE LOT!
OUI.
THAT'S GREAT... JUST GREAT. SAY, UH, ANT--THERE'VE BEEN A LOT OF REUNIONS SINCE WE BEAT 'ROBUTTNIK,' Y'KNOW...
OF COURSE--YOU WITH YOUR PARENTS--SALLY WITH HER FAMILY--AND EVEN ZIS NATE MORGAN WITH ZEE KINGDOM HE HELPED TO ERECT!
EET MAKES ME QUESTION ZEE FATE OF MY OWN FATHER WHO HAS BEEN MISSING SINCE ROBOTNIK'S REIGN BEGAN--(SIGH) WILL I NEVE SEE HIM AGAIN?
ANT--TAILS AND I ENCOUNTERED A LOT O' HOSTILE AND DANGEROUS ROBIANS* WHILE WE WERE AWAY. YOUR DAD--YOUR DAD WAS--
--BREAK IT GENTLY, SONIC--
*Roboticized citizens of Mobius-Editor
AH WONDER WHAT THOSE TWO COULD BE YAMMERIN' ON ABOUT FOR SO LONG. WHATEVER IT IS...
...IT DON'T SEEM TO BE MAKIN' TWAN TOO HAPPY! I'D BETTER--

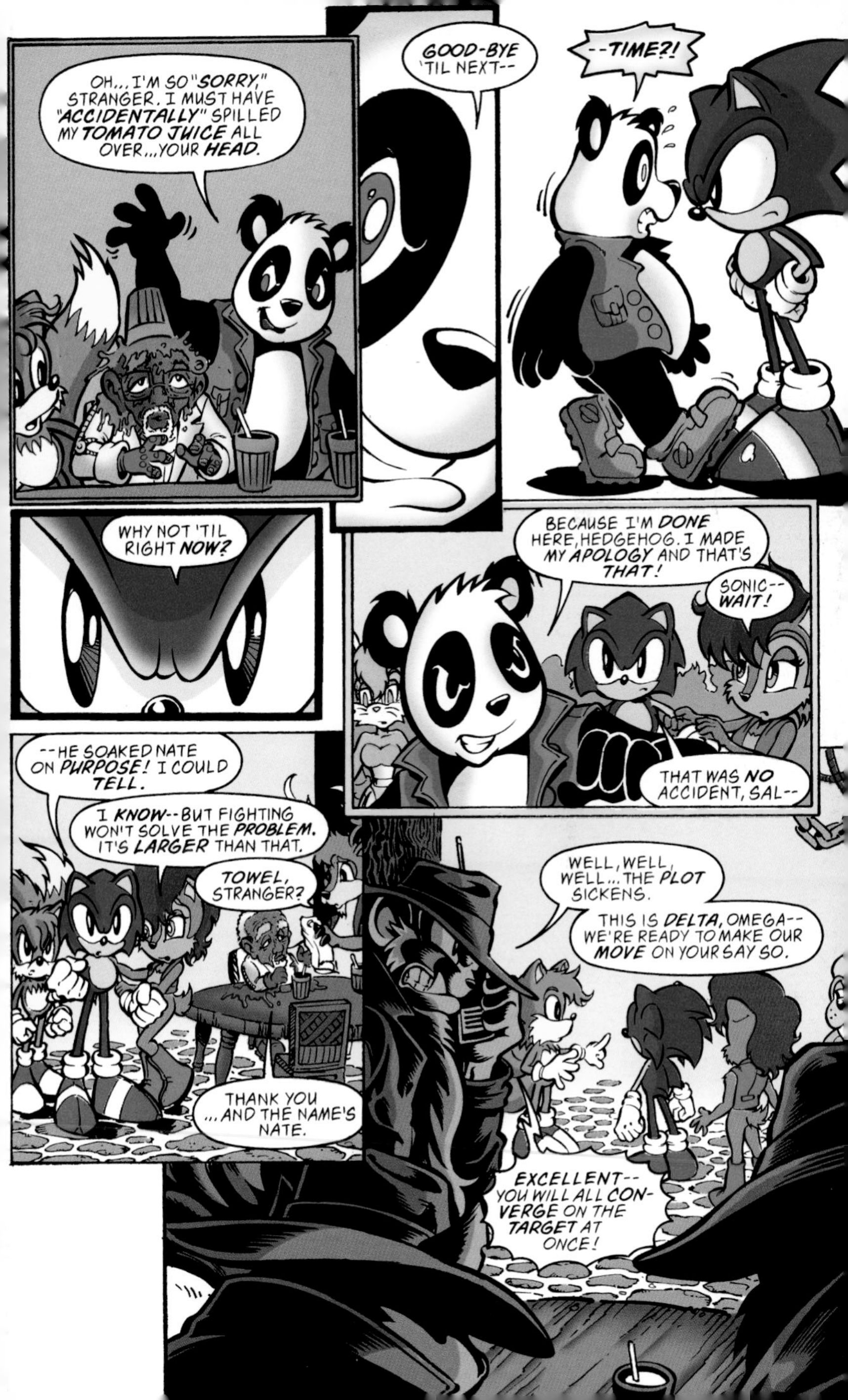
OH... I'M SO "SORRY," STRANGER. I MUST HAVE "ACCIDENTALLY" SPILLED MY TOMATO JUICE ALL OVER... YOUR HEAD.
GOOD-BYE 'TIL NEXT--
--TIME?!
WHY NOT 'TIL RIGHT NOW?
BECAUSE I'M DONE HERE, HEDGEHOG. I MADE MY APOLOGY AND THAT'S THAT!
SONIC-- WAIT!
THAT WAS NO ACCIDENT, SAL--
--HE SOAKED NATE ON PURPOSE! I COULD TELL.
I KNOW--BUT FIGHTING WON'T SOLVE THE PROBLEM. IT'S LARGER THAN THAT.
TOWEL, STRANGER?
THANK YOU ...AND THE NAME'S NATE.
WELL, WELL, WELL... THE PLOT SICKENS.
THIS IS DELTA, OMEGA-- WE'RE READY TO MAKE OUR MOVE ON YOUR SAY SO.
EXCELLENT-- YOU WILL ALL CONVERGE ON THE TARGET AT ONCE!

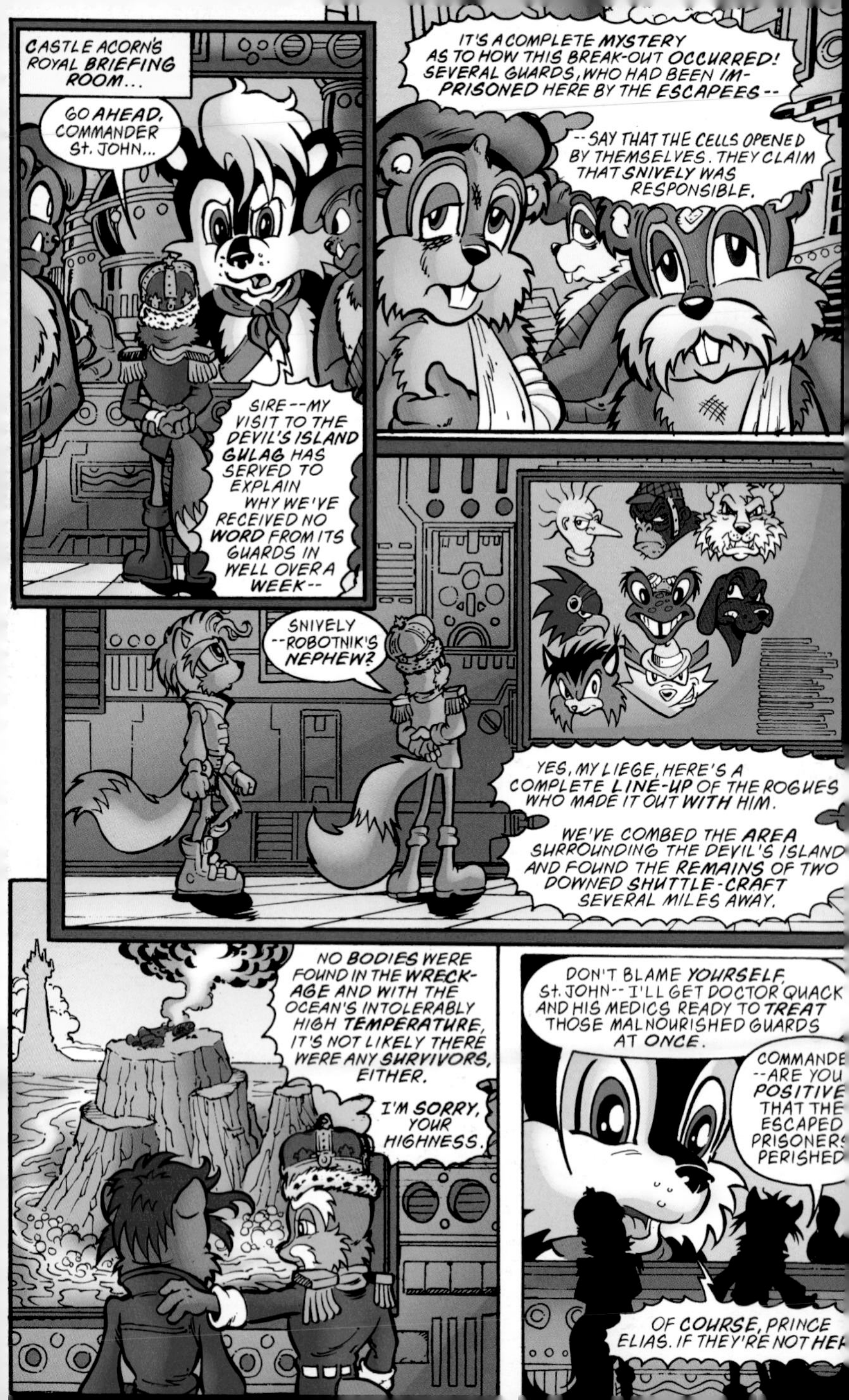

CASTLE ACORN'S ROYAL BRIEFING ROOM...
GO AHEAD, COMMANDER St. JOHN...
SIRE--MY VISIT TO THE DEVIL'S ISLAND GULAG HAS SERVED TO EXPLAIN WHY WE'VE RECEIVED NO WORD FROM ITS GUARDS IN WELL OVER A WEEK--
IT'S A COMPLETE MYSTERY AS TO HOW THIS BREAK-OUT OCCURRED! SEVERAL GUARDS, WHO HAD BEEN IMPRISONED HERE BY THE ESCAPEES--
--SAY THAT THE CELLS OPENED BY THEMSELVES. THEY CLAIM THAT SNIVELY WAS RESPONSIBLE.
SNIVELY --ROBOTNIK'S NEPHEW?
YES, MY LIEGE, HERE'S A COMPLETE LINE-UP OF THE ROGUES WHO MADE IT OUT WITH HIM.
WE'VE COMBED THE AREA SURROUNDING THE DEVIL'S ISLAND AND FOUND THE REMAINS OF TWO DOWNED SHUTTLE-CRAFT SEVERAL MILES AWAY.
NO BODIES WERE FOUND IN THE WRECKAGE AND WITH THE OCEAN'S INTOLERABLY HIGH TEMPERATURE, IT'S NOT LIKELY THERE WERE ANY SURVIVORS, EITHER.
I'M SORRY, YOUR HIGHNESS.
DON'T BLAME YOURSELF, St. JOHN-- I'LL GET DOCTOR QUACK AND HIS MEDICS READY TO TREAT THOSE MALNOURISHED GUARDS AT ONCE.
COMMANDE --ARE YOU POSITIVE THAT THE ESCAPED PRISONERS PERISHED
OF COURSE, PRINCE ELIAS. IF THEY'RE NOT HER

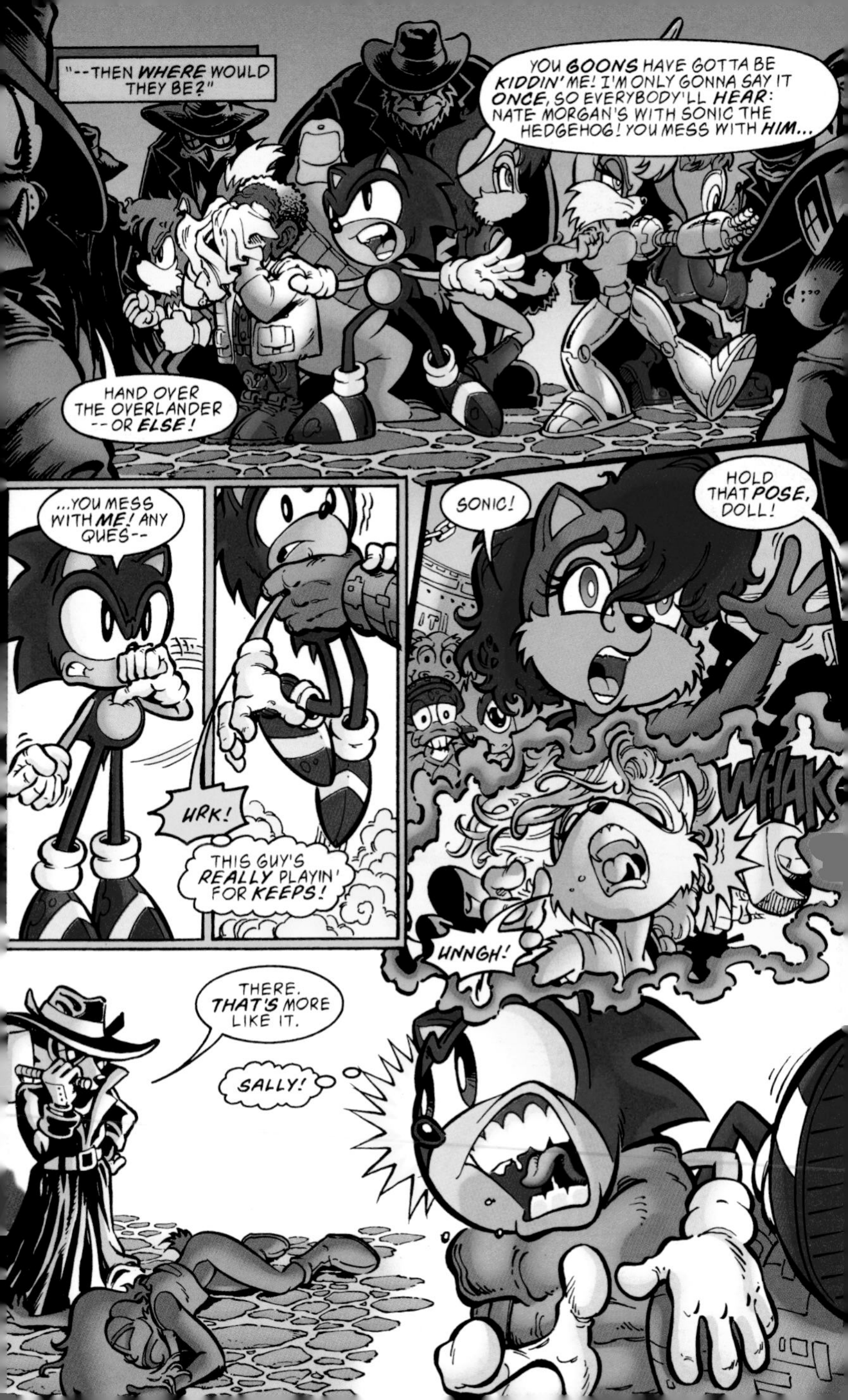
"--THEN WHERE WOULD THEY BE?"
YOU GOONS HAVE GOTTA BE KIDDIN' ME! I'M ONLY GONNA SAY IT ONCE, SO EVERYBODY'LL HEAR: NATE MORGAN'S WITH SONIC THE HEDGEHOG! YOU MESS WITH HIM...
HAND OVER THE OVERLANDER --OR ELSE!
...YOU MESS WITH ME! ANY QUES--
URK!
THIS GUY'S REALLY PLAYIN' FOR KEEPS!
SONIC!
HOLD THAT POSE, DOLL!
WHAK
UNNGH!
THERE. THAT'S MORE LIKE IT.
SALLY!

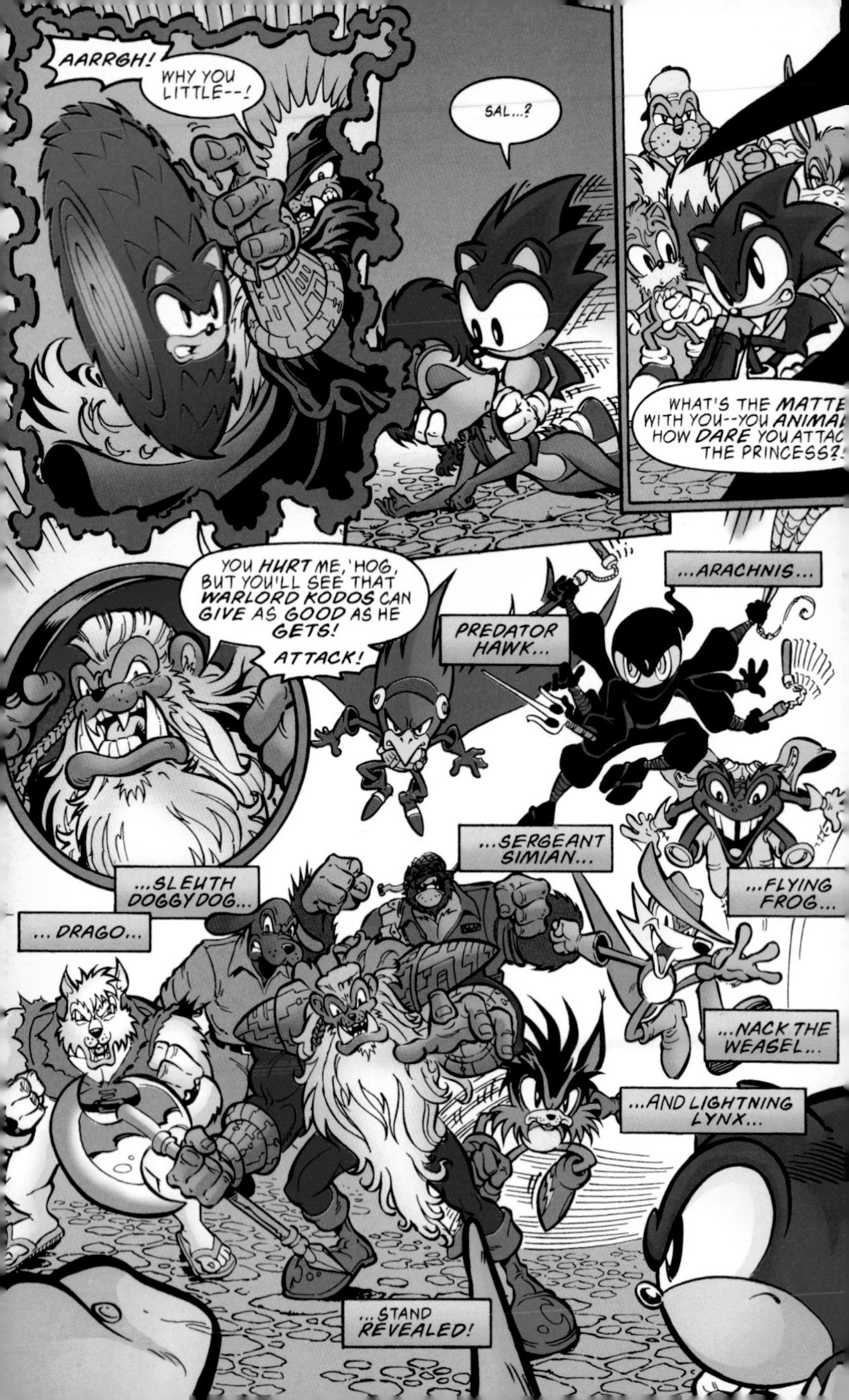
AARRGH!
WHY YOU LITTLE--!
SAL...?
WHAT'S THE MATTE WITH YOU--YOU ANIMA HOW DARE YOU ATTAC THE PRINCESS?!
YOU HURT ME, 'HOG, BUT YOU'LL SEE THAT WARLORD KODOS CAN GIVE AS GOOD AS HE GETS!
ATTACK!
PREDATOR HAWK...
...ARACHNIS...
...SERGEANT SIMIAN...
...FLYING FROG...
...SLEUTH DOGGYDOG...
... DRAGO...
...NACK THE WEASEL...
...AND LIGHTNING LYNX...
...STAND REVEALED!

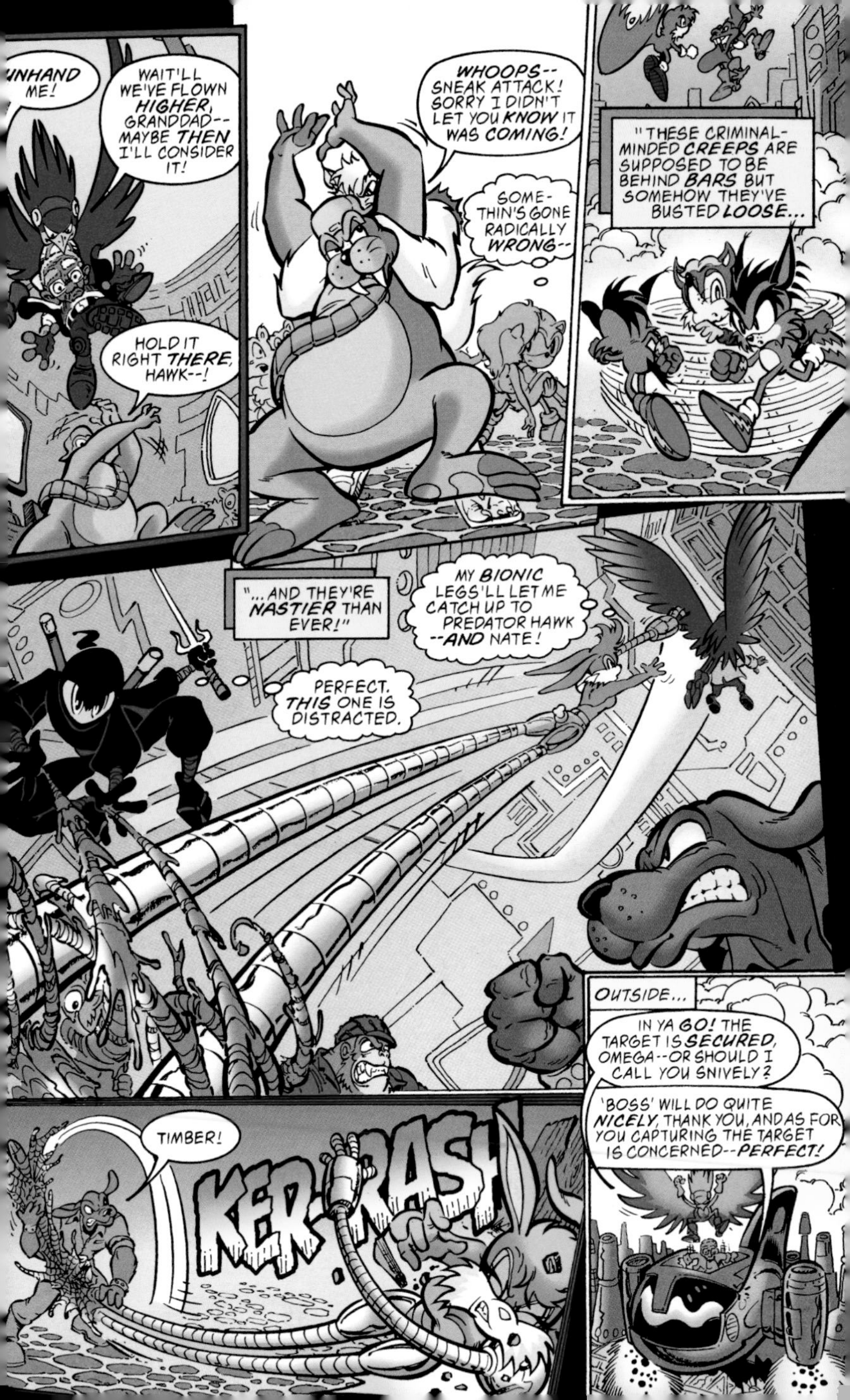
UNHAND ME!
WAIT'LL WE'VE FLOWN HIGHER, GRANDDAD--MAYBE THEN I'LL CONSIDER IT!
HOLD IT RIGHT THERE, HAWK--!
WHOOPS--SNEAK ATTACK! SORRY I DIDN'T LET YOU KNOW IT WAS COMING!
SOME-THIN'S GONE RADICALLY WRONG--
"THESE CRIMINAL-MINDED CREEPS ARE SUPPOSED TO BE BEHIND BARS BUT SOMEHOW THEY'VE BUSTED LOOSE...
"...AND THEY'RE NASTIER THAN EVER!"
MY BIONIC LEGS'LL LET ME CATCH UP TO PREDATOR HAWK --AND NATE!
PERFECT. THIS ONE IS DISTRACTED.
OUTSIDE...
IN YA GO! THE TARGET IS SECURED, OMEGA--OR SHOULD I CALL YOU SNIVELY?
'BOSS' WILL DO QUITE NICELY, THANK YOU, AND AS FOR YOU CAPTURING THE TARGET IS CONCERNED--PERFECT!
TIMBER!
KER-RASH

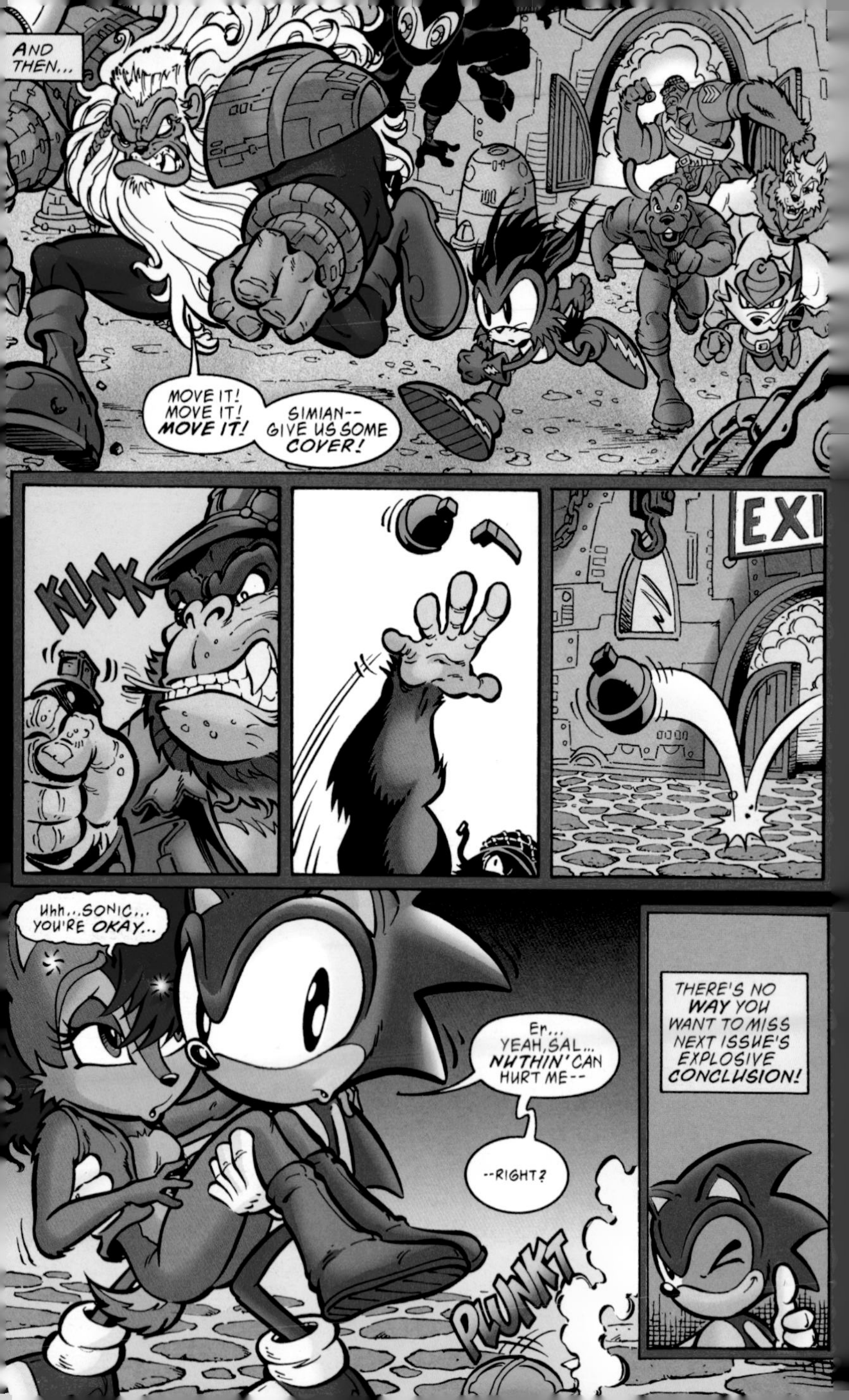
AND THEN...
MOVE IT! MOVE IT! MOVE IT!
SIMIAN-- GIVE US SOME COVER!
KLINK
EXI
Uhh...SONIC... YOU'RE OKAY...
Er... YEAH, SAL... NUTHIN' CAN HURT ME--
--RIGHT?
PLUNKT
THERE'S NO WAY YOU WANT TO MISS NEXT ISSUE'S EXPLOSIVE CONCLUSION!

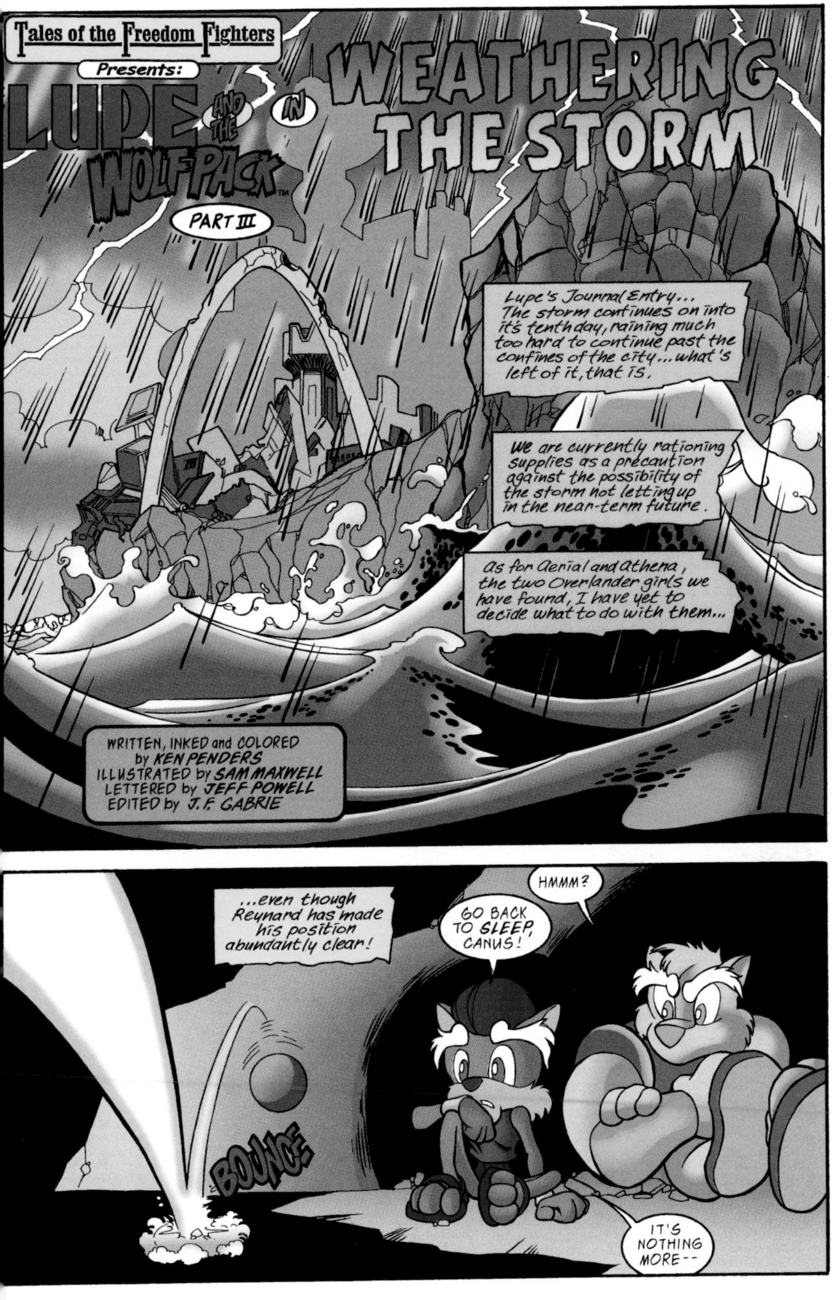

Tales of the Freedom Fighters
Presents:
LUPE AND THE WOLFPACK™ IN
WEATHERING THE STORM
PART III
Lupe's Journal Entry... The storm continues on into it's tenth day, raining much too hard to continue past the confines of the city... what's left of it, that is.
We are currently rationing supplies as a precaution against the possibility of the storm not letting up in the near-term future.
As for Aerial and Athena, the two Overlander girls we have found, I have yet to decide what to do with them...
WRITTEN, INKED and COLORED by KEN PENDERS
ILLUSTRATED by SAM MAXWELL
LETTERED by JEFF POWELL
EDITED by J.F. GABRIE
...even though Reynard has made his position abundantly clear!
HMMM?
GO BACK TO SLEEP, CANUS!
BOUNCE
IT'S NOTHING MORE--

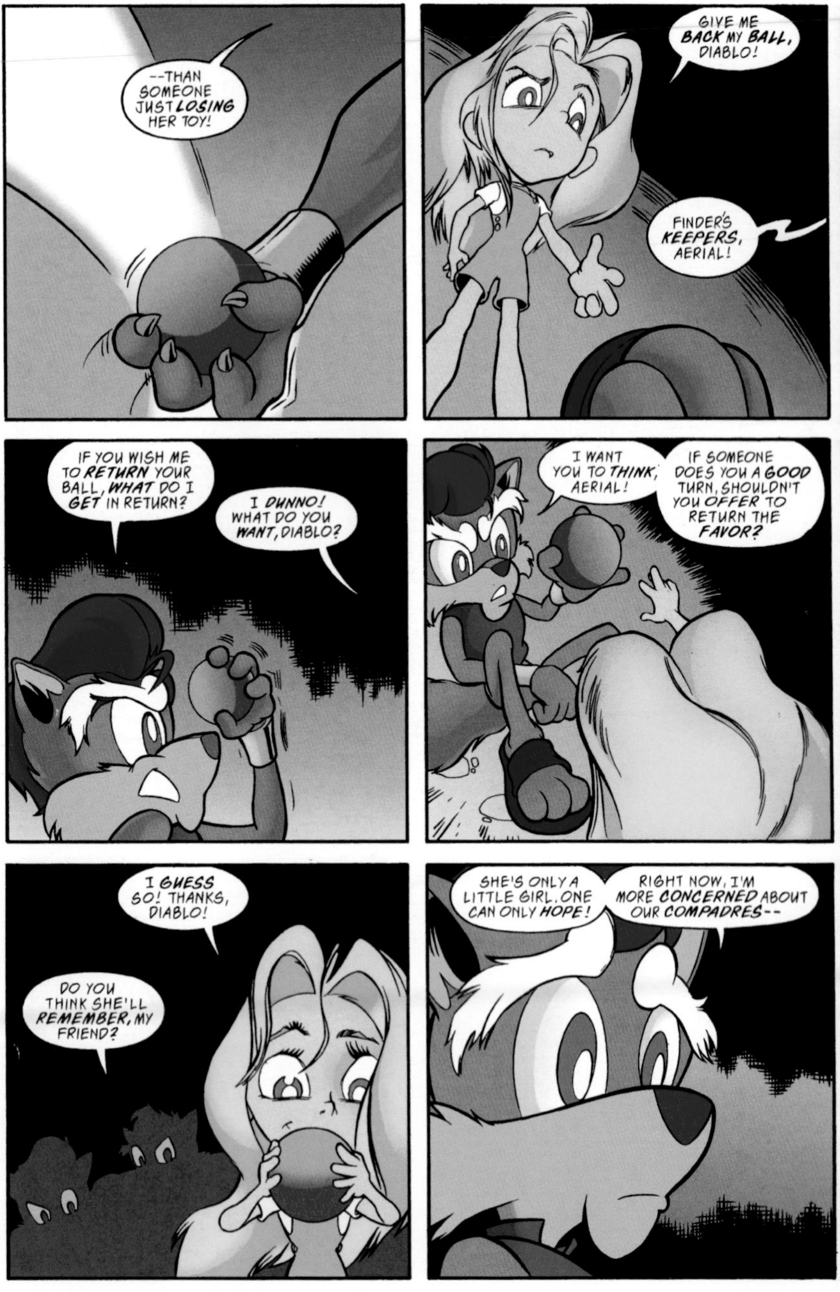
--THAN SOMEONE JUST LOSING HER TOY!
GIVE ME BACK MY BALL, DIABLO!
FINDER'S KEEPERS, AERIAL!
IF YOU WISH ME TO RETURN YOUR BALL, WHAT DO I GET IN RETURN?
I DUNNO! WHAT DO YOU WANT, DIABLO?
I WANT YOU TO THINK, AERIAL!
IF SOMEONE DOES YOU A GOOD TURN, SHOULDN'T YOU OFFER TO RETURN THE FAVOR?
I GUESS SO! THANKS, DIABLO!
DO YOU THINK SHE'LL REMEMBER, MY FRIEND?
SHE'S ONLY A LITTLE GIRL. ONE CAN ONLY HOPE!
RIGHT NOW, I'M MORE CONCERNED ABOUT OUR COMPADRES--

" --AND WONDERING WHAT'S TAKING THEM SO LONG."

JUST BECAUSE THEIR *PARENTS* MET WITH AN *UNFORTUNATE* END IS NO *REASON* FOR YOU TO ASSUME THE *RESPONSIBILITY*, LUPE!

OUR *PRESENT* SITUATION IS *DIFFICULT* ENOUGH WITHOUT TAKING ON THAT *BURDEN!*

THERE'S WHERE YOU'RE *WRONG*, REYNARD!

I WOULD LIKE TO BELIEVE *OTHERS* WOULD SHOW THE SAME *COMPASSION* TO *WOLF CUBS* IF THEY WERE DISCOVERED IN *SIMILAR* CIRCUMSTANCES!

TURNING OUR BACKS ON THE GIRLS WOULD MAKE US NO BETTER THAN THOSE WE FOUGHT TO PRESERVE OUR KIND!

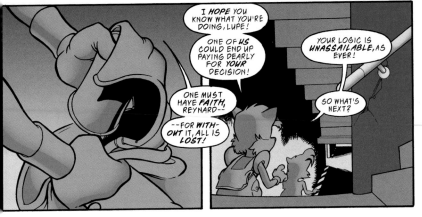

I *HOPE* YOU KNOW WHAT YOU'RE DOING, LUPE!

ONE OF *US* COULD END UP PAYING DEARLY FOR *YOUR* DECISION!

ONE MUST HAVE *FAITH*, REYNARD--

--FOR *WITHOUT* IT, ALL IS *LOST!*

YOUR LOGIC IS *UNASSAILABLE*, AS EVER!

SO WHAT'S NEXT?

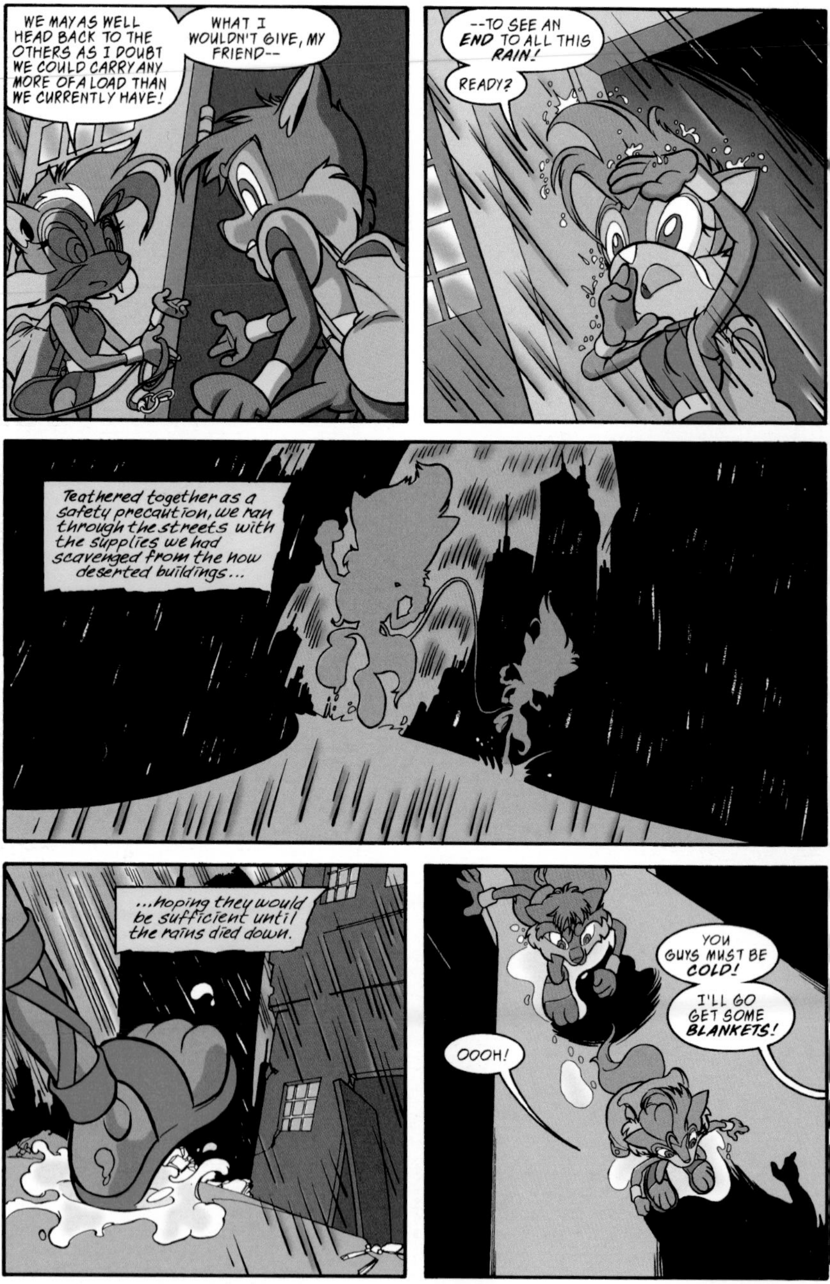
WE MAY AS WELL HEAD BACK TO THE OTHERS AS I DOUBT WE COULD CARRY ANY MORE OF A LOAD THAN WE CURRENTLY HAVE!
WHAT I WOULDN'T GIVE, MY FRIEND--
--TO SEE AN END TO ALL THIS RAIN!
READY?
Teathered together as a safety precaution, we ran through the streets with the supplies we had scavenged from the now deserted buildings...
...hoping they would be sufficient until the rains died down.
YOU GUYS MUST BE COLD!
I'LL GO GET SOME BLANKETS!
OOOH!

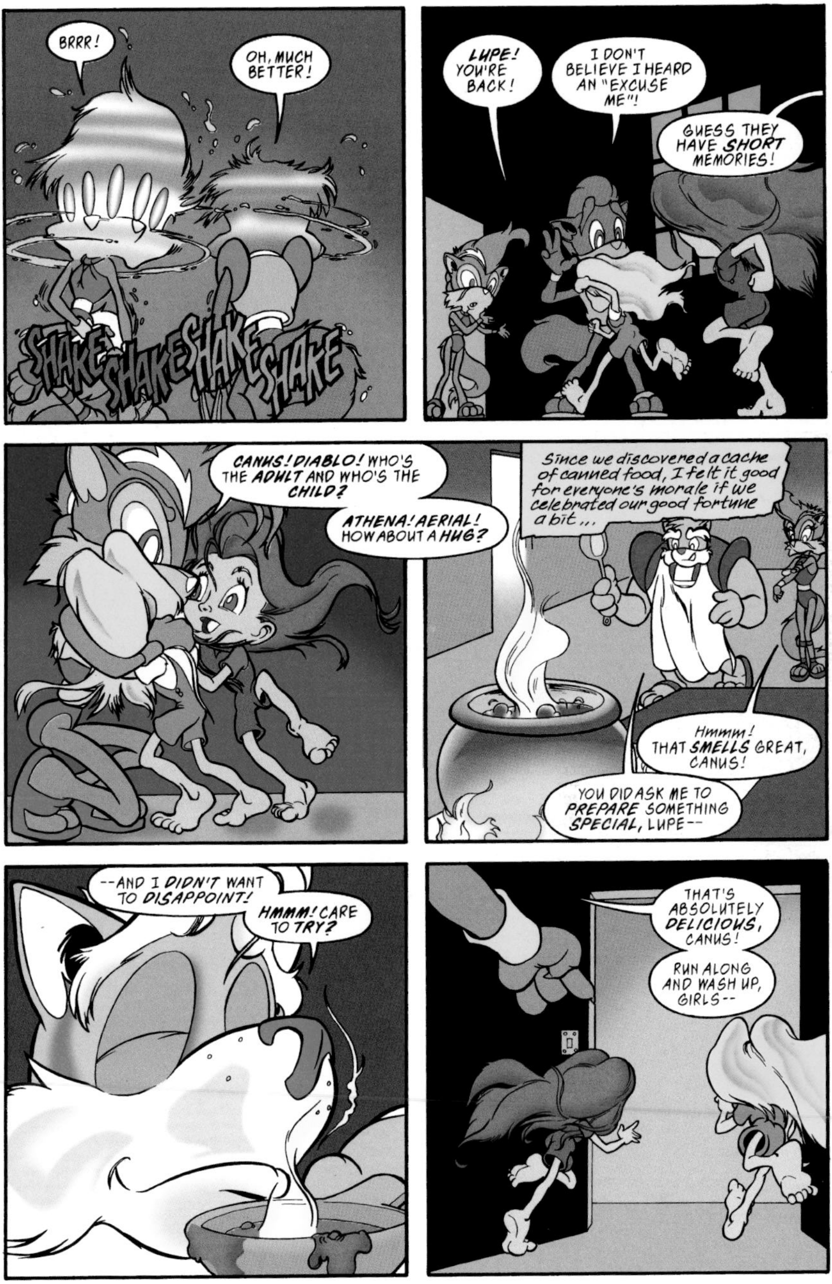
BRRR!
OH, MUCH BETTER!
SHAKE SHAKE SHAKE SHAKE
LUPE! YOU'RE BACK!
I DON'T BELIEVE I HEARD AN "EXCUSE ME"!
GUESS THEY HAVE SHORT MEMORIES!
CANUS! DIABLO! WHO'S THE ADULT AND WHO'S THE CHILD?
ATHENA! AERIAL! HOW ABOUT A HUG?
Since we discovered a cache of canned food, I felt it good for everyone's morale if we celebrated our good fortune a bit...
Hmmm! THAT SMELLS GREAT, CANUS!
YOU DID ASK ME TO PREPARE SOMETHING SPECIAL, LUPE--
--AND I DIDN'T WANT TO DISAPPOINT!
HMMM! CARE TO TRY?
THAT'S ABSOLUTELY DELICIOUS, CANUS!
RUN ALONG AND WASH UP, GIRLS--

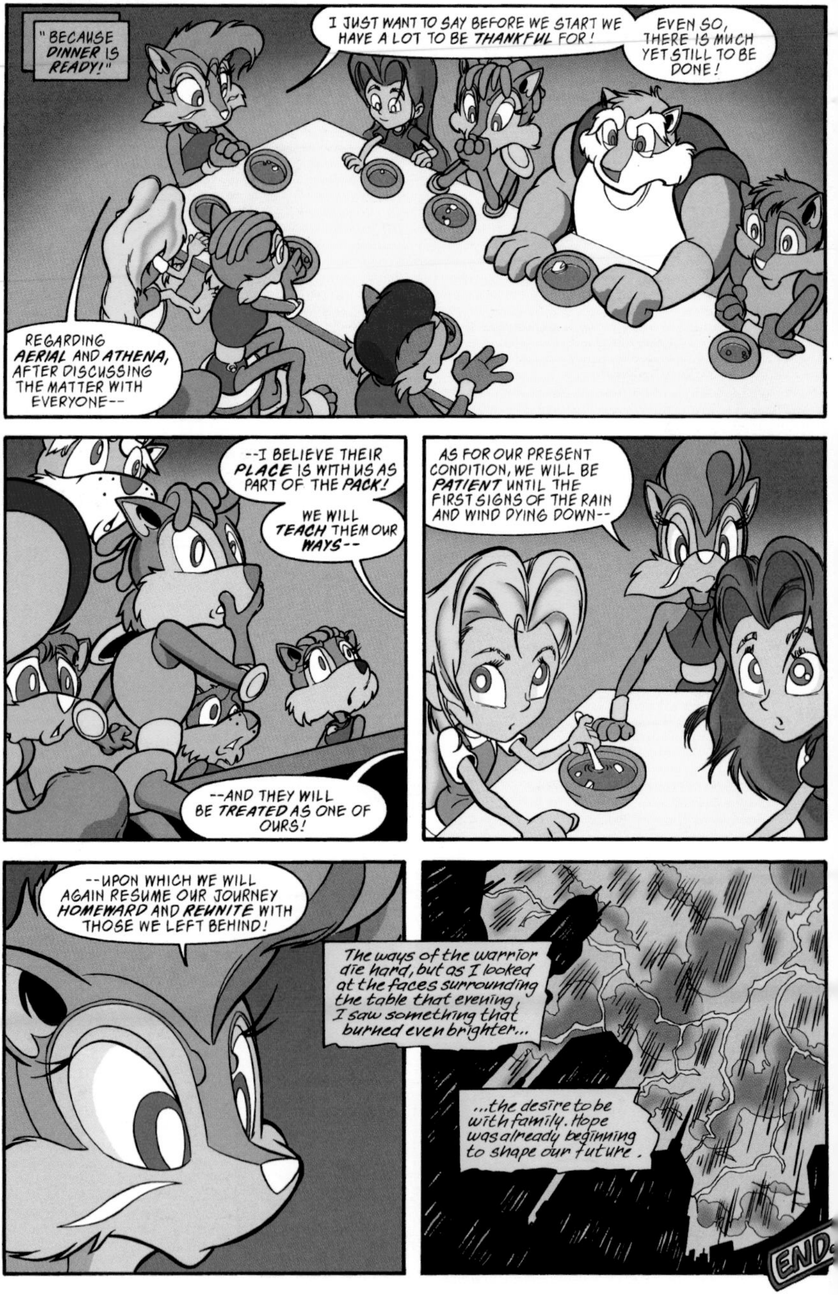
"BECAUSE DINNER IS READY!"
I JUST WANT TO SAY BEFORE WE START WE HAVE A LOT TO BE THANKFUL FOR!
EVEN SO, THERE IS MUCH YET STILL TO BE DONE!
REGARDING AERIAL AND ATHENA, AFTER DISCUSSING THE MATTER WITH EVERYONE--
--I BELIEVE THEIR PLACE IS WITH US AS PART OF THE PACK!
WE WILL TEACH THEM OUR WAYS--
--AND THEY WILL BE TREATED AS ONE OF OURS!
AS FOR OUR PRESENT CONDITION, WE WILL BE PATIENT UNTIL THE FIRST SIGNS OF THE RAIN AND WIND DYING DOWN--
--UPON WHICH WE WILL AGAIN RESUME OUR JOURNEY HOMEWARD AND REUNITE WITH THOSE WE LEFT BEHIND!
The ways of the warrior die hard, but as I looked at the faces surrounding the table that evening, I saw something that burned even brighter...
...the desire to be with family. Hope was already beginning to shape our future.
END

BONUS PIN-UP

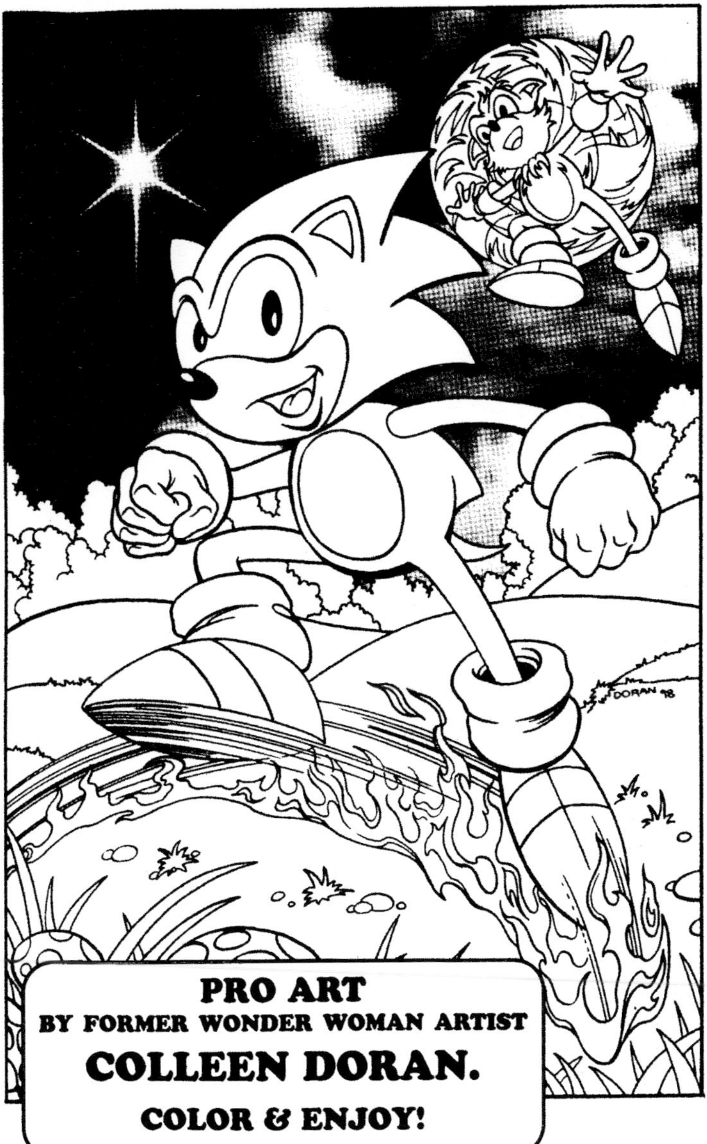
DORAN '98

PRO ART
BY FORMER WONDER WOMAN ARTIST
COLLEEN DORAN.
COLOR & ENJOY!

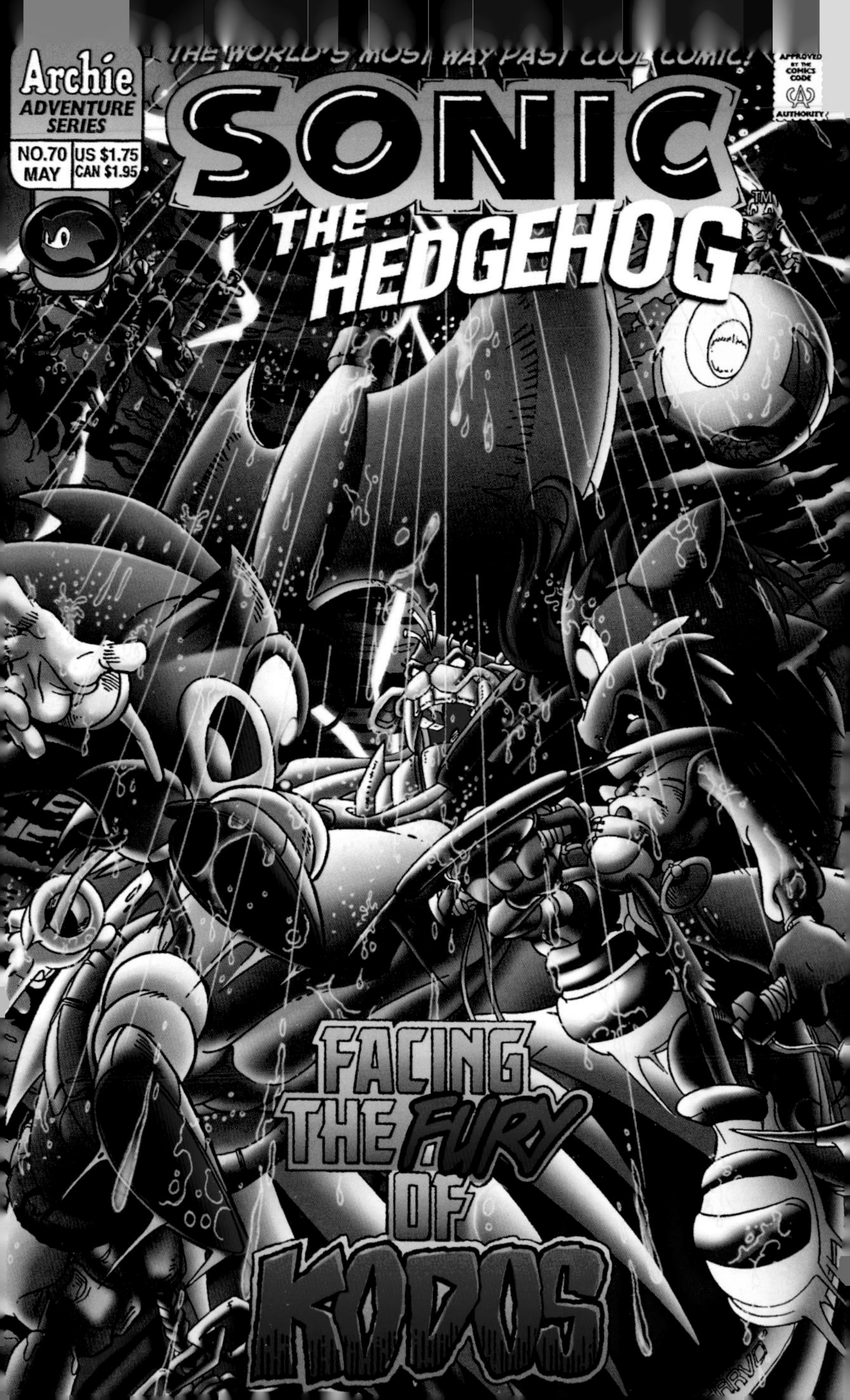
THE WORLD'S MOST WAY PAST COOL COMIC!
Archie
ADVENTURE SERIES
NO.70
MAY
US $1.75
CAN $1.95
APPROVED BY THE COMICS CODE AUTHORITY
SONIC
THE HEDGEHOG
FACING THE FURY OF KODOS

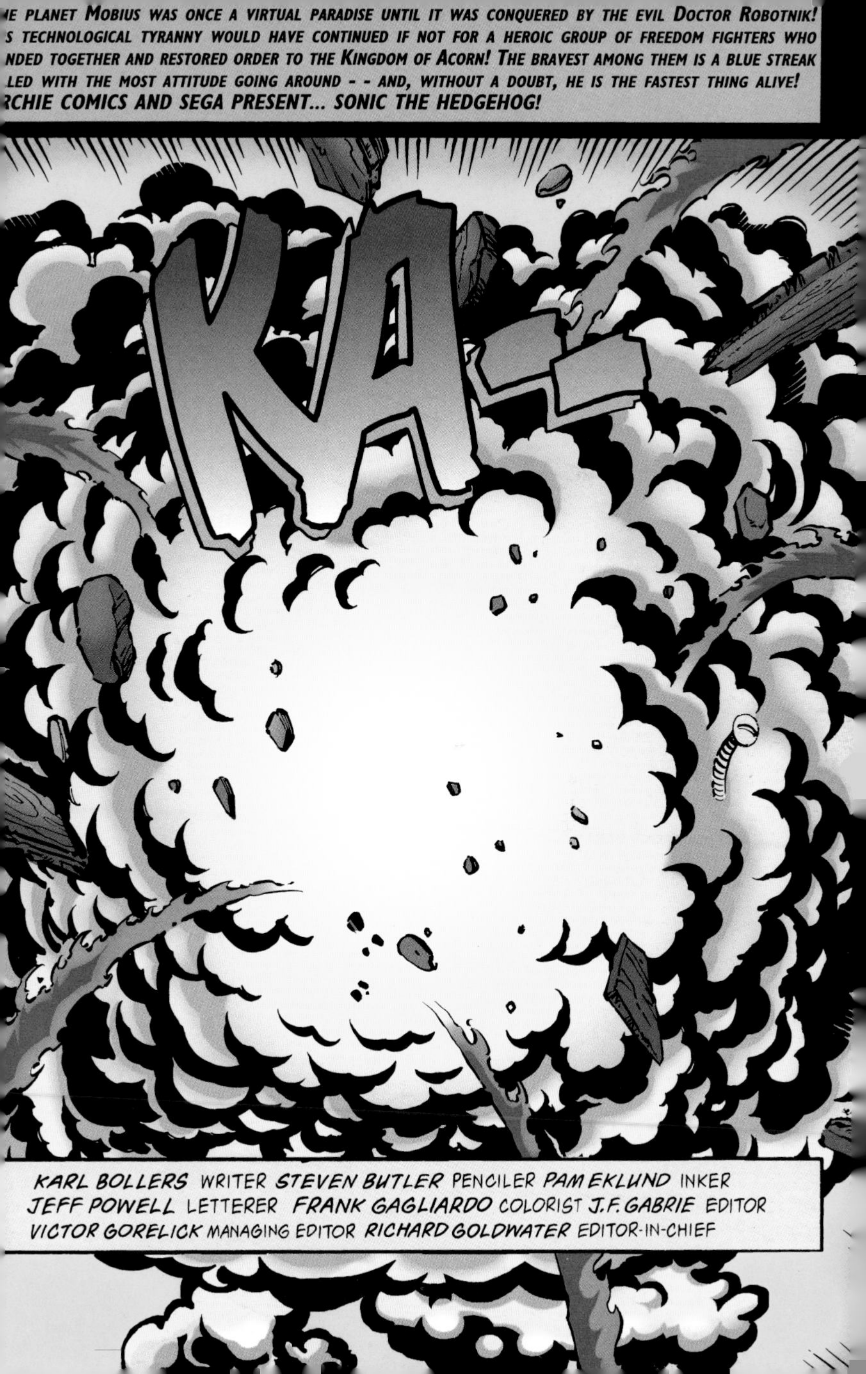
E PLANET MOBIUS WAS ONCE A VIRTUAL PARADISE UNTIL IT WAS CONQUERED BY THE EVIL DOCTOR ROBOTNIK! S TECHNOLOGICAL TYRANNY WOULD HAVE CONTINUED IF NOT FOR A HEROIC GROUP OF FREEDOM FIGHTERS WHO NDED TOGETHER AND RESTORED ORDER TO THE KINGDOM OF ACORN! THE BRAVEST AMONG THEM IS A BLUE STREAK LED WITH THE MOST ATTITUDE GOING AROUND - - AND, WITHOUT A DOUBT, HE IS THE FASTEST THING ALIVE!
RCHIE COMICS AND SEGA PRESENT... SONIC THE HEDGEHOG!
KA-
KARL BOLLERS WRITER STEVEN BUTLER PENCILER PAM EKLUND INKER JEFF POWELL LETTERER FRANK GAGLIARDO COLORIST J.F. GABRIE EDITOR VICTOR GORELICK MANAGING EDITOR RICHARD GOLDWATER EDITOR-IN-CHIEF

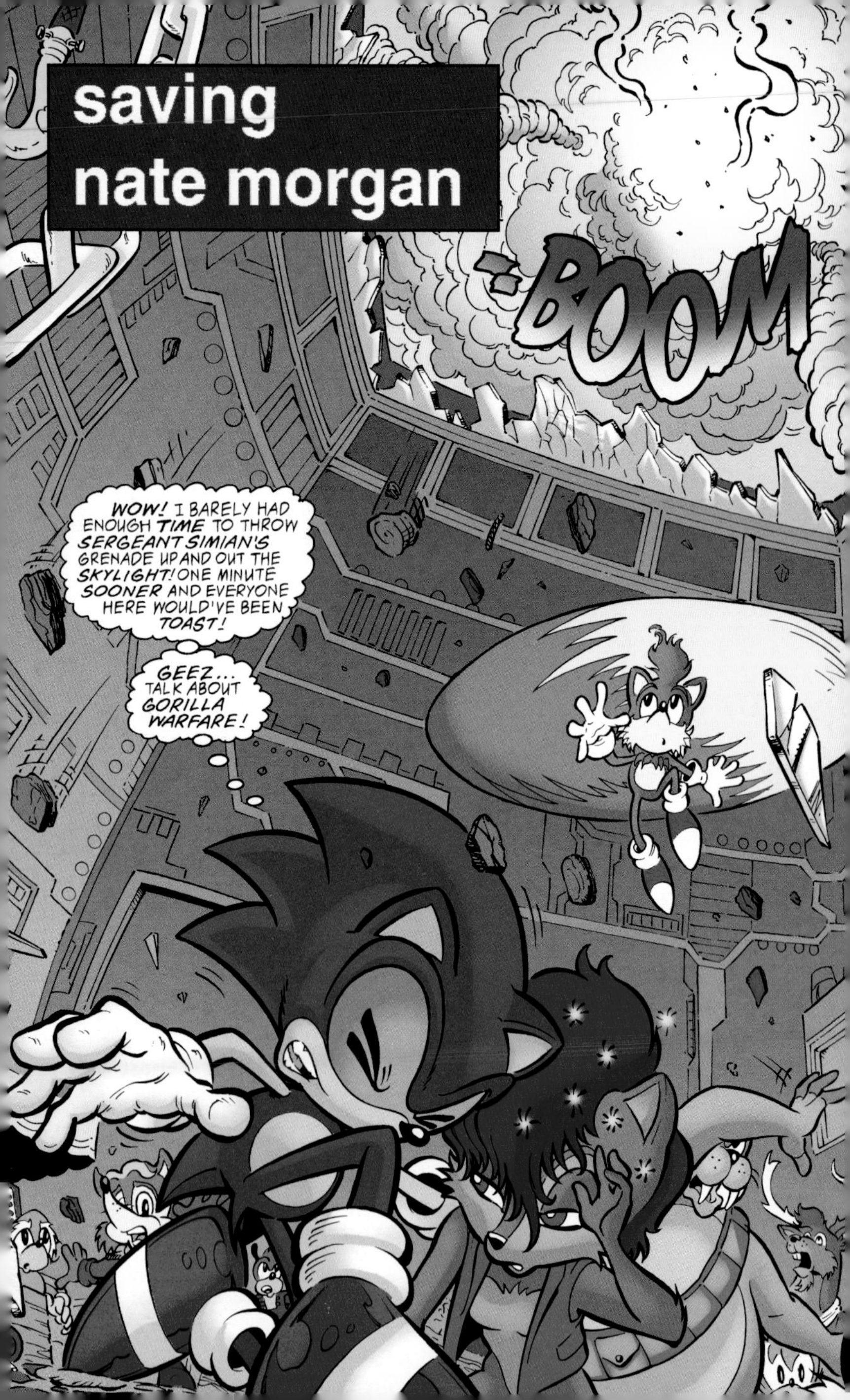
saving
nate morgan
BOOM
WOW! I BARELY HAD ENOUGH TIME TO THROW SERGEANT SIMIAN'S GRENADE UP AND OUT THE SKYLIGHT! ONE MINUTE SOONER AND EVERYONE HERE WOULD'VE BEEN TOAST!
GEEZ... TALK ABOUT GORILLA WARFARE!

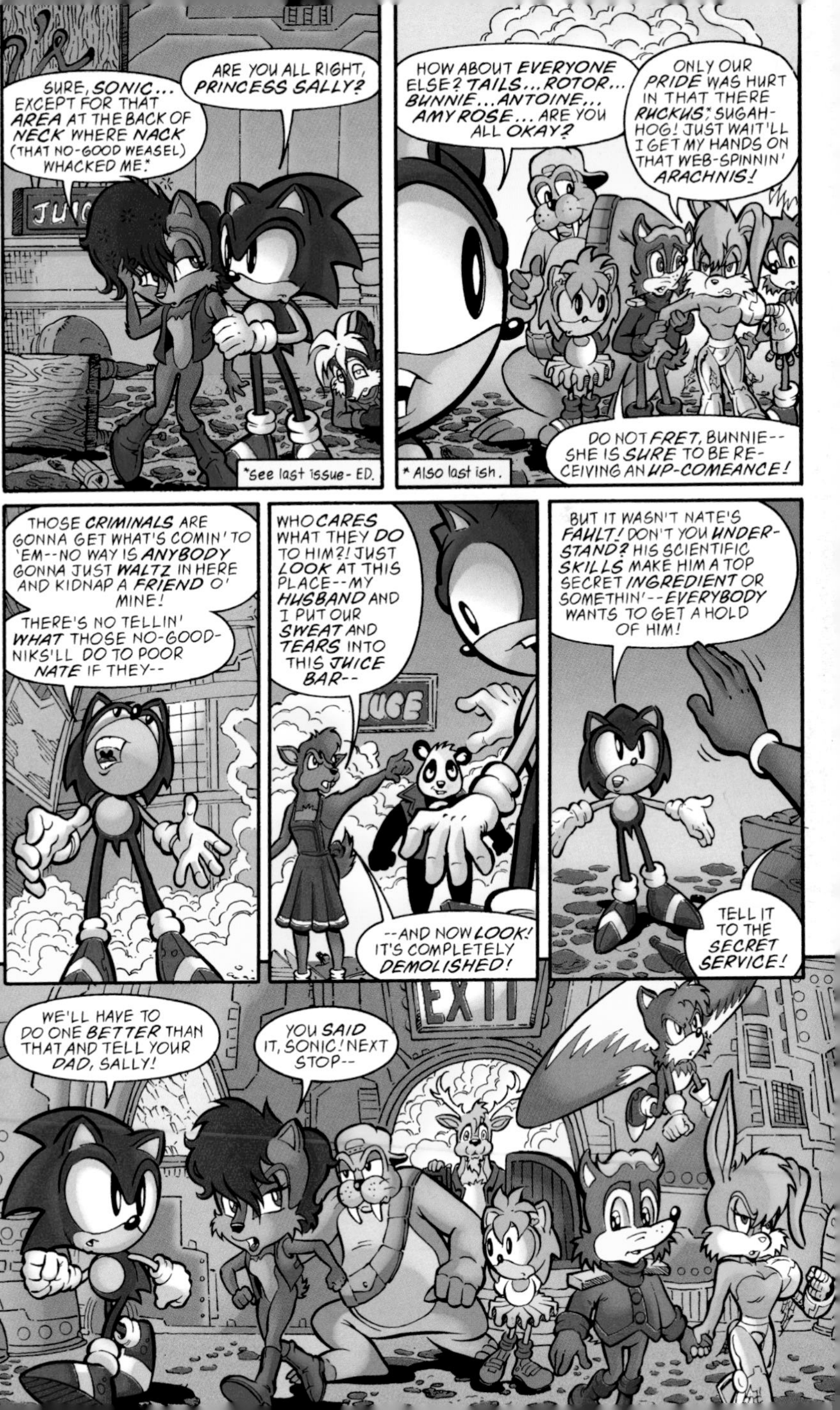
ARE YOU ALL RIGHT, PRINCESS SALLY?
SURE, SONIC... EXCEPT FOR THAT AREA AT THE BACK OF NECK WHERE NACK (THAT NO-GOOD WEASEL) WHACKED ME!*
JUIC
*See last issue - ED.
HOW ABOUT EVERYONE ELSE? TAILS... ROTOR... BUNNIE... ANTOINE... AMY ROSE... ARE YOU ALL OKAY?
ONLY OUR PRIDE WAS HURT IN THAT THERE RUCKUS,* SUGAH-HOG! JUST WAIT'LL I GET MY HANDS ON THAT WEB-SPINNIN' ARACHNIS!
DO NOT FRET, BUNNIE-- SHE IS SURE TO BE RE-CEIVING AN UP-COMEANCE!
* Also last ish.
THOSE CRIMINALS ARE GONNA GET WHAT'S COMIN' TO 'EM--NO WAY IS ANYBODY GONNA JUST WALTZ IN HERE AND KIDNAP A FRIEND O' MINE!
THERE'S NO TELLIN' WHAT THOSE NO-GOOD-NIKS'LL DO TO POOR NATE IF THEY--
WHO CARES WHAT THEY DO TO HIM?! JUST LOOK AT THIS PLACE--MY HUSBAND AND I PUT OUR SWEAT AND TEARS INTO THIS JUICE BAR--
JUCE
--AND NOW LOOK! IT'S COMPLETELY DEMOLISHED!
BUT IT WASN'T NATE'S FAULT! DON'T YOU UNDER-STAND? HIS SCIENTIFIC SKILLS MAKE HIM A TOP SECRET INGREDIENT OR SOMETHIN'--EVERYBODY WANTS TO GET A HOLD OF HIM!
TELL IT TO THE SECRET SERVICE!
EXIT
WE'LL HAVE TO DO ONE BETTER THAN THAT AND TELL YOUR DAD, SALLY!
YOU SAID IT, SONIC! NEXT STOP--

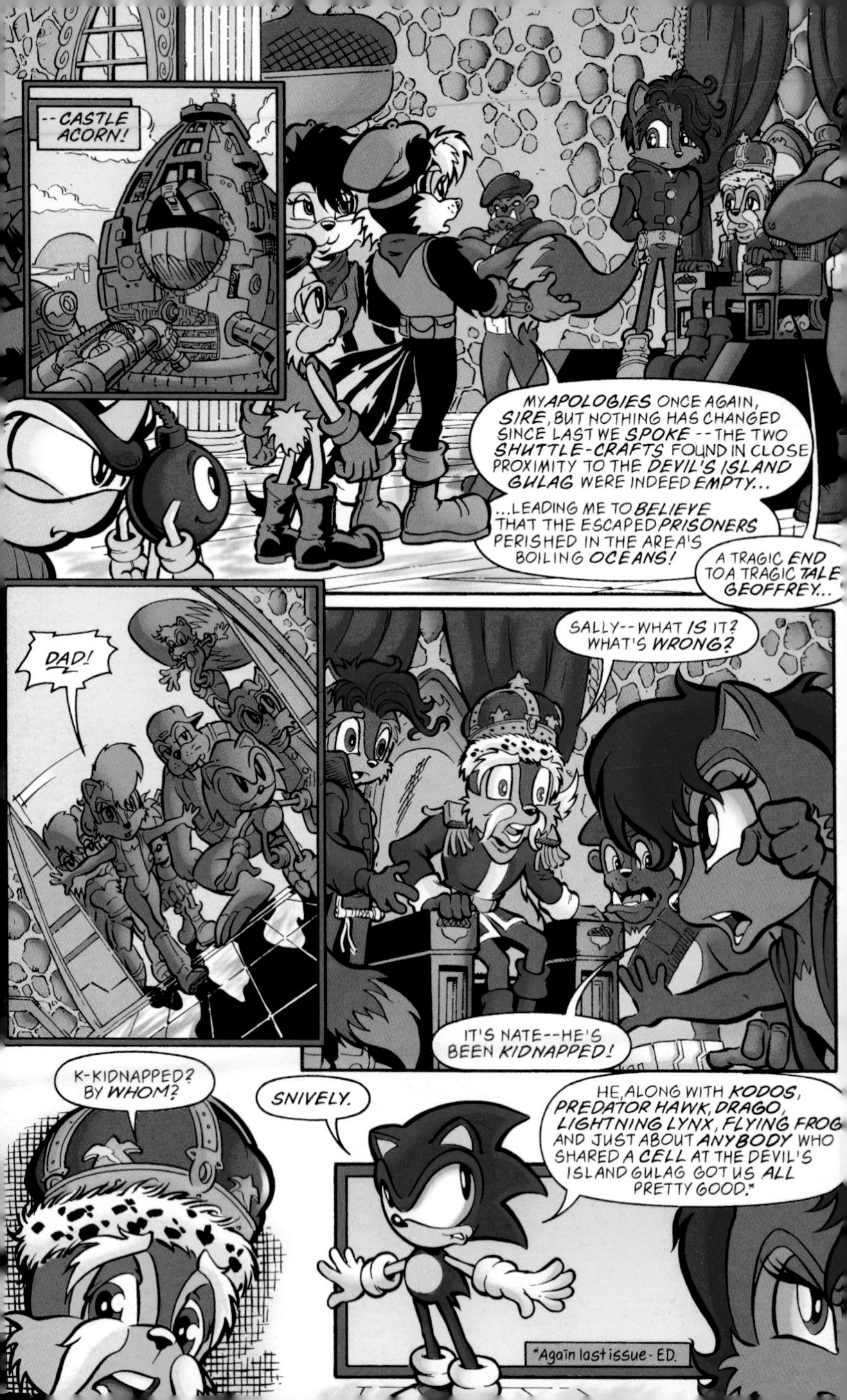
--CASTLE ACORN!
MY APOLOGIES ONCE AGAIN, SIRE, BUT NOTHING HAS CHANGED SINCE LAST WE SPOKE--THE TWO SHUTTLE-CRAFTS FOUND IN CLOSE PROXIMITY TO THE DEVIL'S ISLAND GULAG WERE INDEED EMPTY...
...LEADING ME TO BELIEVE THAT THE ESCAPED PRISONERS PERISHED IN THE AREA'S BOILING OCEANS!
A TRAGIC END TO A TRAGIC TALE GEOFFREY...
DAD!
SALLY--WHAT IS IT? WHAT'S WRONG?
IT'S NATE--HE'S BEEN KIDNAPPED!
K-KIDNAPPED? BY WHOM?
SNIVELY.
HE, ALONG WITH KODOS, PREDATOR HAWK, DRAGO, LIGHTNING LYNX, FLYING FROG AND JUST ABOUT ANYBODY WHO SHARED A CELL AT THE DEVIL'S ISLAND GULAG GOT US ALL PRETTY GOOD.*
*Again last issue - ED.

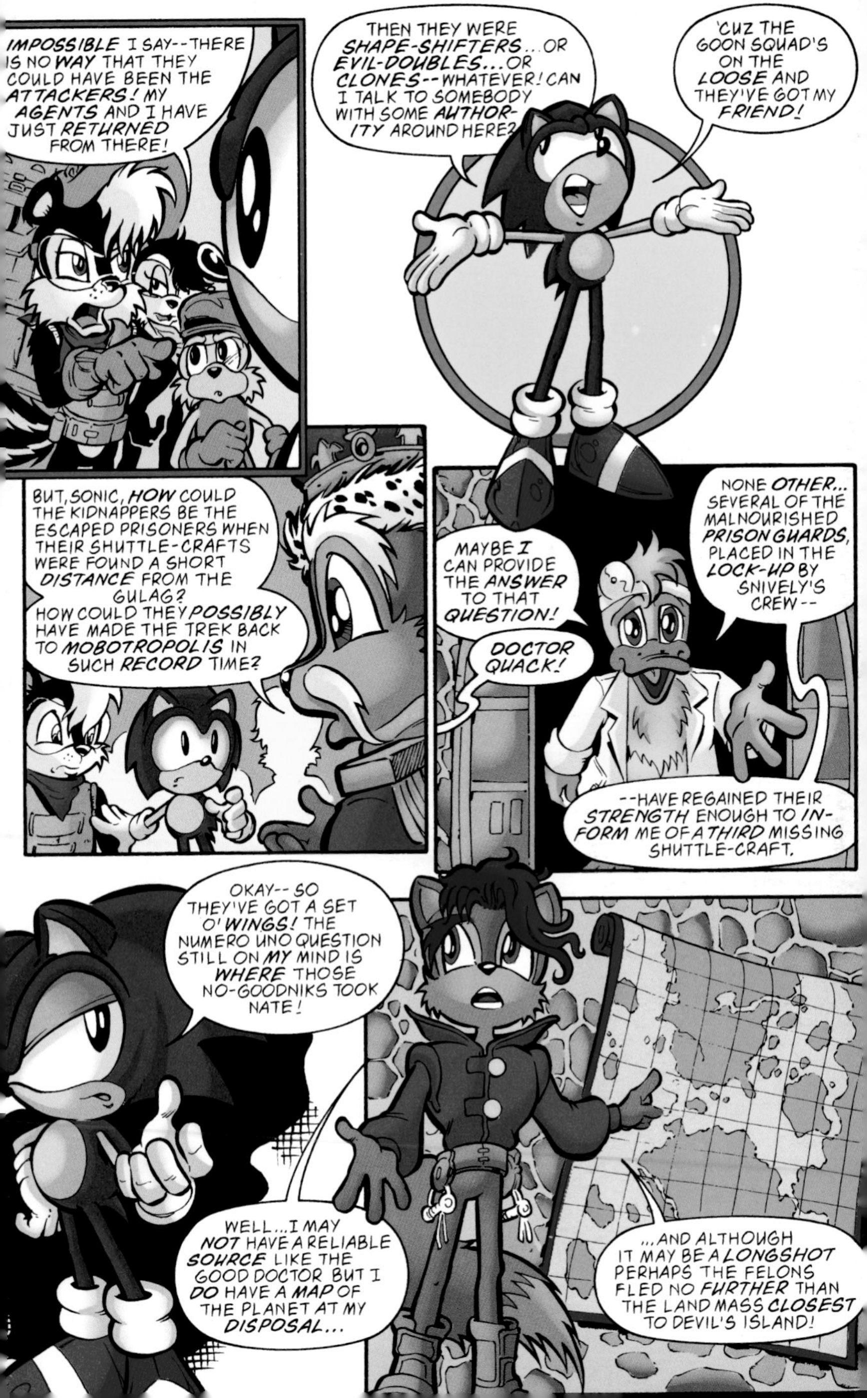

IMPOSSIBLE I SAY--THERE IS NO WAY THAT THEY COULD HAVE BEEN THE ATTACKERS! MY AGENTS AND I HAVE JUST RETURNED FROM THERE!
THEN THEY WERE SHAPE-SHIFTERS...OR EVIL-DOUBLES...OR CLONES--WHATEVER! CAN I TALK TO SOMEBODY WITH SOME AUTHOR-ITY AROUND HERE?
'CUZ THE GOON SQUAD'S ON THE LOOSE AND THEY'VE GOT MY FRIEND!
BUT, SONIC, HOW COULD THE KIDNAPPERS BE THE ESCAPED PRISONERS WHEN THEIR SHUTTLE-CRAFTS WERE FOUND A SHORT DISTANCE FROM THE GULAG? HOW COULD THEY POSSIBLY HAVE MADE THE TREK BACK TO MOBOTROPOLIS IN SUCH RECORD TIME?
MAYBE I CAN PROVIDE THE ANSWER TO THAT QUESTION!
DOCTOR QUACK!
NONE OTHER... SEVERAL OF THE MALNOURISHED PRISON GUARDS, PLACED IN THE LOCK-UP BY SNIVELY'S CREW --
--HAVE REGAINED THEIR STRENGTH ENOUGH TO IN-FORM ME OF A THIRD MISSING SHUTTLE-CRAFT.
OKAY-- SO THEY'VE GOT A SET O' WINGS! THE NUMERO UNO QUESTION STILL ON MY MIND IS WHERE THOSE NO-GOODNIKS TOOK NATE!
WELL...I MAY NOT HAVE A RELIABLE SOURCE LIKE THE GOOD DOCTOR BUT I DO HAVE A MAP OF THE PLANET AT MY DISPOSAL...
...AND ALTHOUGH IT MAY BE A LONGSHOT PERHAPS THE FELONS FLED NO FURTHER THAN THE LAND MASS CLOSEST TO DEVIL'S ISLAND!

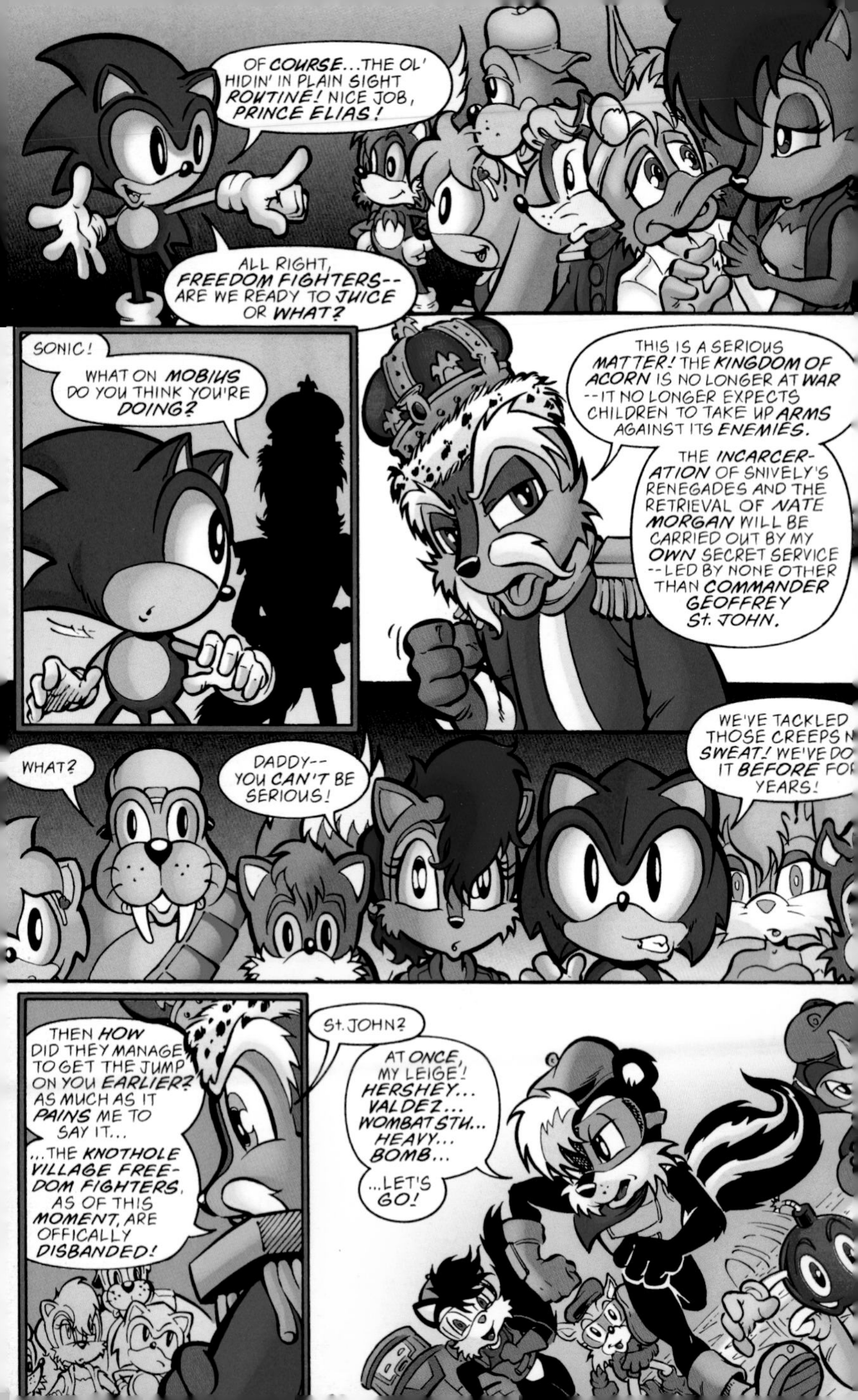
OF COURSE...THE OL' HIDIN' IN PLAIN SIGHT ROUTINE! NICE JOB, PRINCE ELIAS!
ALL RIGHT, FREEDOM FIGHTERS--ARE WE READY TO JUICE OR WHAT?
SONIC!
WHAT ON MOBIUS DO YOU THINK YOU'RE DOING?
THIS IS A SERIOUS MATTER! THE KINGDOM OF ACORN IS NO LONGER AT WAR --IT NO LONGER EXPECTS CHILDREN TO TAKE UP ARMS AGAINST ITS ENEMIES.
THE INCARCER-ATION OF SNIVELY'S RENEGADES AND THE RETRIEVAL OF NATE MORGAN WILL BE CARRIED OUT BY MY OWN SECRET SERVICE --LED BY NONE OTHER THAN COMMANDER GEOFFREY St. JOHN.
WHAT?
DADDY--YOU CAN'T BE SERIOUS!
WE'VE TACKLED THOSE CREEPS N SWEAT! WE'VE DO IT BEFORE FO YEARS!
THEN HOW DID THEY MANAGE TO GET THE JUMP ON YOU EARLIER? AS MUCH AS IT PAINS ME TO SAY IT...
...THE KNOTHOLE VILLAGE FREE-DOM FIGHTERS, AS OF THIS MOMENT, ARE OFFICALLY DISBANDED!
St. JOHN?
AT ONCE, MY LEIGE! HERSHEY... VALDEZ... WOMBAT STU... HEAVY... BOMB...
...LET'S GO!

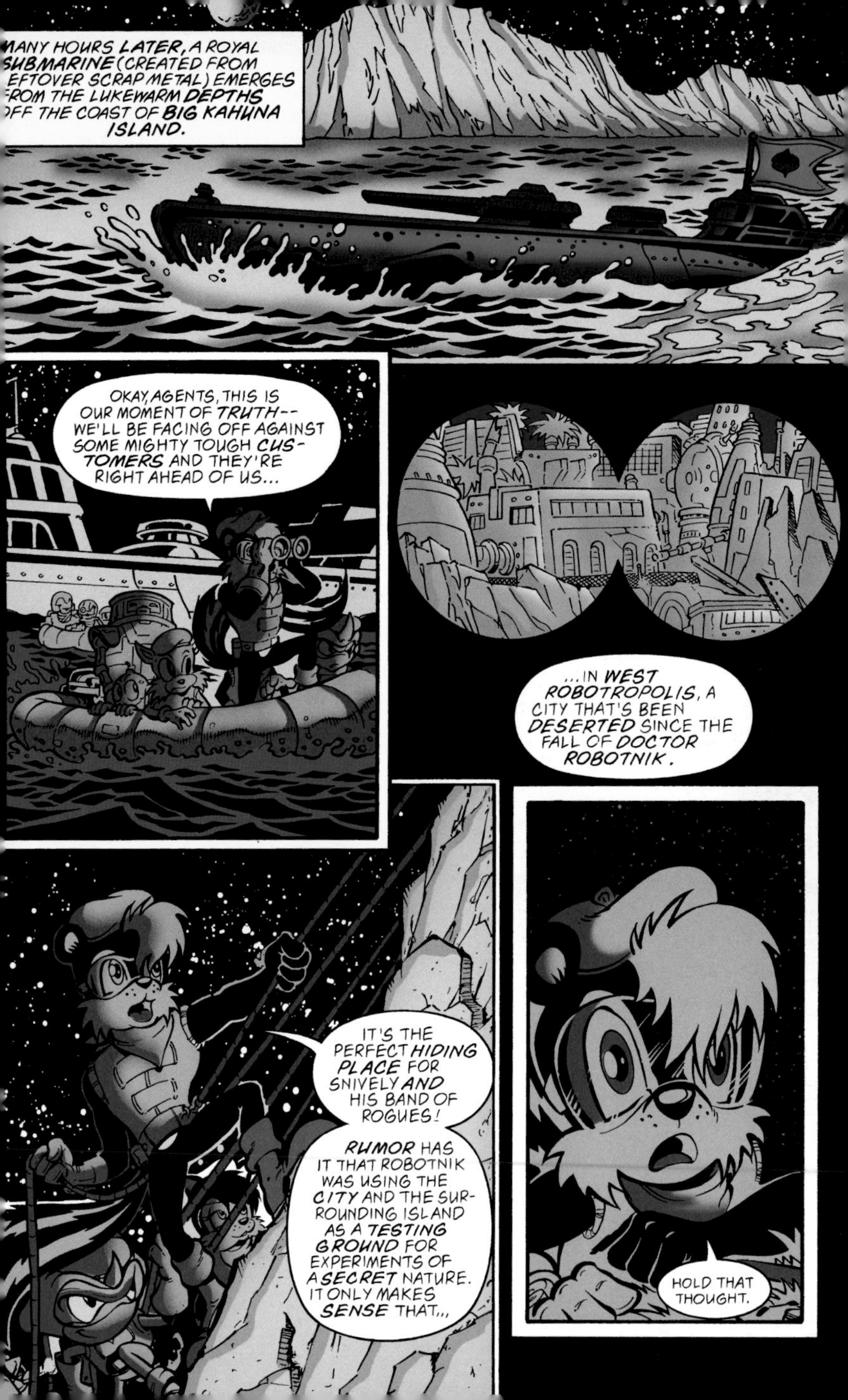
MANY HOURS LATER, A ROYAL SUBMARINE (CREATED FROM LEFTOVER SCRAP METAL) EMERGES FROM THE LUKEWARM DEPTHS OFF THE COAST OF BIG KAHUNA ISLAND.
OKAY, AGENTS, THIS IS OUR MOMENT OF TRUTH-- WE'LL BE FACING OFF AGAINST SOME MIGHTY TOUGH CUSTOMERS AND THEY'RE RIGHT AHEAD OF US...
...IN WEST ROBOTROPOLIS, A CITY THAT'S BEEN DESERTED SINCE THE FALL OF DOCTOR ROBOTNIK.
IT'S THE PERFECT HIDING PLACE FOR SNIVELY AND HIS BAND OF ROGUES!
RUMOR HAS IT THAT ROBOTNIK WAS USING THE CITY AND THE SURROUNDING ISLAND AS A TESTING GROUND FOR EXPERIMENTS OF A SECRET NATURE. IT ONLY MAKES SENSE THAT...
HOLD THAT THOUGHT.

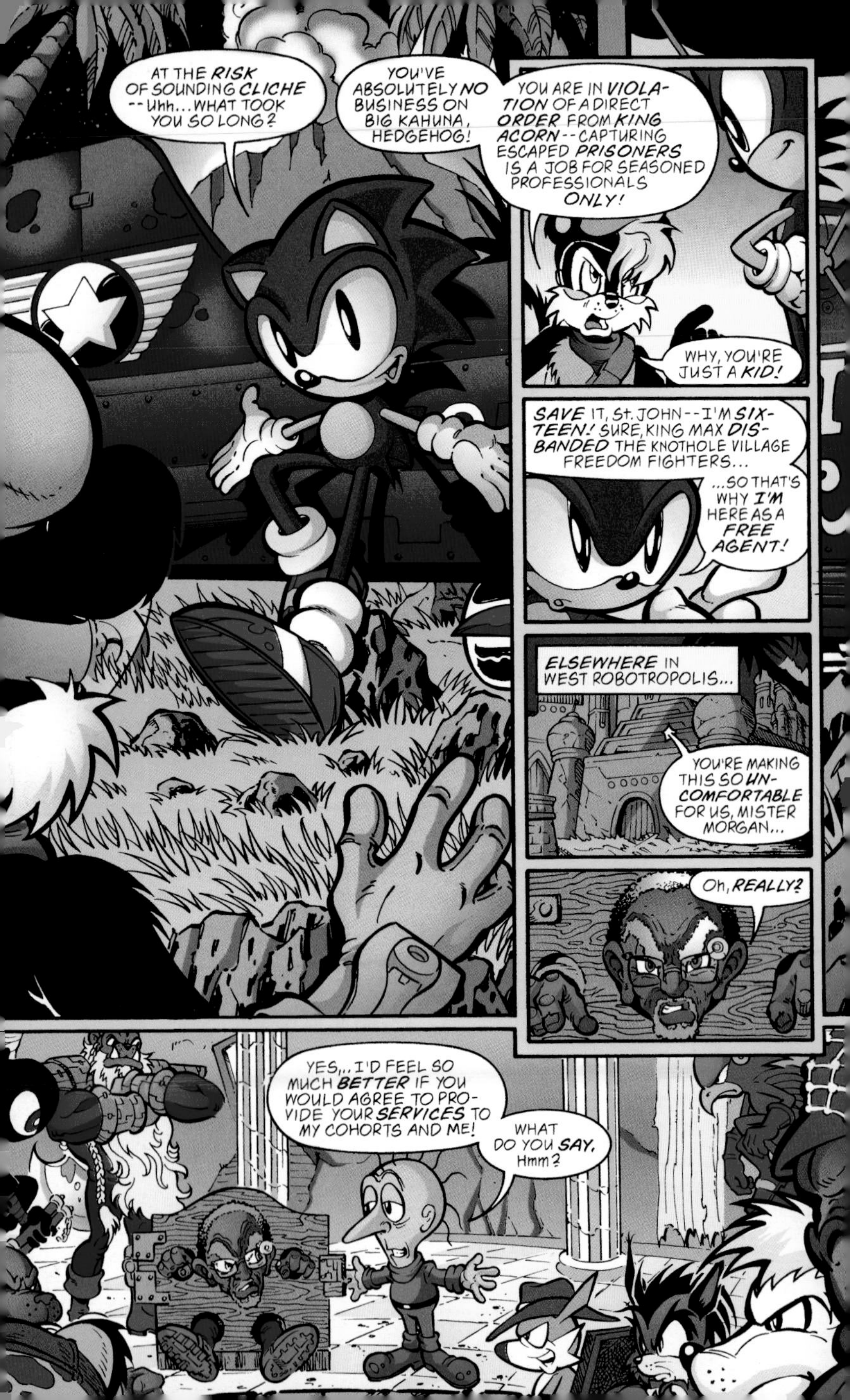
AT THE RISK OF SOUNDING CLICHE --Uhh... WHAT TOOK YOU SO LONG?
YOU'VE ABSOLUTELY NO BUSINESS ON BIG KAHUNA, HEDGEHOG!
YOU ARE IN VIOLATION OF A DIRECT ORDER FROM KING ACORN--CAPTURING ESCAPED PRISONERS IS A JOB FOR SEASONED PROFESSIONALS ONLY!
WHY, YOU'RE JUST A KID!
SAVE IT, St. JOHN--I'M SIXTEEN! SURE, KING MAX DISBANDED THE KNOTHOLE VILLAGE FREEDOM FIGHTERS...
...SO THAT'S WHY I'M HERE AS A FREE AGENT!
ELSEWHERE IN WEST ROBOTROPOLIS...
YOU'RE MAKING THIS SO UNCOMFORTABLE FOR US, MISTER MORGAN...
Oh, REALLY?
YES,.. I'D FEEL SO MUCH BETTER IF YOU WOULD AGREE TO PROVIDE YOUR SERVICES TO MY COHORTS AND ME!
WHAT DO YOU SAY. Hmm?

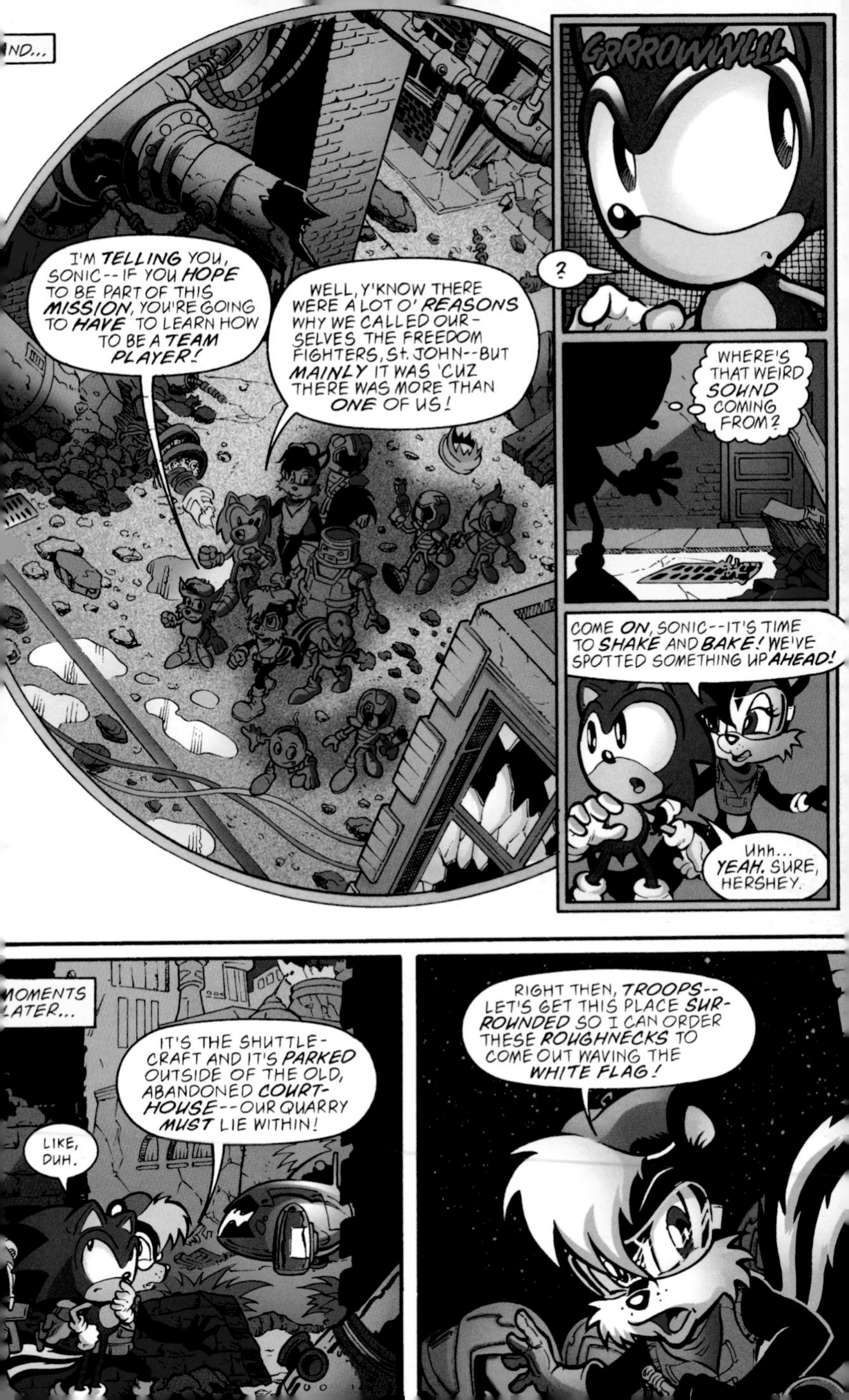
...ND...
I'M TELLING YOU, SONIC--IF YOU HOPE TO BE PART OF THIS MISSION, YOU'RE GOING TO HAVE TO LEARN HOW TO BE A TEAM PLAYER!
WELL, Y'KNOW THERE WERE A LOT O' REASONS WHY WE CALLED OUR-SELVES THE FREEDOM FIGHTERS, St. JOHN--BUT MAINLY IT WAS 'CUZ THERE WAS MORE THAN ONE OF US!
GRRROWWWLLL
?
WHERE'S THAT WEIRD SOUND COMING FROM?
COME ON, SONIC--IT'S TIME TO SHAKE AND BAKE! WE'VE SPOTTED SOMETHING UP AHEAD!
Uhh... YEAH. SURE, HERSHEY.
MOMENTS LATER...
IT'S THE SHUTTLE-CRAFT AND IT'S PARKED OUTSIDE OF THE OLD, ABANDONED COURT-HOUSE--OUR QUARRY MUST LIE WITHIN!
LIKE, DUH.
RIGHT THEN, TROOPS--LET'S GET THIS PLACE SUR-ROUNDED SO I CAN ORDER THESE ROUGHNECKS TO COME OUT WAVING THE WHITE FLAG!

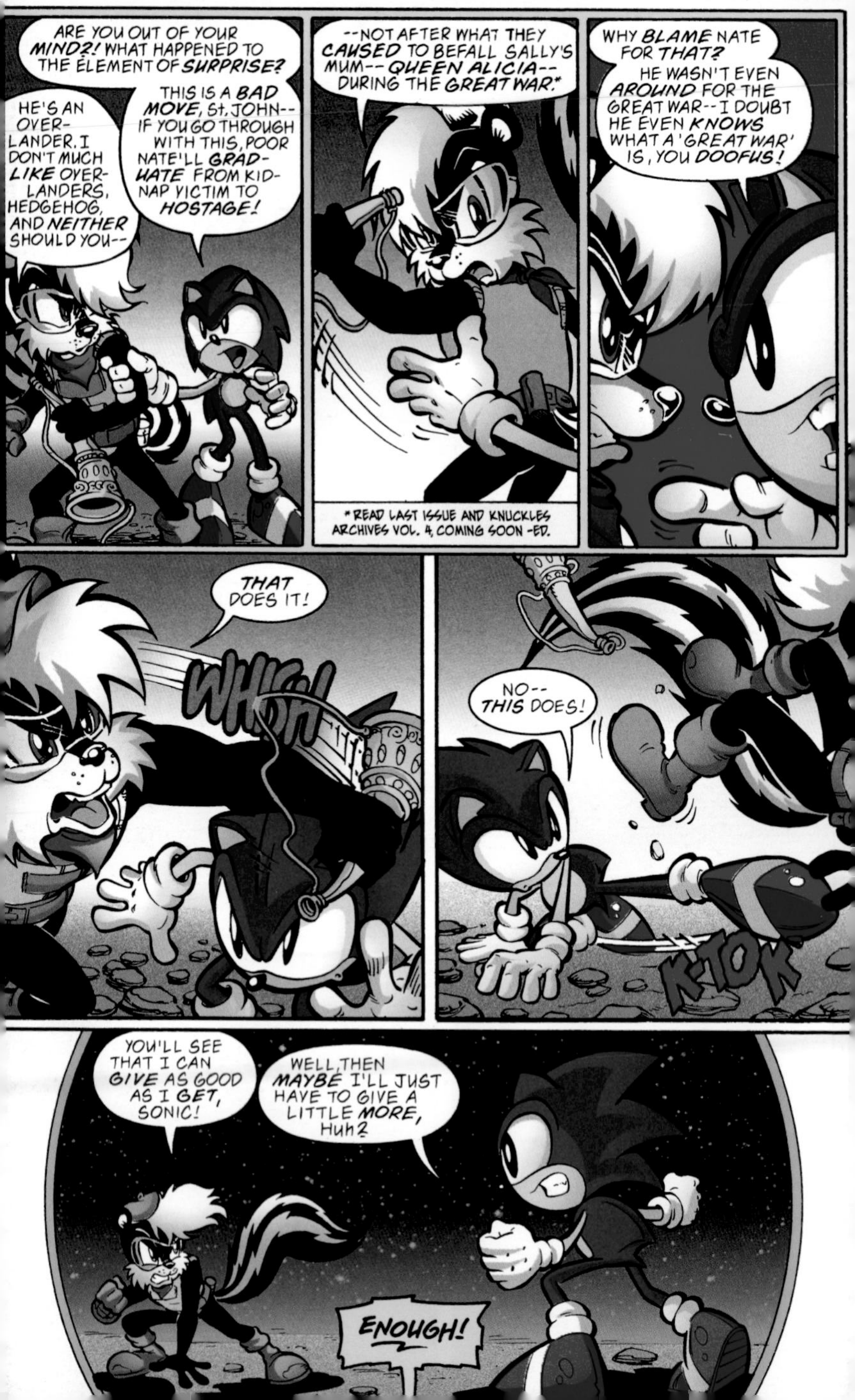
ARE YOU OUT OF YOUR MIND?! WHAT HAPPENED TO THE ÉLEMENT OF SURPRISE?
HE'S AN OVER-LANDER. I DON'T MUCH LIKE OVER-LANDERS, HEDGEHOG, AND NEITHER SHOULD YOU--
THIS IS A BAD MOVE, St. JOHN-- IF YOU GO THROUGH WITH THIS, POOR NATE'LL GRAD-UATE FROM KID-NAP VICTIM TO HOSTAGE!
--NOT AFTER WHAT THEY CAUSED TO BEFALL SALLY'S MUM-- QUEEN ALICIA-- DURING THE GREAT WAR.*
*READ LAST ISSUE AND KNUCKLES ARCHIVES VOL. 4, COMING SOON -ED.
WHY BLAME NATE FOR THAT?
HE WASN'T EVEN AROUND FOR THE GREAT WAR-- I DOUBT HE EVEN KNOWS WHAT A 'GREAT WAR' IS, YOU DOOFUS!
THAT DOES IT!
WHISH
NO-- THIS DOES!
K-TOK
YOU'LL SEE THAT I CAN GIVE AS GOOD AS I GET, SONIC!
WELL, THEN MAYBE I'LL JUST HAVE TO GIVE A LITTLE MORE, Huh?
ENOUGH!

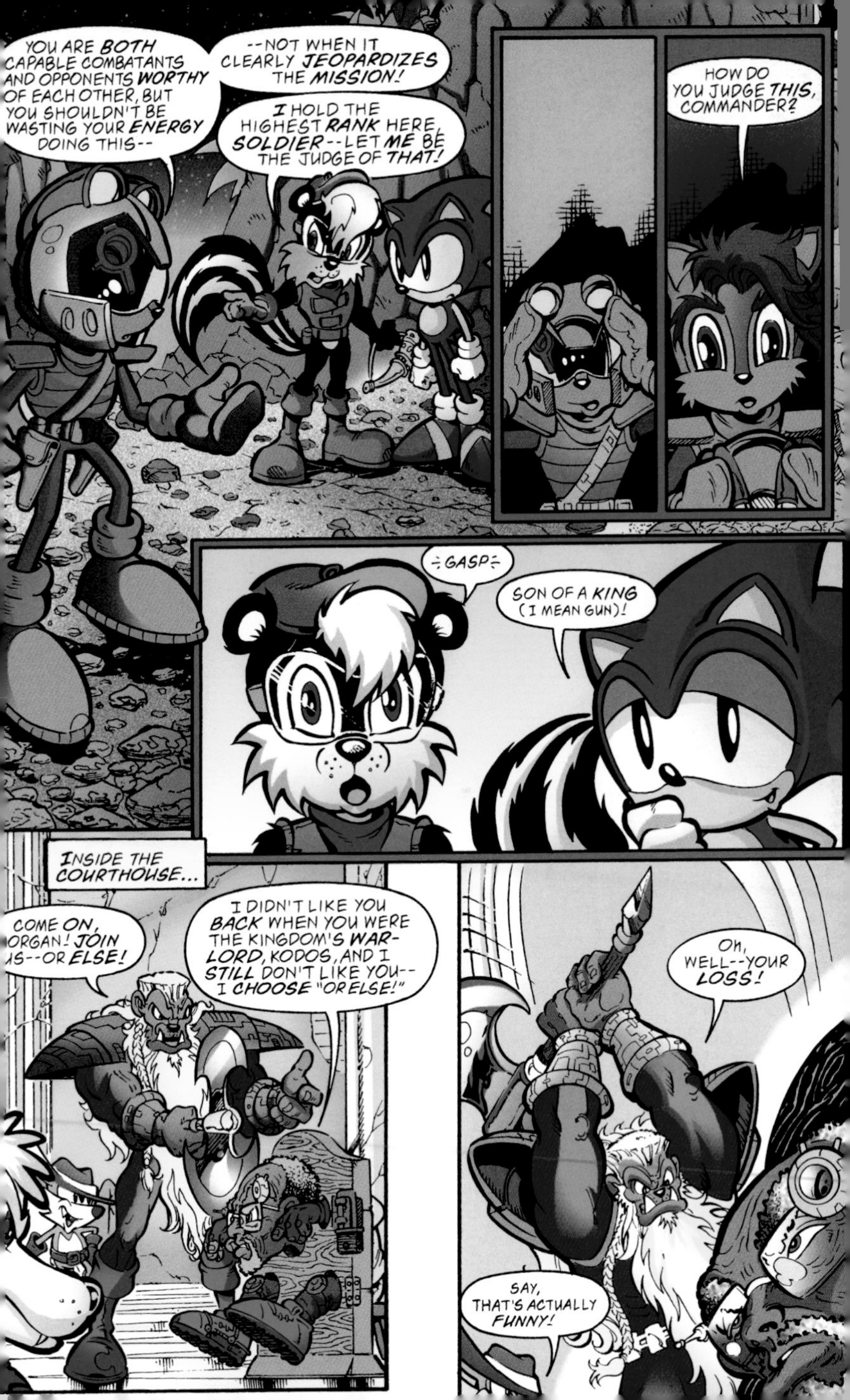
YOU ARE BOTH CAPABLE COMBATANTS AND OPPONENTS WORTHY OF EACH OTHER, BUT YOU SHOULDN'T BE WASTING YOUR ENERGY DOING THIS--
--NOT WHEN IT CLEARLY JEOPARDIZES THE MISSION!
I HOLD THE HIGHEST RANK HERE, SOLDIER--LET ME BE THE JUDGE OF THAT!
HOW DO YOU JUDGE THIS, COMMANDER?
÷GASP÷
SON OF A KING (I MEAN GUN)!
INSIDE THE COURTHOUSE...
COME ON, ORGAN! JOIN US--OR ELSE!
I DIDN'T LIKE YOU BACK WHEN YOU WERE THE KINGDOM'S WAR-LORD, KODOS, AND I STILL DON'T LIKE YOU--I CHOOSE "OR ELSE!"
OH, WELL--YOUR LOSS!
SAY, THAT'S ACTUALLY FUNNY!

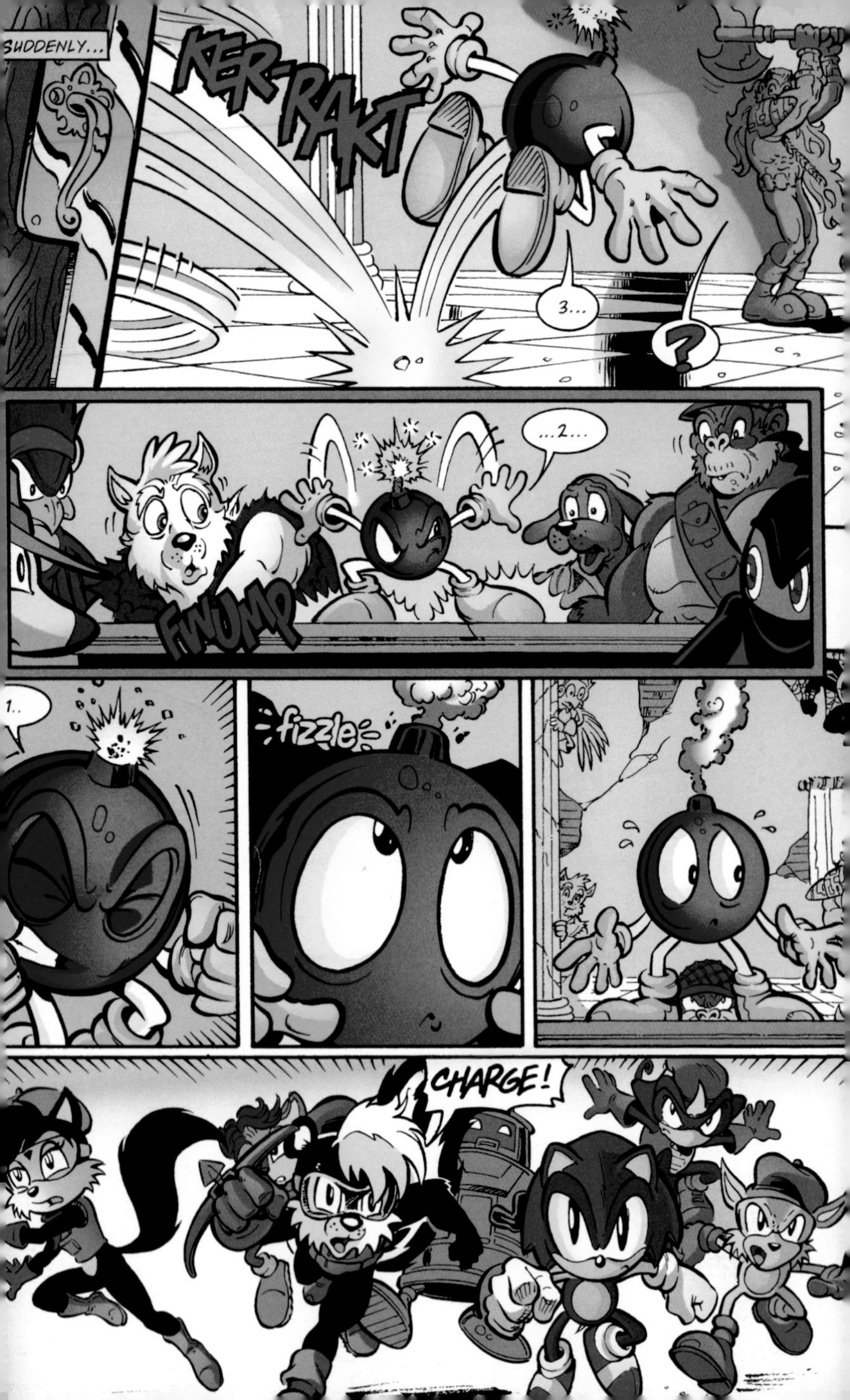
SUDDENLY...
KER-RAKT
3...
?
...2...
FWUMP
1..
fizzle
CHARGE!

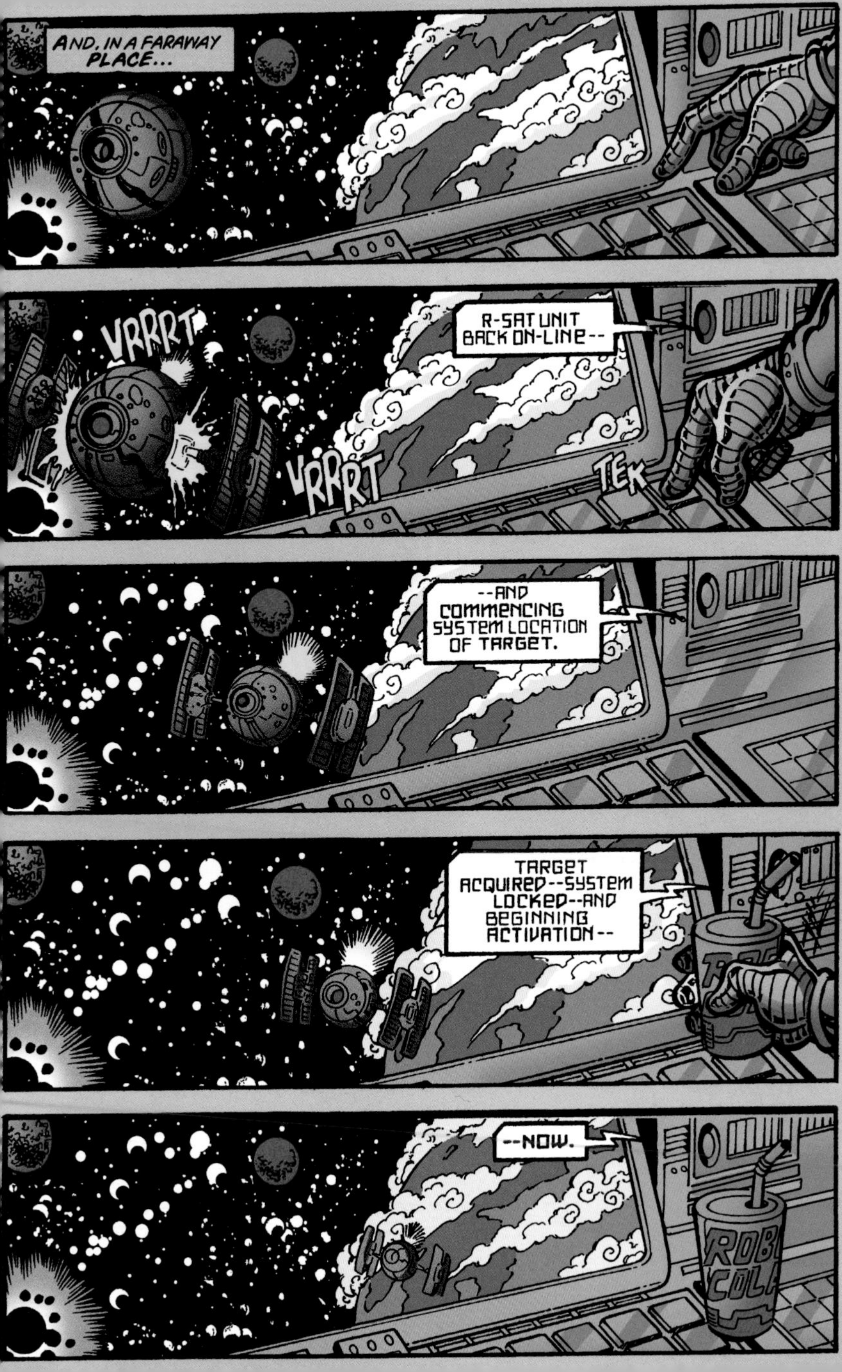
AND, IN A FARAWAY PLACE...
VRRRT
R-SAT UNIT BACK ON-LINE--
VRRRT
TEK
--AND COMMENCING SYSTEM LOCATION OF TARGET.
TARGET ACQUIRED--SYSTEM LOCKED--AND BEGINNING ACTIVATION--
--NOW.

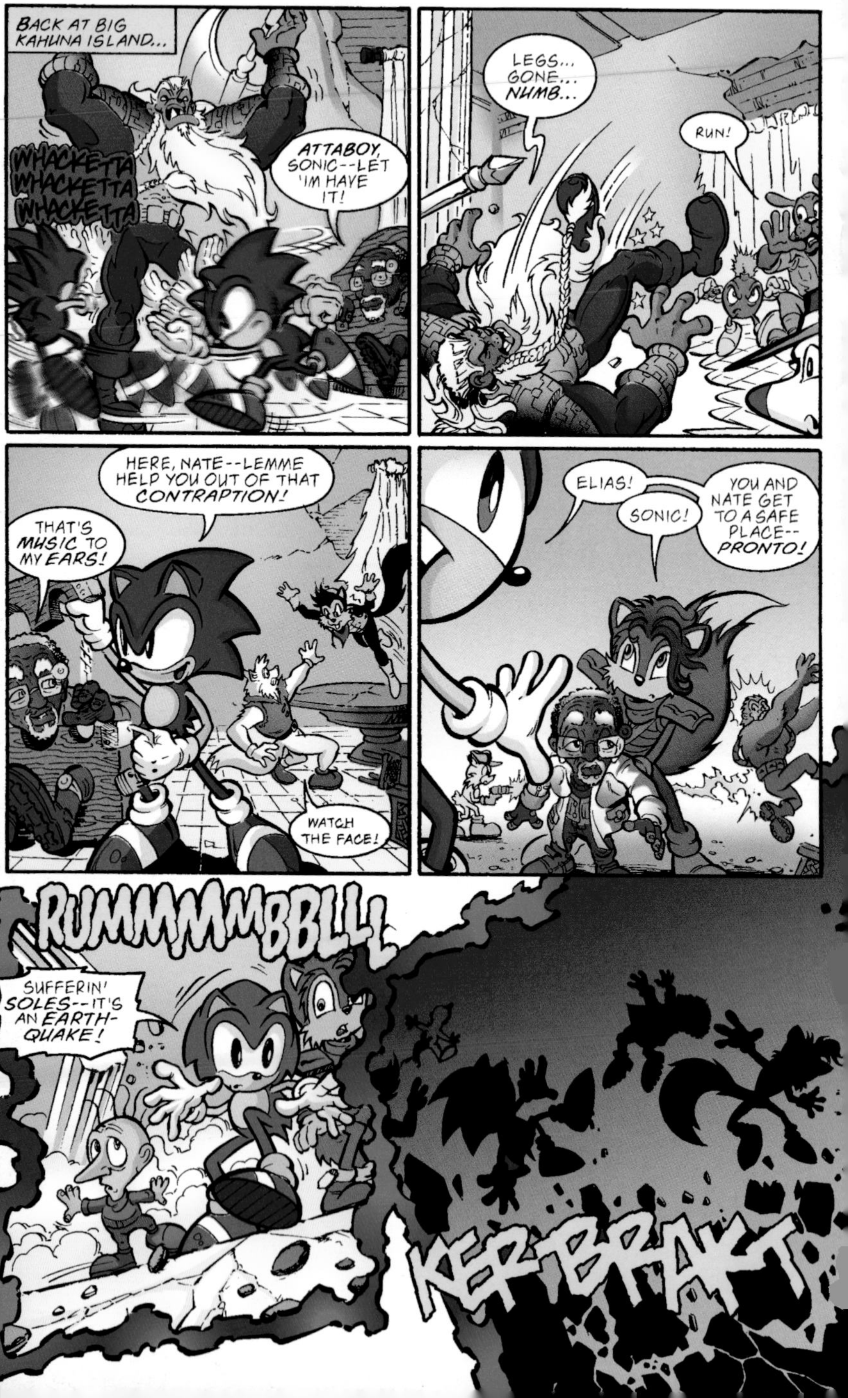
BACK AT BIG KAHUNA ISLAND...
WHACKETTA WHACKETTA WHACKETTA
ATTABOY, SONIC--LET 'IM HAVE IT!
LEGS... GONE... NUMB...
RUN!
HERE, NATE--LEMME HELP YOU OUT OF THAT CONTRAPTION!
THAT'S MUSIC TO MY EARS!
WATCH THE FACE!
ELIAS!
SONIC!
YOU AND NATE GET TO A SAFE PLACE--PRONTO!
RUMMMMMBBLLL
SUFFERIN' SOLES--IT'S AN EARTH-QUAKE!
KER-BRAKT!

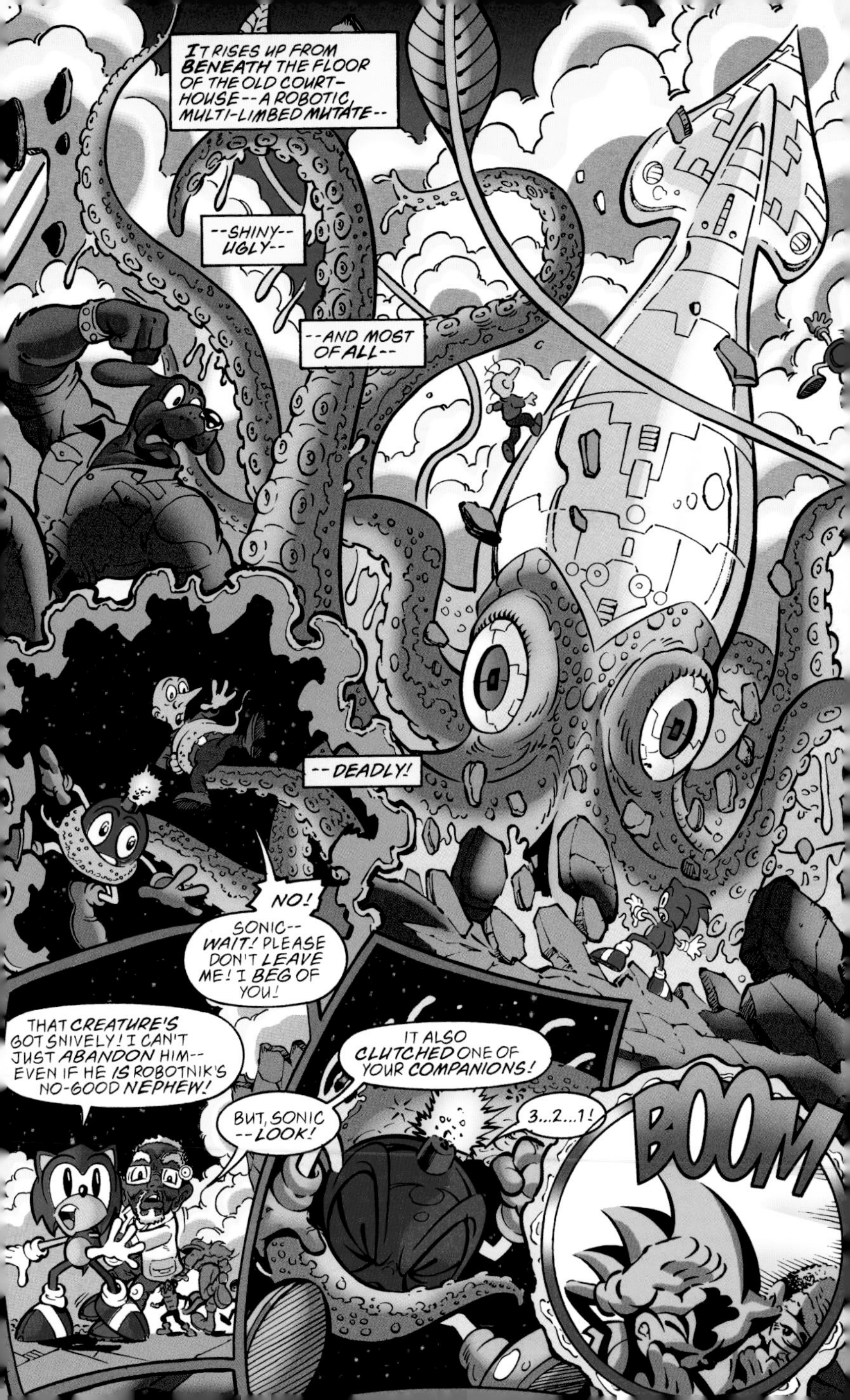
IT RISES UP FROM BENEATH THE FLOOR OF THE OLD COURT-HOUSE--A ROBOTIC, MULTI-LIMBED MUTATE--
--SHINY-- UGLY--
--AND MOST OF ALL--
--DEADLY!
NO!
SONIC-- WAIT! PLEASE DON'T LEAVE ME! I BEG OF YOU!
THAT CREATURE'S GOT SNIVELY! I CAN'T JUST ABANDON HIM-- EVEN IF HE IS ROBOTNIK'S NO-GOOD NEPHEW!
BUT, SONIC --LOOK!
IT ALSO CLUTCHED ONE OF YOUR COMPANIONS!
3...2...1!
BOOM

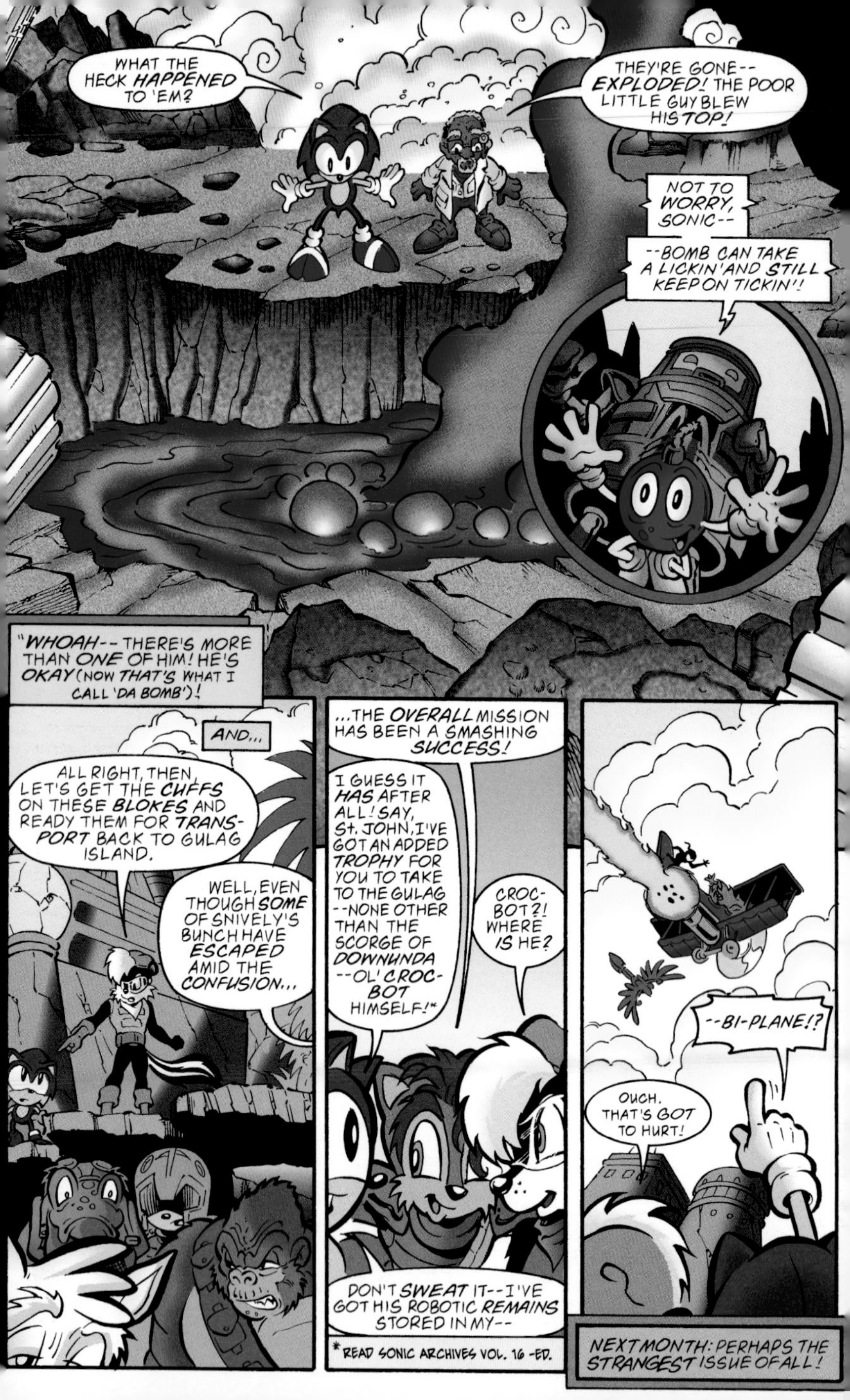
WHAT THE HECK HAPPENED TO 'EM?
THEY'RE GONE--EXPLODED! THE POOR LITTLE GUY BLEW HIS TOP!
NOT TO WORRY, SONIC--
--BOMB CAN TAKE A LICKIN' AND STILL KEEP ON TICKIN'!
"WHOAH--THERE'S MORE THAN ONE OF HIM! HE'S OKAY (NOW THAT'S WHAT I CALL 'DA BOMB')!
AND...
ALL RIGHT, THEN, LET'S GET THE CUFFS ON THESE BLOKES AND READY THEM FOR TRANS-PORT BACK TO GULAG ISLAND.
WELL, EVEN THOUGH SOME OF SNIVELY'S BUNCH HAVE ESCAPED AMID THE CONFUSION...
...THE OVERALL MISSION HAS BEEN A SMASHING SUCCESS!
I GUESS IT HAS AFTER ALL! SAY, St. JOHN, I'VE GOT AN ADDED TROPHY FOR YOU TO TAKE TO THE GULAG --NONE OTHER THAN THE SCORGE OF DOWNUNDA --OL' CROC-BOT HIMSELF!*
CROC-BOT?! WHERE IS HE?
DON'T SWEAT IT--I'VE GOT HIS ROBOTIC REMAINS STORED IN MY--
* READ SONIC ARCHIVES VOL. 16 -ED.
--BI-PLANE!?
OUCH. THAT'S GOT TO HURT!
NEXT MONTH: PERHAPS THE STRANGEST ISSUE OF ALL!

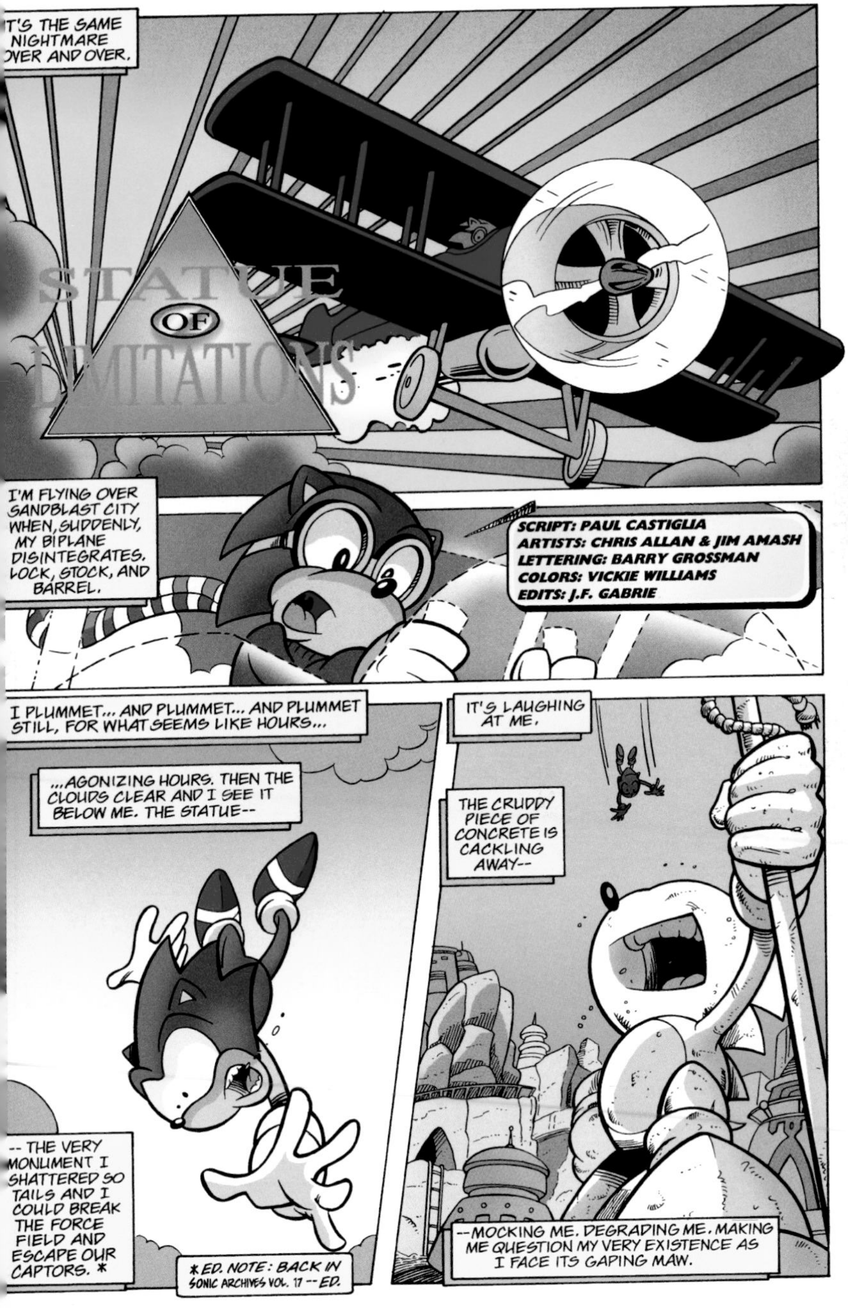
T'S THE SAME NIGHTMARE OVER AND OVER.
STATUE OF LIMITATIONS
I'M FLYING OVER SANDBLAST CITY WHEN, SUDDENLY, MY BIPLANE DISINTEGRATES. LOCK, STOCK, AND BARREL.
SCRIPT: PAUL CASTIGLIA
ARTISTS: CHRIS ALLAN & JIM AMASH
LETTERING: BARRY GROSSMAN
COLORS: VICKIE WILLIAMS
EDITS: J.F. GABRIE
I PLUMMET... AND PLUMMET... AND PLUMMET STILL, FOR WHAT SEEMS LIKE HOURS...
...AGONIZING HOURS. THEN THE CLOUDS CLEAR AND I SEE IT BELOW ME. THE STATUE--
-- THE VERY MONUMENT I SHATTERED SO TAILS AND I COULD BREAK THE FORCE FIELD AND ESCAPE OUR CAPTORS. *
* ED. NOTE: BACK IN SONIC ARCHIVES VOL. 17 -- ED.
IT'S LAUGHING AT ME.
THE CRUDDY PIECE OF CONCRETE IS CACKLING AWAY--
--MOCKING ME. DEGRADING ME. MAKING ME QUESTION MY VERY EXISTENCE AS I FACE ITS GAPING MAW.

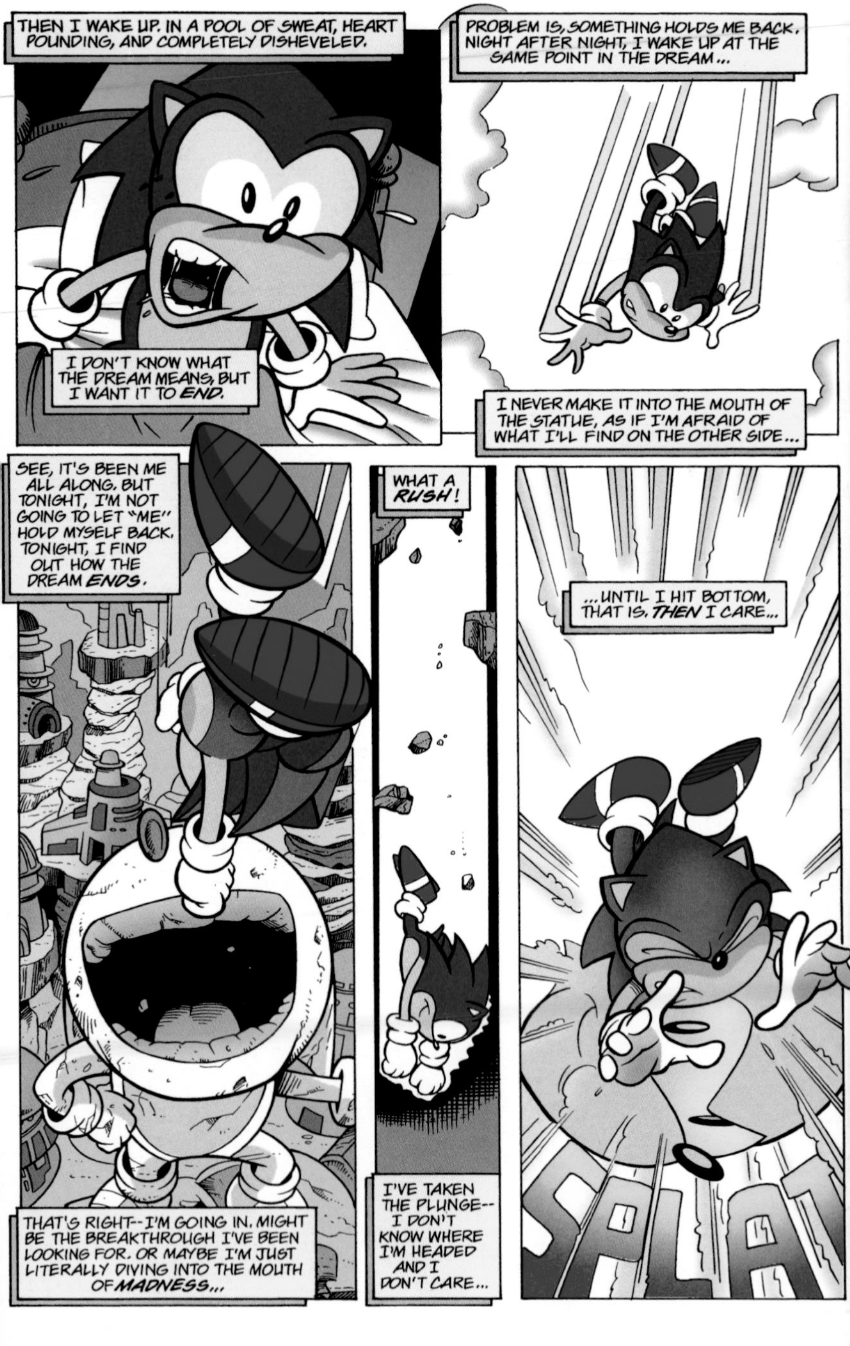
THEN I WAKE UP. IN A POOL OF SWEAT, HEART POUNDING, AND COMPLETELY DISHEVELED.
I DON'T KNOW WHAT THE DREAM MEANS, BUT I WANT IT TO END.
PROBLEM IS, SOMETHING HOLDS ME BACK. NIGHT AFTER NIGHT, I WAKE UP AT THE SAME POINT IN THE DREAM...
I NEVER MAKE IT INTO THE MOUTH OF THE STATUE, AS IF I'M AFRAID OF WHAT I'LL FIND ON THE OTHER SIDE...
SEE, IT'S BEEN ME ALL ALONG. BUT TONIGHT, I'M NOT GOING TO LET "ME" HOLD MYSELF BACK. TONIGHT, I FIND OUT HOW THE DREAM ENDS.
THAT'S RIGHT--I'M GOING IN. MIGHT BE THE BREAKTHROUGH I'VE BEEN LOOKING FOR. OR MAYBE I'M JUST LITERALLY DIVING INTO THE MOUTH OF MADNESS...
WHAT A RUSH!
I'VE TAKEN THE PLUNGE-- I DON'T KNOW WHERE I'M HEADED AND I DON'T CARE...
...UNTIL I HIT BOTTOM, THAT IS. THEN I CARE...
SPLAT

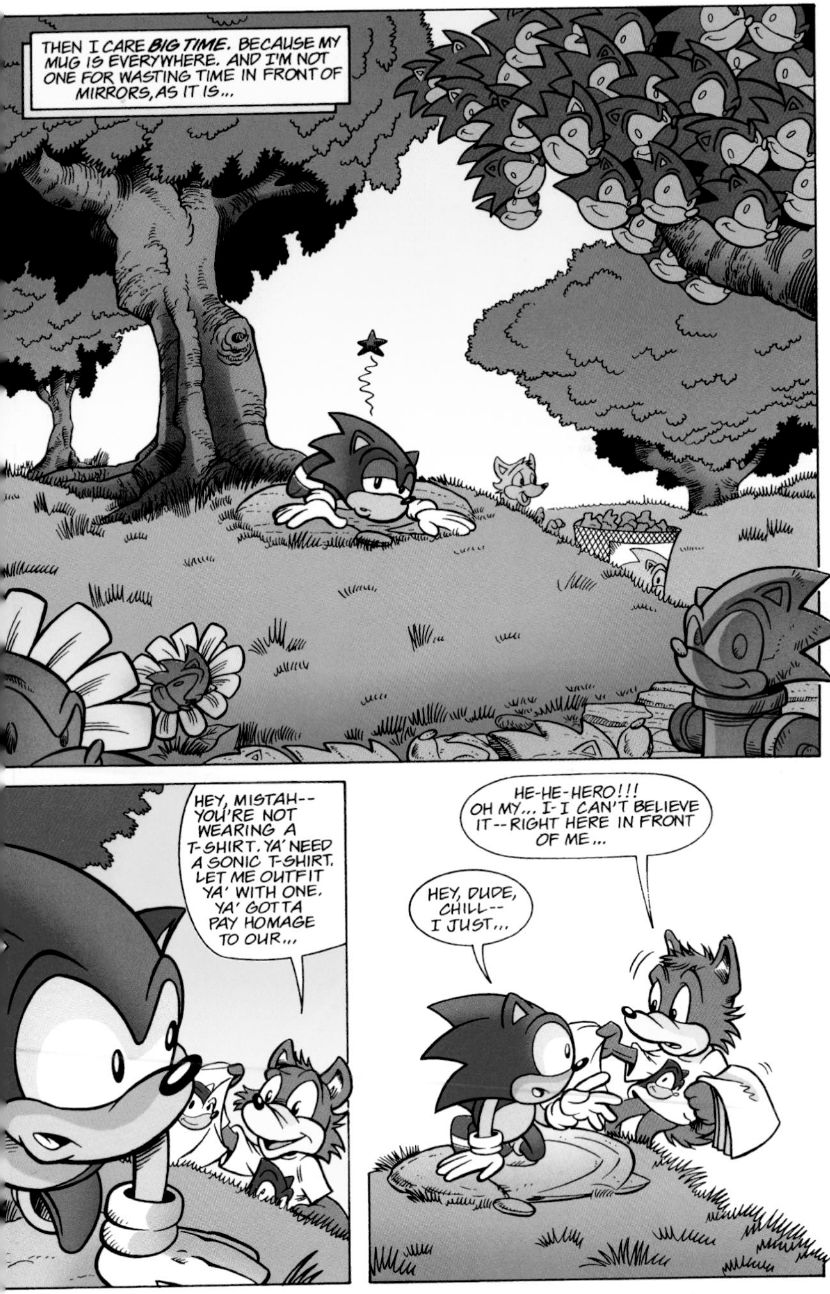
THEN I CARE BIG TIME. BECAUSE MY MUG IS EVERYWHERE. AND I'M NOT ONE FOR WASTING TIME IN FRONT OF MIRRORS, AS IT IS...
HEY, MISTAH-- YOU'RE NOT WEARING A T-SHIRT. YA' NEED A SONIC T-SHIRT. LET ME OUTFIT YA' WITH ONE. YA' GOTTA PAY HOMAGE TO OUR...
HE-HE-HERO!!! OH MY... I-I CAN'T BELIEVE IT--RIGHT HERE IN FRONT OF ME...
HEY, DUDE, CHILL-- I JUST...

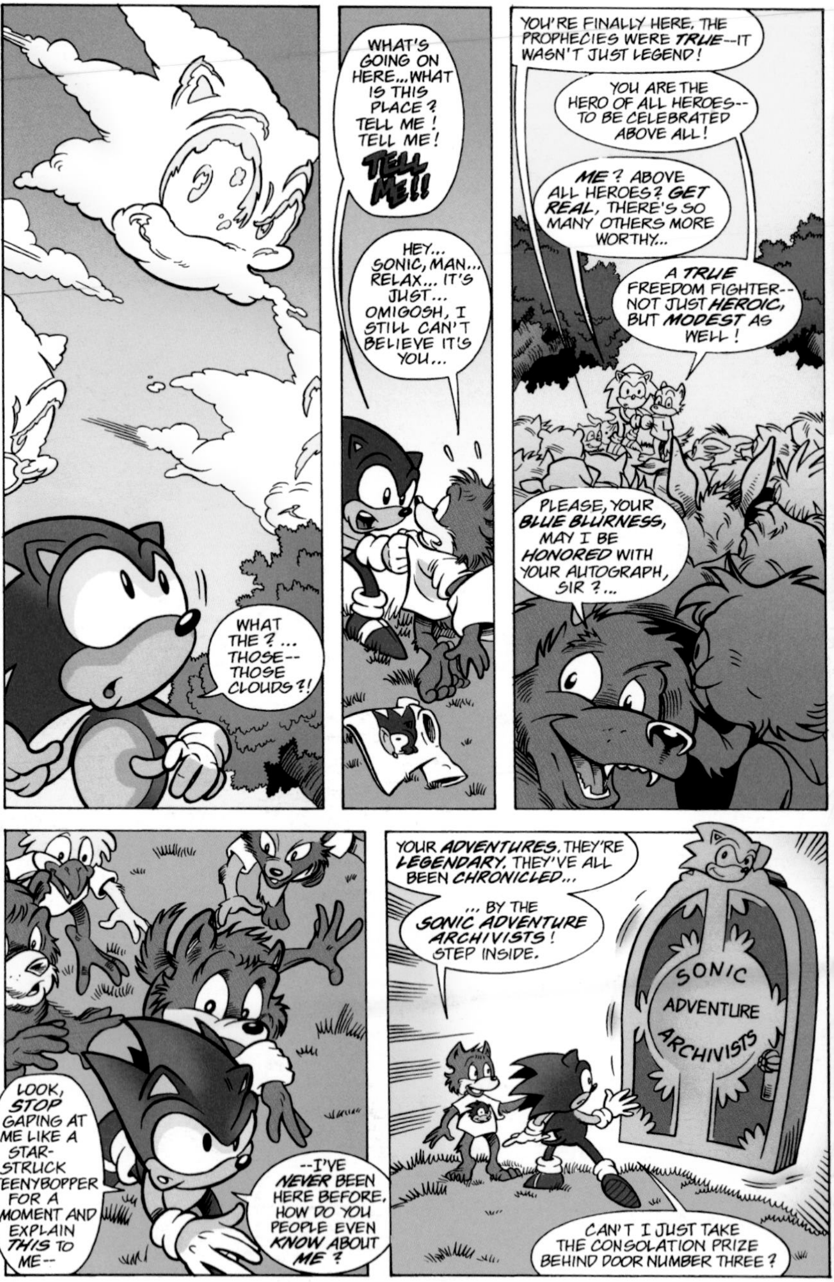
WHAT THE ? ... THOSE-- THOSE CLOUDS ?!
WHAT'S GOING ON HERE... WHAT IS THIS PLACE ? TELL ME ! TELL ME ! TELL ME!!
HEY... SONIC, MAN... RELAX... IT'S JUST... OMIGOSH, I STILL CAN'T BELIEVE IT'S YOU...
YOU'RE FINALLY HERE. THE PROPHECIES WERE TRUE--IT WASN'T JUST LEGEND !
YOU ARE THE HERO OF ALL HEROES-- TO BE CELEBRATED ABOVE ALL !
ME ? ABOVE ALL HEROES ? GET REAL, THERE'S SO MANY OTHERS MORE WORTHY...
A TRUE FREEDOM FIGHTER-- NOT JUST HEROIC, BUT MODEST AS WELL !
PLEASE, YOUR BLUE BLURNESS, MAY I BE HONORED WITH YOUR AUTOGRAPH, SIR ?...
LOOK, STOP GAPING AT ME LIKE A STAR-STRUCK TEENYBOPPER FOR A MOMENT AND EXPLAIN THIS TO ME--
--I'VE NEVER BEEN HERE BEFORE, HOW DO YOU PEOPLE EVEN KNOW ABOUT ME ?
YOUR ADVENTURES. THEY'RE LEGENDARY. THEY'VE ALL BEEN CHRONICLED...
... BY THE SONIC ADVENTURE ARCHIVISTS ! STEP INSIDE.
SONIC ADVENTURE ARCHIVISTS
CAN'T I JUST TAKE THE CONSOLATION PRIZE BEHIND DOOR NUMBER THREE ?

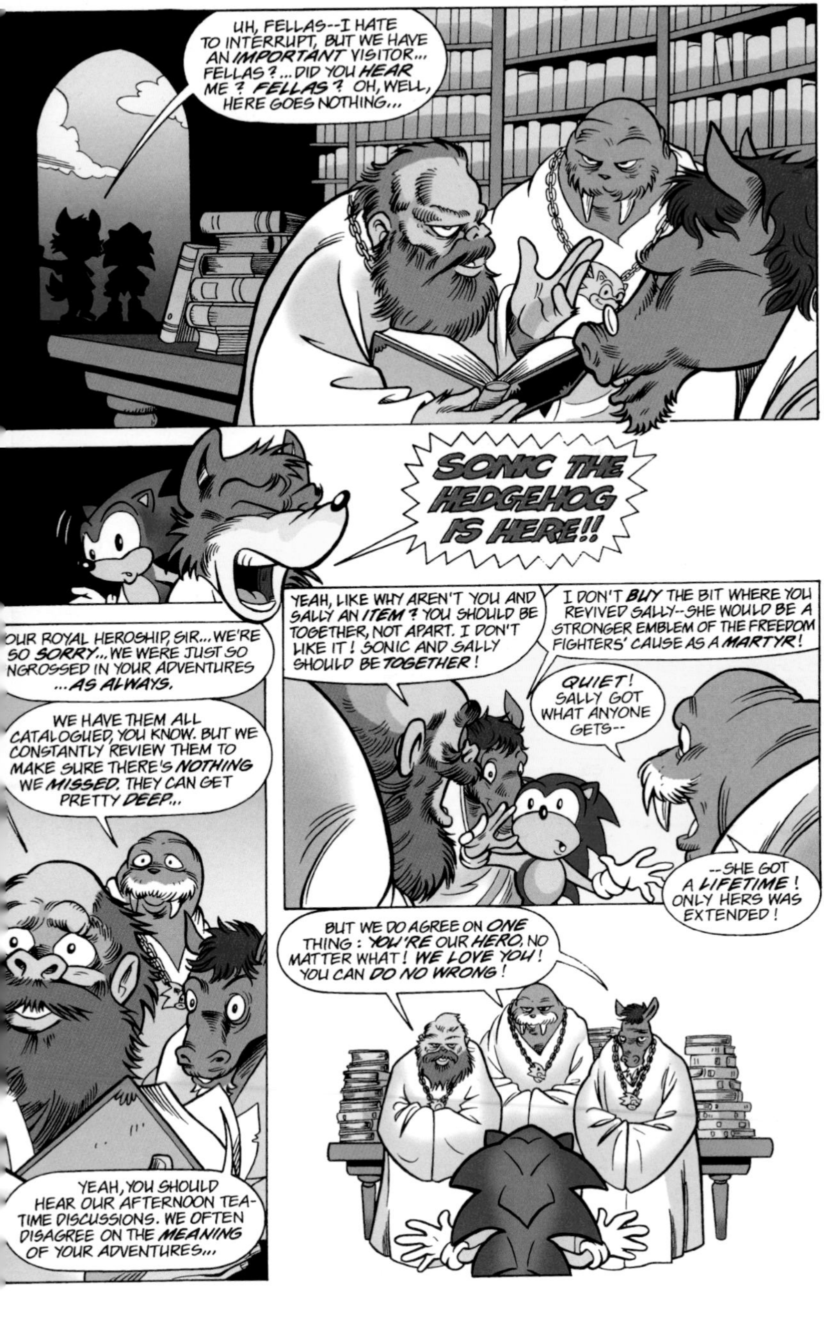
UH, FELLAS--I HATE TO INTERRUPT, BUT WE HAVE AN IMPORTANT VISITOR... FELLAS? ...DID YOU HEAR ME? FELLAS? OH, WELL, HERE GOES NOTHING...
SONIC THE HEDGEHOG IS HERE!!
OUR ROYAL HEROSHIP, SIR... WE'RE SO SORRY... WE WERE JUST SO NGROSSED IN YOUR ADVENTURES ...AS ALWAYS.
WE HAVE THEM ALL CATALOGUED, YOU KNOW. BUT WE CONSTANTLY REVIEW THEM TO MAKE SURE THERE'S NOTHING WE MISSED. THEY CAN GET PRETTY DEEP...
YEAH, YOU SHOULD HEAR OUR AFTERNOON TEA-TIME DISCUSSIONS. WE OFTEN DISAGREE ON THE MEANING OF YOUR ADVENTURES...
YEAH, LIKE WHY AREN'T YOU AND SALLY AN ITEM? YOU SHOULD BE TOGETHER, NOT APART. I DON'T LIKE IT! SONIC AND SALLY SHOULD BE TOGETHER!
I DON'T BUY THE BIT WHERE YOU REVIVED SALLY--SHE WOULD BE A STRONGER EMBLEM OF THE FREEDOM FIGHTERS' CAUSE AS A MARTYR!
QUIET! SALLY GOT WHAT ANYONE GETS--
--SHE GOT A LIFETIME! ONLY HERS WAS EXTENDED!
BUT WE DO AGREE ON ONE THING: YOU'RE OUR HERO, NO MATTER WHAT! WE LOVE YOU! YOU CAN DO NO WRONG!

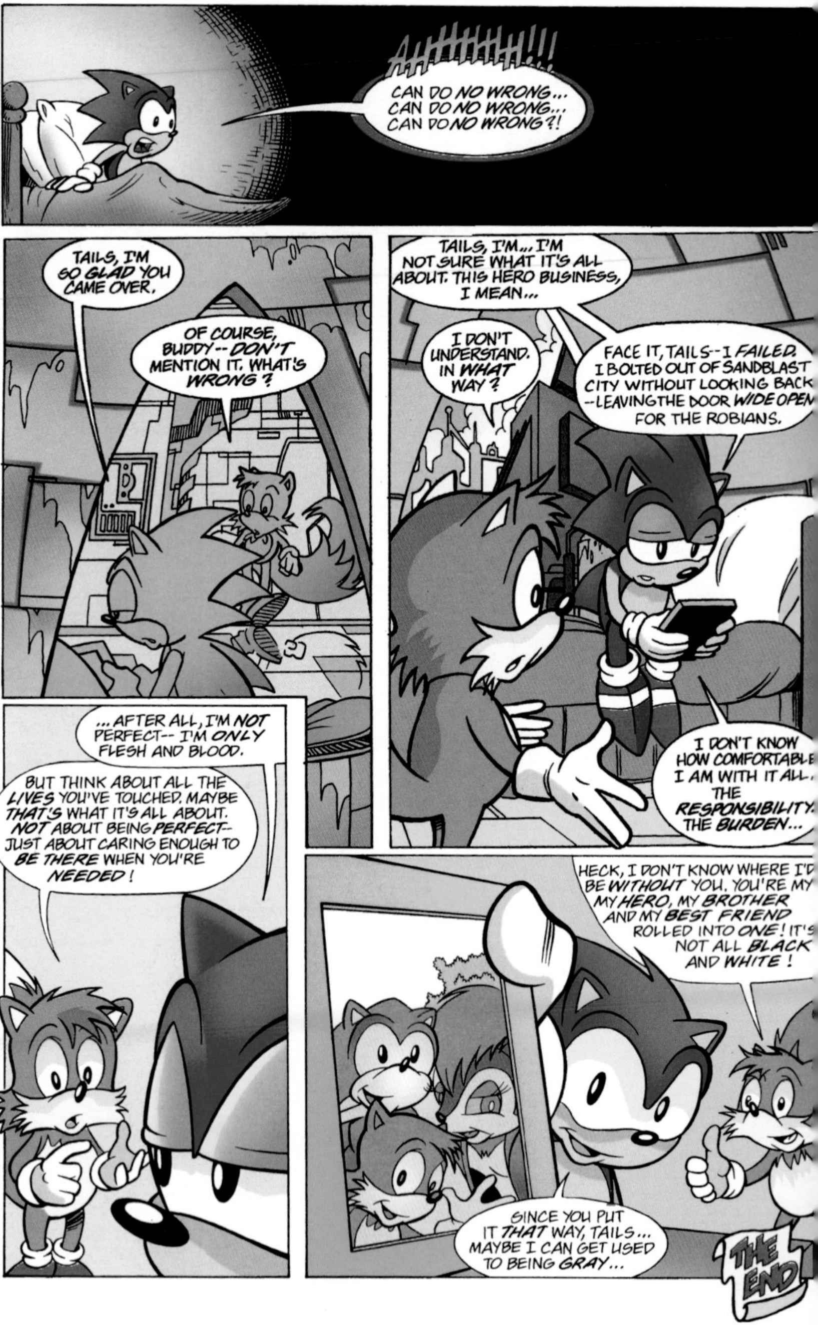
AHHHHHHH!!!
CAN DO NO WRONG... CAN DO NO WRONG... CAN DO NO WRONG?!
TAILS, I'M SO GLAD YOU CAME OVER.
OF COURSE, BUDDY--DON'T MENTION IT. WHAT'S WRONG?
TAILS, I'M... I'M NOT SURE WHAT IT'S ALL ABOUT. THIS HERO BUSINESS, I MEAN...
I DON'T UNDERSTAND. IN WHAT WAY?
FACE IT, TAILS--I FAILED. I BOLTED OUT OF SANDBLAST CITY WITHOUT LOOKING BACK --LEAVING THE DOOR WIDE OPEN FOR THE ROBIANS.
I DON'T KNOW HOW COMFORTABLE I AM WITH IT ALL... THE RESPONSIBILITY. THE BURDEN...
...AFTER ALL, I'M NOT PERFECT-- I'M ONLY FLESH AND BLOOD.
BUT THINK ABOUT ALL THE LIVES YOU'VE TOUCHED. MAYBE THAT'S WHAT IT'S ALL ABOUT. NOT ABOUT BEING PERFECT-- JUST ABOUT CARING ENOUGH TO BE THERE WHEN YOU'RE NEEDED!
HECK, I DON'T KNOW WHERE I'D BE WITHOUT YOU. YOU'RE MY MY HERO, MY BROTHER AND MY BEST FRIEND ROLLED INTO ONE! IT'S NOT ALL BLACK AND WHITE!
SINCE YOU PUT IT THAT WAY, TAILS... MAYBE I CAN GET USED TO BEING GRAY...
THE END

SONIC THE HEDGEHOG™

Welcome to a brief who's who
of the Sonic universe. You have
just read some of the earliest
and most loved stories from the
Sonic comic. We thought
you'd like to learn a little extra
about a few of our
favorite Sonic characters!

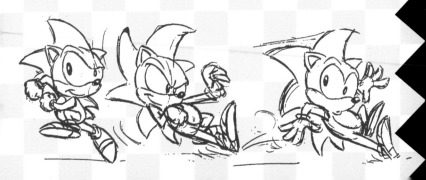

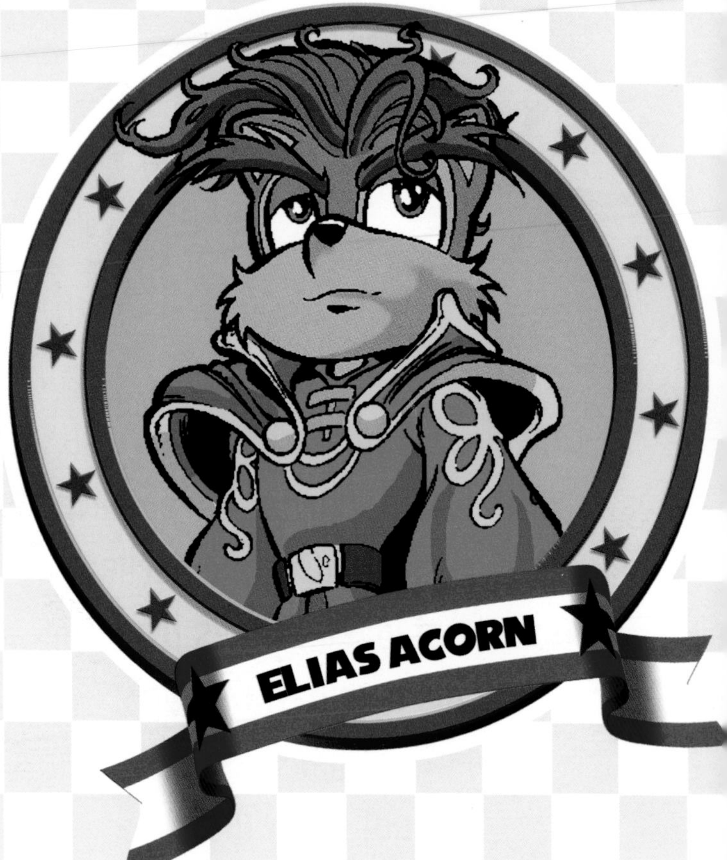
ELIAS ACORN

ELIAS ACORN

The crown prince of the Kingdom of Acorn! Elias was thought long-lost during the Great War when the Overland shot down the escape shuttle carrying him and his mother. Instead, he was rescued by the Brotherhood of Guardians and raised as an adventurer!

ALICIA ACORN

ALICIA ACORN

The Queen of Acorns! She was supposed
to be whisked to safety during the Great
War, but her shuttle was shot down over
Angel Island. The Brotherhood of
Guardians could not sufficiently heal her,
and so she remains in a state of
suspended animation.

AERIAL & ATHENA

AERIAL & ATHENA

These twin Overlander girls are orphans!
Aerial does all the talking for her mute twin
sister, Athena. They lived in a ruined
Overlander city until found by Lupe and the
Wolf Pack. To everyone's shock, Lupe adopted
them as her own daughters!

SONIC THE HEDGEHOG ™

Welcome to a brief what's what
of the Sonic universe. You have
just read some of the earliest
and most loved stories from the
Sonic comic. We thought
you'd like to learn a little extra
about a few of the items and places
that make the Sonic universe so
awesome!

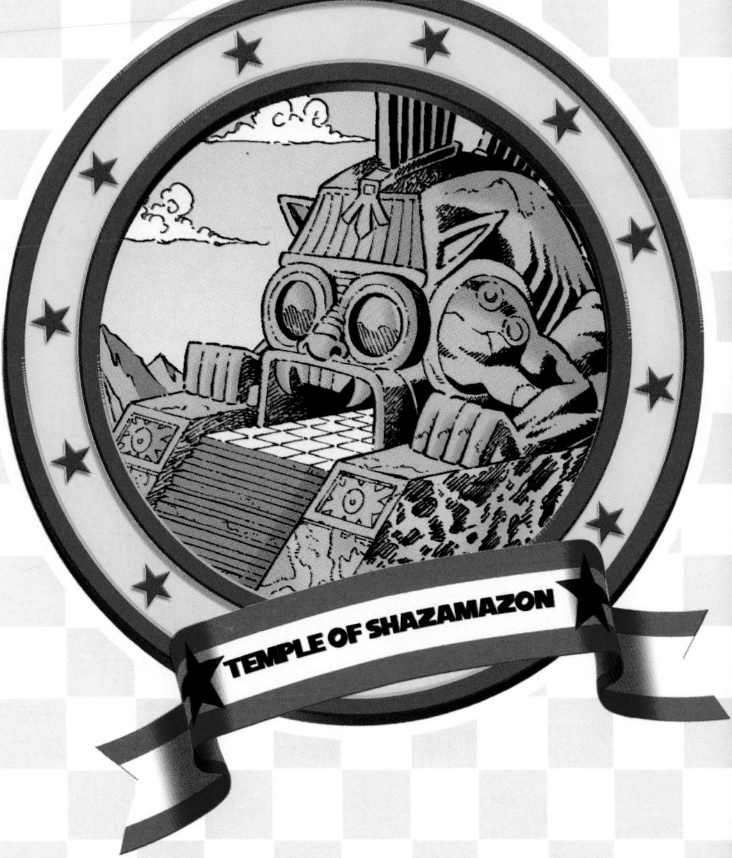
TEMPLE OF SHAZAMAZON

TEMPLE OF SHAZAMAZON

An ancient and spooky temple hidden deep in the Great Rainforest. Who built it, and when, and why? Nobody knows! It once was home to the Green Super Emerald, and then the Ring of Acorns. It was also home to a terrible mutate from the Forgotten Wars!

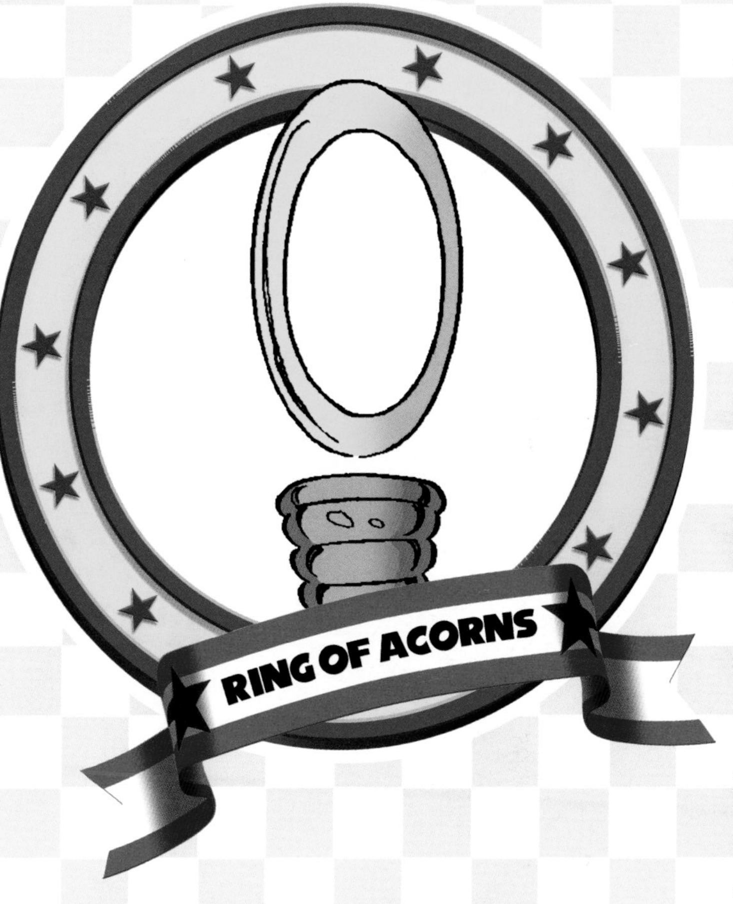
RING OF ACORNS

RING OF ACORNS

A normal power ring can give Sonic an edge in battle, but the Ring of Acorns is something special! Created by Nate Morgan using the Green Super Emerald, the Ring of Acorns can grant any wish -- but only a finite number of them!

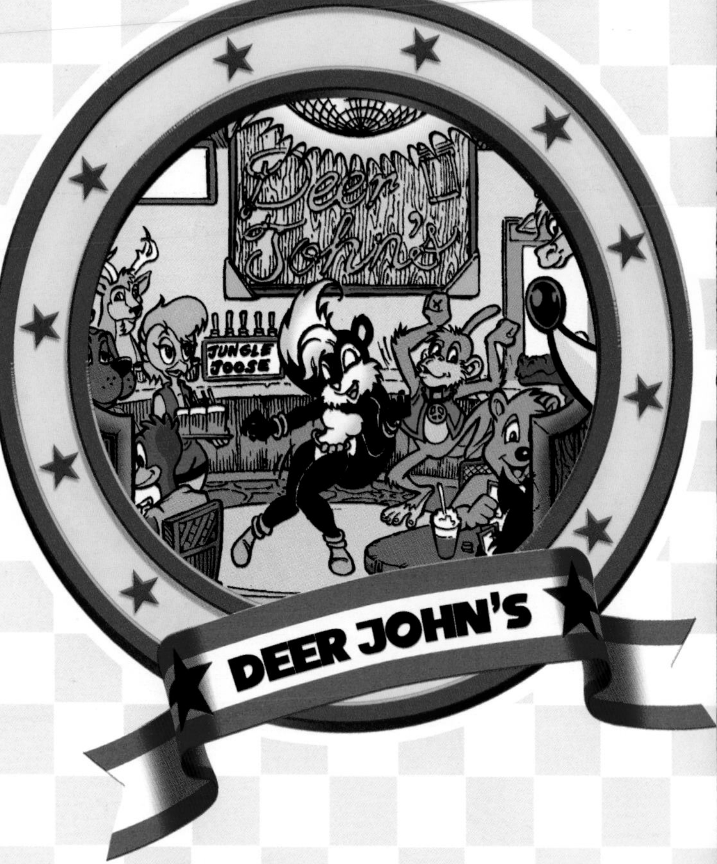
Deer John's
JUNGLE JOOSE
DEER JOHN'S

DEER JOHN'S

This is the place to be! Run by Joe and Jane Doe, this juice bar is the premiere hangout in Mobotropolis. Tired of rebuilding the city? Just need to unwind? Come on down to Deer John's and relax with all your friends!

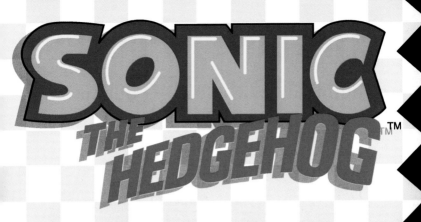

The Cover Process

Welcome to a brief look on how
Sonic comic artist, Patrick "Spaz" Spaziante,
created the cover for Sonic Archives Vol. 18.

See how a cover develops from
a quick thumbnail sketch, to a completed
illustration, and all of the changes
in between!

The Cover Process

-Thumbnail sketches by Paul Kaminski-

SONIC ARCHIVES VOL18
major themes:
- SONIC+TAILS return to home after their world tour
- The Royal heirarchy is set-up
Speed sequence
WELCOME HOME
Maxx on the throne, bemused
OPTION A
Tails
Sally + Elias
Sky writing "welcome Back" in the sky
Nate Morgan
Maxx on the throne, NOT AMUSED
Sally + Elias
pose similar to STH 226 (Genesis pt 1) pg 6, panel 4
OPTION B
SONIC "Borrows" Steals MAXX'S Crown to pose

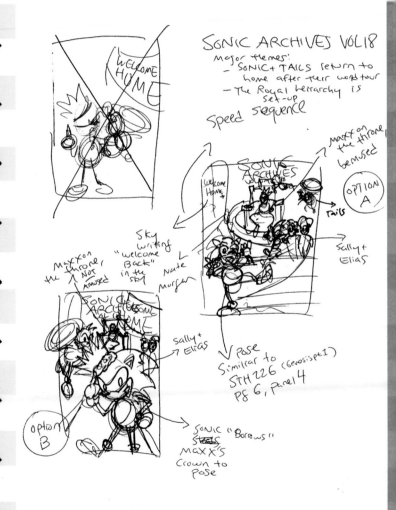

The Cover Process

-Cover sketch "A" by Patrick Spaziante-

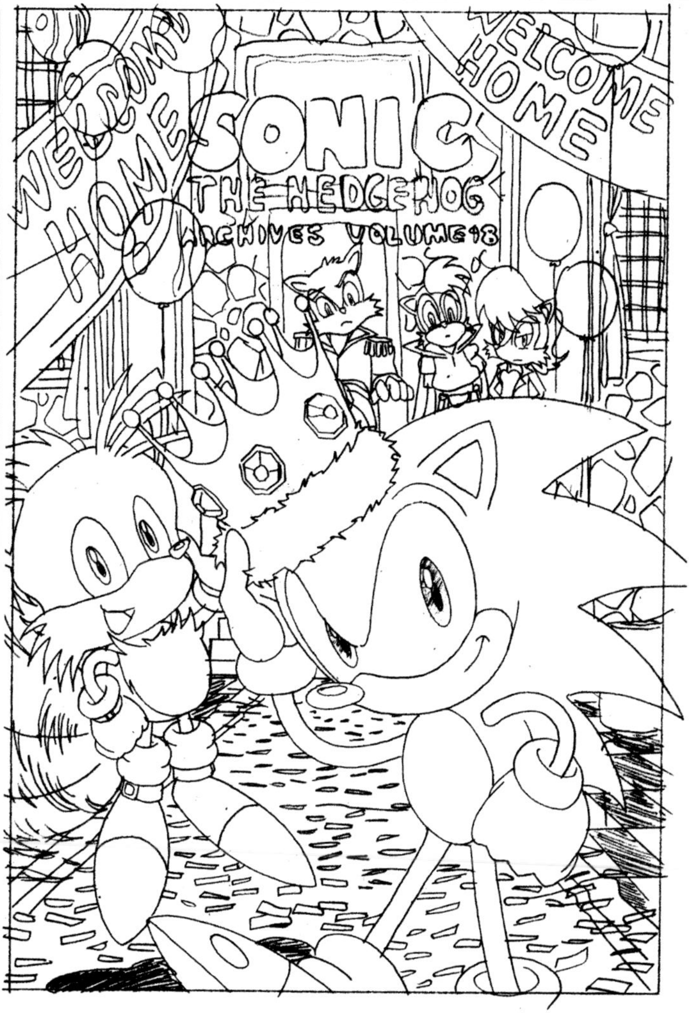
WELCOME HOME
WELCOME HOME
SONIC
THE HEDGEHOG
ARCHIVES VOLUME 18
WELCOME HOME

The Cover Process